the
fiction
between
us

JULIE OLIVIA

Author's Note

The Fiction Between Us is the second book in the *Honeywood Fun Park* Series. This book is a standalone and does not need to be read with the series. However, there will be spoilers for previous books.

Please be advised that this book is a **slow burn, open-door** romance, meaning there is **on-page** sexual content. Mature readers only.

Also, while this rom-com is 98% laugh-out-loud, exciting theme park moments, there is also about 2% angst, including mentions of depression. Be kind to your heart when you read, friends.

For everyone who thinks they're not enough.

Playlist

"Here You Come Again" - Dolly Parton
"Someday My Prince Will Come" - Emile Pandolfi
"Ophelia" - The Lumineers
"Crop Circles" - Odie Leigh
"Meet Me in the Woods" - Lord Huron
"cardigan" - Taylor Swift
"Summertime Sadness" - Lana Del Rey
"Fall With Me" - The Wild Reeds
"Love" - Nancy Adams
"Everybody Loves Somebody" - Dean Martin

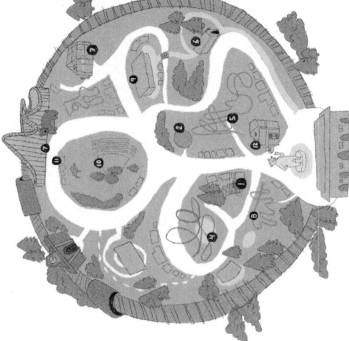

Honeywood
FUN PARK

1. The Bee-fast Stop
2. The Beesting
3. Bumblebee Greenhouse
4. Bumblebee's Flight
5. Buzzard of Death
6. Canoodler
7. The Grizzly
8. Little Pecker's Joyride
9. The Romping Meadow
10. Honey Pleasure Stage
11. Security Office
12. Main Office

1

Quinn

Once upon a time, in the hot humidity of a late Georgia summer, a queen ices her swollen lip. Or rather, a theme park employee masquerading as a queen. An employee who, currently, can't tell if the metallic tang in her mouth is from leftover summer rainfall or blood.

I promise this is a funny story, but every fairy tale has a few stepsisters with plucked-out eyes or an old woman tricking children. Trust me, I'm in the business of happily ever afters. And mine starts with a bloody lip.

I'm backstage at Honeywood Fun Park's outdoor amphitheater, staring at a rickety folding chair in the corner. I want nothing more than to collapse into it, but I've worked as Queen Bee for almost ten years. I know better than to sit down while wearing the poofy pink ball gown. Costuming would have my head.

The walkie-talkie in my non-ice-holding fist scratches to life. My blood pressure spikes, and it's not because I'm overwhelmed by stomach butterflies or dreamy, lovey-dovey thoughts vignetted in peachy pinks and creams. No, it is due to stress from the other voice coming over the walkie's line—Landon Arden.

"Your heels are hiding from me," he says.

I can hear the smile in his tone. Everything he says is with a laugh, or a chuckle, or a grin. Even if I can't see it, I know it's there.

I push the button on the side to talk back. "No, they're in the corner, under the tulle."

"That word means nothing to me," he responds.

My heart pounds in my ears—once again, and very notably, *not* from love. If this type of annoyance is love, no wonder the divorce rate is so high.

"It's the poofy skirt that looks like fishing—"

"Yep. Got 'em!" he says with a light *ha*. "Weird name. Tulle."

"The name's been around forever," I say.

"Then, why haven't I heard of it?"

"It's not my job to keep a log of your shortcomings."

I hear him chuckle, a sound so low that the walkie-talkie practically vibrates.

"Surprising," he says. "I'll be at the stage in five, Barbie."

Barbie.

Cue steam coming out of my ears.

I don't respond to him, instead groaning when I hand the walkie-talkie back to our stagehand, Emily, who giggles when she takes it.

"Barbie," she echoes, almost a whisper to herself.

"I'm Queen Bee to you, ma'am," I say with a pointed finger and a smile.

"Ah, so only Landon can call you Barbie?" Emily asks.

"No, nobody can," I grumble as my smile falls. "He just does it anyway."

As head of security, Landon thinks he can get away

with anything. Honestly, with that dimpled smile of his, skirting murder might be possible for him. But I see right through it. I have since I was fifteen when he and his brood of friends taunted me in the high school halls.

My best friend's twin brother and my old high school bully receives zero extra privileges from me.

The stage's side door opens, and Honeywood Fun Park's general manager, Fred, walks through. He takes one look at me and sighs.

It's a fair reaction. On one hand, I'm dressed as Queen Bee, elegant and graceful in a pink ballroom dress, complete with delicate tulle sleeves hanging off my shoulders. On the other hand, I've got a busted lip and bare feet with black toenail polish on display—the antithesis of Queen Bee's color palette. I look like she's completed her villain origin story.

"It's not as bad as it looks," I automatically respond.

"It doesn't look great," he says.

"Landon is bringing my shoes."

"And why aren't they here to begin with?" he asks.

"It's a long story."

"And the ice?" he asks.

"You don't wanna know." I cringe at my own words.

Yeah, okay, so this isn't a good look for me.

"Emily, what happened?" he asks, turning to the eighteen-year-old next to me.

Emily tugs at her blonde braid, wincing.

She's totally gonna break.

"Quinn got into it with a guest again," says my once-loyal coworker.

Fred's eyes widen, and his hands go to his hips in the pose that stretches his yellow Honeywood polo across his stomach.

3

"Okay, wait! That's not why I have a bloody lip though," I quickly say. "I wouldn't openly *fight* a guest. Jeez. Give me more credit than that."

But Fred leans in for the whole truth.

"But Buzzy did try to defend me," I say. "And he did faint."

"Christ," Fred says, wiping his meaty hand over his face, pulling down at his thick mustache.

Some of the park's summer newbies think they're invincible. The teen dressed as Buzzy the Bear was trying to distract the guest who was bothering me. But he got too fancy with cartwheels and wheeled himself right into heat exhaustion.

One minute, we had been taking pictures with kids, and the next minute, Buzzy the Bear was prostrate on the ground, his big bobblehead detached next to him, revealing the red-faced teenager underneath. Every kid screamed. I guess I would have, too, if I had seen my hero beheaded.

"I caught him when he fell," I say. "But his costume zipper got my lip."

I lower my bag of ice to display my small battle scar. Fred hisses in air.

"I carried him to the dressing room with the medics. And then it started raining, and it was just a whole thing. See? Told you it wasn't as bad as it seemed!"

"Quinn ..." Fred starts.

"Let's focus on the here and now instead," I say, holding out my hands. "I left my shoes in the dressing room. I ran here in my slides because of the rain—no, don't give me that face, Fred—and security is bringing them now. No harm, no foul!"

"No, go back to the then and when," Fred says. "Who

4

was Buzzy defending you from? Do we need to get a chaperone for you again? One who *isn't* Buzzy?"

I normally have staff members accompany me to signings. They help mitigate the bold men who like my exposed shoulders and flighty fake laugh. But with our staff shortage lately, we've been utilizing Buzzy the Bear as my bodyguard instead. Kids love seeing him, so it knocks out two birds with one stone. Sort of. Buzzy is not effective with intimidation. His huge smile is too cute and welcoming.

"No," I say, ignoring his question of *who* Buzzy defended me from. "I'm capable of handling myself."

I am. Mostly because I'm getting too old for the shenanigans of older male guests. I'm almost thirty years old. If I can't do anything else, I can at least manage grabby men with a queenly smile.

"We can always bring back Ranger Randy," Fred suggests.

"*God*, no."

Ranger Randy is another Honeywood character known for his thick thighs and short shorts. We pulled him from rotation when one too many women slipped their number in his pocket. Plus, we always hire the cheesiest Ken doll–looking dudes with dead eyes, plastic smiles, and super-white teeth.

"I don't want Ranger Randy again," I say.

"Hey, Em, is Her Majesty still there?" Landon's voice crackles through the walkie.

I take it back; I'd rather have Ranger Randy than this man.

Emily's eyes dart up to me, and I roll my eyes dramatically.

"Yes," she says into the walkie with a laugh. "Quinn's here."

"Can you put her on?" Landon asks, his tone sweet yet oddly firm.

I shake my head and mouth, *No*, but Emily holds out the walkie to me with a grin anyway. I swear she gets a kick out of our bickering.

I take it and press the button. "Yes, Master of the Underworld?"

I toss a smile at Emily, who giggles back. Landon chuckles through the walkie, too, and my face falls.

"I kind of like that one," he says.

"It was for Emily's benefit. Go on."

"Honest question for you," Landon says.

"I might be dishonest with my answer."

"I'd expect nothing less."

I snort.

No. Don't laugh with him.

"Ahem, your question?" I ask.

"Did you steal my shorts?"

"Pardon?"

"I said, did you steal my shorts?"

"Why in the world would I steal your shorts?"

"That's a question I asked myself too."

"Then, you have your answer."

"I don't believe that answer," he says.

"I wouldn't either."

I *did* in fact steal his security uniform shorts. Or at least, the only clean pair in his size. I knew he would have to wear one size up. I liked the idea of him being annoyed all day.

Emily curls her lips in, hiding a not-so-hidden smile. Fred grunts out a mix between a chuckle and a scoff. At least my boss finds me funny.

I peer out the small hole cut into the stage curtains.

Our outdoor amphitheater is filling up. It's only because

6

it rained, and people are escaping under the canopy tarp, trying to bypass the errant raindrops falling from the trees. Plus, it's the last week before our theme park switches to its fall season schedule. Kids are taking advantage of what feels like the last days of summer.

But is our park as packed as it could be right before autumn? As packed as it has been in years past?

No. Not really.

"Big crowd?" Fred asks. I can hear the hopefulness in his voice.

"Bigger than usual," I lie. I don't like seeing him sad.

Honeywood Fun Park isn't perfect. I've worked here in some capacity since I was a teenager, and I don't think we have a single perfect roller coaster bone in our theme park body. Our bear mascot costumes have slightly matted fur, we still play '70s rock tunes over the speakers, and we're based on some kooky woman's children's book series that is barely in the cultural consciousness.

But despite its shortcomings, Honeywood has heart. You can see it in the way the sun rises over our stone Buzzy the Bear statue fountain. You can hear it in the tinkling bell of the gift shop or the symphony of employees' laughter. You can smell it in the bumblebee-shaped pancakes and syrup.

It's familiar. It's home.

We're just going through a rough time, is all.

Fred's mustache tilts downward at my answer.

"We'll be fine," I reassure, patting his arm.

"You're right," he says. His smile returns slowly, then all at once, jollier than before. "It's fine. It'll all be fine."

"Okay, well, let's not get *too* optimistic," I say.

He shrugs like a mother who just got asked if Santa was real, complete with a cheeky smile.

Ah, so he's got secrets today.

"What are you hiding, Fred?"

His smile only gets bigger.

The walkie-talkie buzzes to life.

"I'm here," Landon says.

I look through the curtain again, and there he is, in all his glory.

Landon Arden's tall frame crests over the hill to the outdoor amphitheater like he's freaking Prince Charming on a white horse. My sparkly high heels are in his hand, and from here, they look like a shining beacon of light. His button-up security shirt spans across his broad chest and—

Wait a second.

What is he wearing?

His shorts.

They're ...

Tight.

Real tight.

Oh crap.

Instead of picking one size up for his shorts, he chose one size *down*. Thick, very toned, *definitely doesn't skip leg day* thighs look like they're about to bust out of his brown shorts, Hulk-style. A UPS man gone wild.

My face heats. My jaw tenses. And it isn't until after the shame from my unbroken stare washes over me that I realize I've been gripping the curtain tight in my fist. Emily takes my place, peering through the hole. Her mouth gapes open.

"Oh my *God*."

"Keep it in your pants, Em," I say, leaning so that I have a clear view again.

With each step Landon takes, his shorts cling tighter, and with each inch they ride up, many women's eyes follow.

Good Lord.

"Stage left," I croak through the walkie. "And maybe wear work-appropriate shorts."

I see him tilt his chin to the side and press the walkie clipped to his shirt.

"I don't know what stage left means," he says. "And it's funny; I actually thought you'd be nicer to me, considering I'm the one bringing your shoes."

"Bribery doesn't work on me."

He doesn't reply, but I see him grin under that full chestnut-red beard.

Landon navigates through the crowd and makes his way to the opposite side of the stage.

"*Stage left, stage left,*" I hiss into the walkie.

"That means nothing," he answers.

I look across the stage right as he appears, notably on the *wrong* side of the backstage area. He glances out over the set pieces. The big wooden honeycomb standee spans from floor to ceiling.

"Dang, that's huge," he says.

"Wow, a sentence you haven't heard often, huh?" I quip.

"Thanks, Barb. You know how self-conscious I can be *down there.*"

I grind my jaw at his shortening of my nickname.

I practically smash the walkie button. "What you do *down there* is your business."

He chuckles. "Kinda sounds like you think about it enough for the both of us."

I pause, and we meet each other's eyes across the stage. Standing toe to toe—well, with forty feet between us—like a Western showdown. His slow, crooked smile spreads up his mouth, and I almost expect him to tip his hat or place a hand on a holster.

His smile is admittedly pleasant. Dimpled. And so, so happy. Like the world is one giant joke to him. Or maybe I am. Wouldn't be the first time he's laughed at me.

That's it. It's official. I'm gonna need blood pressure medication to stop from losing it with this man.

"Stop staring like a goon and just come around to the other side," I say into my walkie.

He leans toward the walkie clipped on his chest. "Nah, I'll just go behind."

"Behind?!"

He moves, and at that, Emily, Fred, and I rush to the very back of the stage, looking behind the backdrop curtain. On the opposite side, Landon is pressing his bulky chest against the brick wall. From this angle, you can see his muscled curves—the large chest, the tapered waist, the ... *ass.* Jeez, I bet he has some secret social media account where he posts all his stupid gym selfies. I bet he takes nude pictures just to admire them later.

Landon's boot hooks onto the edge of the curtain with his next step. And then I see it all happen in slow motion— the tug, the trip, the fall.

He tears down the curtain, falling on an open stage, tangled in a large pile of black fabric and brown clothes.

I'm cringing.

Emily is cringing.

Fred is grasping his chest, and I fear he might be having a heart attack.

Landon sits up onto his knees, throwing his head back. His hat slings across the stage. His reddish-brown hair hangs limp with a Clark Kent–like curl. The top button of his shirt is popped open. A tuft of amber-colored chest hair peeks out.

He looks like a sacrifice to the sex gods.

My mouth feels like it's been stuffed full of cotton. For a moment, I wonder if it could get worse. But then I notice the large rip just below his belt, exposing pizza-printed underwear.

I cover my mouth with my hand.

And after that, I hear a child yell loudly, "Grammy, look! It's Ranger Randy!"

It just got way, way worse.

2

Landon

I have a recurring nightmare that I'm naked on a stage, making breakfast.

If you look at my current situation from that perspective, I guess I'm not doing too bad. For one, there's no popping bacon threatening my lower bits. And two, I'm not cooking for an audience of over a hundred people.

However, I am on my knees, center stage, in my hometown theme park. Women and children are watching. And now, the crowd is chanting.

So ... not exactly ideal.

"Ran-ger Ran-dy!"

The chant coordinated so quickly that I can't remember when it started.

I reach up to re-button my shirt and cover up *some* parts of me, so I'm not going full Chippendales, but there's only string in its place.

"Ran-ger! Ran-dy!" The chant continues.

I don't like this type of attention. Even when I was on the football field, I wore a helmet that concealed my face. But now, I am openly disarmed with nowhere to go.

So, I do the only thing that makes sense to me in my panicked stupor.

I throw a thumbs-up, grin, and say, "Hi, kids! I'm Ranger Randy!"

My sentence slices through the audience like a fresh blade.

There's deafening silence.

The earth tilts on its axis.

Decades pass.

Centuries.

Then ... the crowd erupts into cheers.

They go absolutely bananas.

And it's not just the kids. *It's everyone.*

Teens are tugging at their hair. Moms are high-fiving. I might as well be headlining for KISS with an electric guitar and leather pants.

The walkie-talkie clipped to my chest pocket scratches on. "Quinn for Bennett."

My back stiffens at the sound of her voice, but there's no time to react before another lower one scratches over.

"Go for Bennett."

I twist the knob at the top, lowering the volume so the audience doesn't hear the faint sound of, "We need maintenance to Honey Pleasure Stage."

Not that they would hear anyway. They're too busy getting swept up in this moment.

I raise my hand, as if to say, *Let's tone it down,* but it only gets more cheers.

As head of security at Honeywood, I have contingency plans for everything. Guest threats. Storms. I even keep all the security uniforms at the park in case my guys forget theirs at home. I try to remain prepared. But this? Children screaming a fictional character's name at my face? This is out of my wheelhouse.

Suddenly, whoops and hollers explode at a volume I didn't know was possible. My heart pounds in my chest, but I quickly realize the cheers aren't for me. They're for *her*.

Stepping out onstage—barefoot with black nail polish— is Queen Bee.

Both my heart and my knees sink onto the wooden stage, melting into the lumps of fabric around me. My shoulders drop, my palms drag against the floor, and I try to keep myself upright. But it's hard to stay composed in the presence of royalty—under the eyes of my sister's best friend, Quinn Sauer.

Even at her pixie-sized height of five foot nothing, her presence is still formidable. The powder blush is worn like war paint on her cheeks, just above the shimmering pink lips. Only Quinn Sauer could make a gentle, bubbly character also look like she'd step on you. But not in a dominatrix way or anything.

Well … maybe.

She looks elegant. Powerful. Gorgeous.

"Ranger Randy?" she asks over the crowd. "Is that you crashing down in my Honeywood Forest?"

Queen Bee's voice is lighter than Quinn's usual low, sarcastic tone. It's airy. Aristocratic, but not too haughty to be unapproachable. It's just right.

A smile twitches at the corner of my lips, and my heart thumps.

There it is. The familiar feeling.

Her head whips to the audience, the elegant blonde curls bouncing with the motion.

"Why, friends of Honeywood, do you think our good

ranger is *startled*?" she asks, blinking out to them with doe eyes.

All the kids laugh at the question.

I clear my throat, realizing I've been sitting here in silence.

"I'm just ..." My voice sounds weird onstage. Echoey. "I'm just patrolling the forest!" I announce. It sounds forced and awful.

Improvisation isn't my strong suit by any stretch of the imagination.

"And is Honeywood safe, Ranger Randy?" Quinn continues.

"Safe as a warm blanket," I say with an immediate cringe.

"A blanket that you seem to be tangled in," she says.

The kids clutch their stomachs in laughter. Quinn holds her hand up to her mouth and smiles back at them.

"And how did you return to our secret forest, Ranger Randy?" Quinn continues, the deceptively sweet voice floating over to me like a kiss from an angel. Before I can answer, she turns to the audience. "Do you think maybe ... he tried to fly in here like Bumble the Bee?" she asks them conspiratorially.

"Yeah!" the kids say through collective giggles.

"Or maybe," she continues, "did he try to growl through the forest like Buzzy the Bear?"

"Yeah!" A more enthusiastic chorus of agreement.

"Well, something tells me," she says, tapping her finger to her chin as she looks back at me, "you've come to bring me a gift?"

It's been so long since I've seen Quinn perform as Queen Bee. I forgot how talented she was.

I can't speak. I'm too distracted by her soft Barbie

blonde hair. Overwhelmed by how much I've missed her. Humbled by how unbelievably *screwed* I am.

I've avoided Quinn for almost two weeks since I moved back. We've talked over the walkies, sure, but this? Her dressed as Queen Bee? It's like a dart to my heart, right on the bull's-eye.

"A gift, Your Majesty?" I barely get out the words.

"Why, I believe you have my shoes," she says. "My *magical* shoes."

She oohs and aahs into the crowd. The kids echo it with giggles.

"Right! Yes," I say, fumbling to grab the sparkling heels near me. "Of course." I stand, shifting out from under the mess I've made. "Your Majesty, if I may ..."

"Oh, good sir, I'll come to you!" Quinn says hurriedly, walking toward me with her hands held out beside her.

When she reaches me, she leans in toward my ear. My heart pounds so loud that I wonder if she can hear it. The scent of her is intoxicating. She smells sweet as honey.

Then, her normal voice comes through with a hiss-whisper of, "Don't move, Pizza Butt."

There's the woman I know.

I smile. "Gotta say, I'm loving these new nicknames."

"No, your *shorts*," she says.

I squint at her for a moment, taking in her big green eyes and the scent of her spearmint breath before the words hit me.

Oh. Pizza butt.

I finally realize why the cool air felt like it was disproportionately hitting my backside.

"I ripped them, didn't I?" I whisper back.

"Bingo."

Yep. Pizza butt.

I wore my lucky pair of pizza-printed underwear.

Or is it the doughnut pair of underwear that's lucky?

Quinn looks at me with a raised eyebrow. I can tell there's an insult at the tip of her tongue, begging to be said. Before she can, I sink down to one knee before her.

The audience gasps. So does she.

I hold out one hand, palm up, with the shoe in my other hand.

"Your Majesty?" I prompt.

Quinn looks from me to the audience, then back down to the shoe.

"What are you doing?" she hisses.

"Literally anything," I whisper. "Give me your foot, Barb."

She hesitates, inhaling sharply, before grabbing a fistful of her skirt and lifting it.

She grits her teeth. "No funny business."

I reach out for her ankle. I run my hand up the back, wrapping my fingers one by one around the bottom of her toned calf. She sucks in air as my other hand slides the glittery shoe onto her foot. It's a perfect fit.

I glance up at her. Quinn stares at me below her lashes, blinking once, twice, a million times. I feel like I can't move under that stare, like my knee is cemented to the floor.

It brings me back to when we were teens—me passing her locker in the hallway, watching her laugh with my sister, only for me to be shepherded away by my teammates. But even if my friends and football weren't so demanding, it wouldn't have mattered. Quinn didn't give me the time of day after sophomore year. If she'd stared at me then how she's staring at me now, I wouldn't have known what to do. Hell, I guess I still don't.

The amphitheater crowd is unmoving and unspeaking.

A camera flashes in the audience. Quinn's fists clench the skirt of her gown with white knuckles.

"Why, thank you," she finally says, her voice an echo in the dead air around us. Her chest slowly breathes in and out.

And I say the only thing that makes sense in my mind at that very moment. "Anything for you, My Queen."

A collective sigh washes over the audience. Goose bumps trail the back of her leg. My fingers twitch against her.

I don't know what to say now. Quinn—opening and closing her mouth, resembling an angelfish—doesn't seem to know either. Thankfully, we're saved.

"Your Majesty!" a loud, goofy voice yells offstage. "Your Majesty!"

The floorboards squeak and moan as someone in a Buzzy the Bear suit comes barreling out, stumbling in front of us onstage.

The crowd bursts into laughter. The tension breaks. I breathe a sigh of relief, but when I look to Quinn, her eyes are narrowed.

My mouth tugs up at the edges into a grin just because I know it'll only make her face get that much redder.

It does.

I remove my hand from her calf, securing her other shoe much faster than I did the first, lest she sacrifice her job and whacks me upside the head.

When I rise, I tower over her. She evaluates me where I stand, as if she's not more than a foot shorter than me. Her presence has all the height she needs.

My lips quirk into a smile, and she rolls her eyes before switching back into Queen Bee mode. She twirls off with the man in the Buzzy suit. Laughing. Giggling. My chest tightens. I try to relax the tension with a sigh.

At least my job here is done.

But that's when I notice that the audience's eyes are still planted on me—Ranger Randy—instead of Buzzy and Queen Bee.

3

Quinn

I slam the newspaper down. "This is ridiculous!"

All three of my friends raise their coffee mugs up to their mouths like they're the *hear no evil, see no evil, speak no evil* monkeys. They don't have to say anything. The *Cedar Cliff Chatter* spells it out clear as day.

IS RANGER RANDY'S ROLLICKING RETURN TO HONEYWOOD TO ROMANCE ROYALTY?

"Ranger Randy isn't rollicking," I bite out, grabbing my mug from the edge of the table.

I pace our kitchen, chugging the coffee. Lorelei winces as I gulp. And, sure, yes, the coffee burns like hell. But I need the fire coursing through me.

"*Romance Royalty*?! Christ."

"Jaymee's good at selling newspapers," Lorelei says, holding out a hand to take my now-empty coffee cup. "You can't deny that."

"She gets better every time too," Theo says, tapping the headline. "I want her to write my obituary."

I lift an eyebrow at Theo. She holds her hands up with a grin and a shrug, then smooths back a piece of her curly black hair behind her ear, which only bounces back into place.

Lorelei gestures again for my mug. I hand it to her.

"I will say," Lorelei says, walking to our coffeepot to refill it, "y'all look super cute together."

I sigh. If she wasn't my best friend, I might throw her a glare. As it is, I would never. But she's wrong about the newspaper.

"The picture isn't cute. It's egregious," I say. "It's insulting."

The newspaper's front page pictures me—or rather, Queen Bee—with my bare foot extended, and on one knee is Landon with his hand on my ankle.

I remember how I felt in that moment—uncomfortable, shocked, irritated ... but in the picture, you see none of that. Instead, I look so deeply in love with Landon that it's sickening.

I groan right as Emory snorts into his coffee.

"What are you laughing at?" I ask, crossing my arms.

Emory shakes his head. "Nothing," he says, feigning innocence.

"Yeah, *right*, nothing," I counter. "I can kick you out, ya know."

Emory is a recent addition to our friend group. He doesn't live here with me and Lorelei, but he might as well with how often he's at our breakfast nook. The two of them started dating a couple of months ago after their lawsuit somehow transformed into a secret love affair that made front-page news. That's when we learned the *Cedar Cliff Chatter* takes no prisoners.

If you overlook Emory's thick, judging eyebrows and

permanent frown, he's not too bad. Plus, he's a goopy mush of feelings for my best friend, and I can't hate a man who looks at Lorelei like she walks on water.

"I hope the Buzzy statue falls on Landon, is all I'm saying," I say.

"Quinn!" Lorelei says, twisting on her heel.

Emory chuckles into his coffee mug.

Another good thing about Emory: I can tell morbid jokes and have someone else in the room laugh.

"You know, I think it's about time Queen Bee had a knight in shining armor," Theo says.

"You don't live here either; I can kick you out too," I say with a smile in her direction. "Queen Bee is an independent woman with a forest to rule over. She doesn't need some silly ranger to help her out."

"Oh, come on, but this is adorable," Theo coos, pointing to the picture of us once more.

"*So* adorable," Lorelei agrees.

A crack signals our front door opening. Nobody in Cedar Cliff knocks unless the door is locked. And in a town where everyone knows everyone, doors are rarely bolted shut, and you're never surprised at who walks through it.

Except now.

The so-called knight in shining armor himself appears.

"Hey, hey," Landon says.

He is too smug. You can tell in the way he poses, how he leans against the doorjamb with his hand sliding into his pocket, and how his eyebrows rise with a *hello*. I want to roll my eyes to the top of my head.

Give me a break.

"Hey, Land-o," Theo chimes at the same time I bite out, "Why are you here?"

His brown eyes sweep over to me.

"Well, I'm here to bug you, of course," Landon says, eyes not leaving mine. He tilts his chin down. "Am I succeeding, Barb?"

I scoff to cover the annoying heartbeat ringing in my ears.

I forget how irritatingly perfect his face is. The straight nose, the full lips, the trimmed chestnut-colored beard. I bet if you folded his face in half, it would be an exact mirror of the other side—immaculately symmetrical aside from the small freckle on his left cheek.

"Go back to Tennessee," I mutter under my breath.

He laughs, as if I'm joking.

I'm not.

"I also came to drop these off," Landon says, holding out a plastic bin with an assortment of muffins, Danishes, and doughnut holes and sliding them toward Emory. "Thanks for helping me move."

"Oh, you show-off!" Lorelei says playfully. "You must have known I had muffins going too."

Landon taps the side of his temple with a grin. "Twin thing."

"Now, mine won't be nearly as good," she says, staring at the oven.

"Nah," he says. "They'll still be perfect."

I click my tongue, and Landon notices. He nudges my elbow with his. I don't return the gesture, though the sparks fly up my shoulder like a current through a wire.

I hate that he still has this effect on me. But more than that, I hate that, at one point, I was naive enough to believe his carefully concocted fantasy. The first time I had dinner at the Ardens' house, fourteen-year-old Landon was leaning against the doorjamb, just as he was moments ago.

"Who invited Barbie?" he asked.

23

I remember how my stomach dropped when he said it. How his mouth tipped up into his crooked smile. How two dimples pressed into his smooth, beardless face like thumbprints in cookie dough. How I, also being fourteen and in awe of his confidence, tried to mirror his charming smile through my pink braces, moving a strand of my blonde hair behind my ear.

"I don't look like Barbie," I answered with an embarrassed laugh.

I still had my prepubescent chubby cheeks and a crippling fear of pool parties. I was far from Barbie.

"It's the hair," he said with his dimpled smile.

That was all it took for me to fall desperately in love with my best friend's twin brother.

I remember going home and writing in my diary, *Mrs. Landon Arden. Mrs. Landon Arden. Mrs. Landon Arden.*

It was the beginning of the end.

Mrs. Landon Arden would haunt me for years—whispered to me in the halls by his friends, scribbled on notes tucked in my locker, written in my yearbook, where I had to use a bottle of whiteout just to make it disappear.

I wish I'd never written it down. I wish that diary had never been found. I wish a lot of things were different, but that's not how life works.

I take an extra step away from Landon, letting the spark through my shoulder simmer. It's not until I'm refocusing on the people around us that I notice Lorelei gaping at us, her jaw dropped. She looks down to the newspaper, then back to us.

"Oh my God, wait, what if they *did*?" Lorelei says, almost in a whisper.

"Who did what?" I ask.

"What if Ranger Randy and Queen Bee were ... you know?" she says, a smile spreading over her face.

My stomach curls in on itself.

"This is a family park, Lorelei," I deadpan, making Theo spit out her coffee.

"Not *that!*" Lorelei says with a laugh. "What if the characters were dating? It'd be sweet."

What if Ranger Randy and Queen Bee were dating?

Lorelei never knew about Landon's friends and their incessant bullying. I couldn't bear to ruin her good opinion of her brother. Not when he was her other best friend. But if she knew about all our history, her sweet self wouldn't be suggesting this.

"Not happening," I say, cutting the air with my palms. "They are not dating."

Landon chuckles. "You make it sound like the end of the world."

I look up to him with a blank expression, and he smiles back.

That's what bothers me the most. Landon acts like nothing ever happened. Like my diary was never found. Like his friends weren't the people who reminded me of it all the time.

"Wait, but she's right!" Theo says, looking between us. "That would be *super* cute."

I slice the air with my palms again. "No, no, no."

"It would just be for show," Lorelei says. "Plus, we need something to get attendance up."

I gesture like a karate kid cutting a block, harder and more definitive. "How many ways can I say a big ol' *no*?"

"Hmm," Lorelei muses, glancing between us.

I don't like this look of hers—a brainstorming look. The

look normally reserved for her role as marketing manager at Honeywood. She has a knack for analyzing roller coasters and intuitively knowing what will make them appealing to guests.

Is she seeing what could make Landon and me appealing?

The oven dings.

"Well, it was a thought," Lorelei says, putting on oven mitts and taking out the muffins. She glances at Emory. "Okay, I'm gonna let these cool, then pack up. Sound good?"

Emory nods, tipping back his coffee mug. "Ready when you are, beautiful."

"They're not for us?" Landon asks.

"We have yours," Theo says, her mouth already full of Emory's gifted baked goods. "We're covered."

"Theo!" Lorelei says through a laugh.

"What? He doesn't use a box recipe!"

"Who are yours for, Lore?" I ask Lorelei, avoiding Landon's pastries that, honest to God, smell like heaven.

She grins. "Well, Fred says we have a special visitor today."

I lift an eyebrow. "Who?"

I almost forgot that beneath all the Ranger Randy drama, Fred *was* acting weird.

"He wouldn't say," Lorelei says. "But I have a sneaking suspicion."

"Well, go on," Theo says, biting into a doughnut hole. "You're dying to say it."

"I think it might be ... Honey Pleasure," Lorelei practically squeals.

Landon snorts out a laugh. "Good God, you're kidding."

But of course, Lorelei, with her love of Honeywood, would be excited about that woman.

Honey Pleasure is the author of *Birds, Bees, and Bears*—the children's book series that birthed Honeywood Fun Park.

Honey is a mystery. I once heard she owns a domesticated grizzly bear. There's also a rumor that two out of her three ex-husbands mysteriously disappeared in the '90s. And then there's the popular theory strictly among Honeywood employees that she's also a porn star. Given her name, I'd buy into that theory. But also, given that she's seventy years old, at minimum, I desperately hope it's just bad gossip.

"That old bird?" I ask.

"Quinn!" Lorelei chastises. "She's a treasure."

"She's practically a *myth*," I say.

"The internet says she's alive," Theo says, turning to display her phone and popping another doughnut hole in her mouth.

Lorelei bounces on the balls of her feet. "Well, I've got the muffins either way!" With an extra squeal, she starts to delicately place the muffins in a plastic container.

My best friend is everything wonderful in the world. If there was anyone who could be a real-life fairy-tale princess, it would be Lorelei with her soft voice and sunny outlook. I love fairy tales, folklore, and classics. They're why I attempted a literature major in college.

Though what society doesn't tell you in those classic stories of princesses, knights, and unicorns is that not everyone deserves that romantic, happy ending. Sometimes, you're saddled with your father's cynicism and your mother's mental predispositions. Sometimes, you're not the woman being kissed out of a deep slumber, but instead, you're the one who succumbed to the rotten apple.

Lorelei got her Prince Charming in Emory. But mine turned out to be a toad.

Landon looks down at his watch, and I can't help but notice the trailing veins up his arm. The defined wrists. The way he exhales as he looks at the time, as if he wishes there were more of it.

An unfairly handsome toad.

His eyes flick over to me, and I look away.

"You carpooling with us?" he asks.

"I start my shift later than the full-timers," I reply, avoiding his gaze.

"Oh," he muses, his face falling. "Right."

Yeah, laugh it up, buddy. I'm still not a salaried employee.

I don't talk to him while Lorelei and Emory grab their bags. I don't say good-bye when he waves to me and Theo. I barely move when the door shuts behind them and the sound of Emory's and Landon's trucks pull out from the driveway.

I dread that sound in the coming months.

With the season ending, I'll start to work at Slow Riser again. It's my full-time coffee shop job that holds me over in the winter while Honeywood is closed. It isn't glamorous, but it is how I keep my seasonal Queen Bee gig year after year.

I'd be lying if I said I didn't want something more—maybe stage managing or writing—but I'm far from qualified. I dropped out of college junior year, and even with all my theater experience, having no degree is still holding me back. I've considered going back to college. But I'm not sure I trust myself not to have a repeat of the last time when I crashed and burned.

"*Romancing royalty*," Theo says, breaking me from my

reverie. She's got the newspaper in her hands again, shaking her head. Her eyes dart to mine with a smile. "I'd pay to see you and Landon pretend to like each other."

We both burst into laughter.

I highly doubt it will come to that.

4

Landon

I've been away from Cedar Cliff for two years, and I almost forgot mountain mornings at Honeywood Fun Park could be this relaxing. I forgot about the smell of coffee brewing at the in-park's restaurant, The Bee-fast Stop. I forgot about The Grizzly's roar as the roller coaster cycles through its test runs. I forgot about the way the rising sun beams across the main strip of walkway at the heart of the park.

The buzzing cicadas and chirping birds serenade my and my sister's morning walk through Honeywood. It's a ritual Lorelei's had for years, and with me tagging along, it gives her the chance to show off new additions since I've been away—the fixed flume for The Canoodler, the new paint job on Little Pecker's Joyride, the repaired windows for the Bumblebee Greenhouse. She'll be Fred's successor for the general manager position once he retires, and her passion for the park is engrained in everything she says.

It's a nice morning, but it is the Deep South after all, and the humidity is still stifling. So, after about an hour into our heat-filled walk, I find relief indoors.

I sit in the security office, creaking in the cracked leather chair. The old desktop boots up, whirring like a rocket bursting into space. I don't know what year this computer is from, but the white square exterior isn't encouraging. I attempt to check my email, but the screen turns blue before I can open the one from Fred.

Wonderful.

I instead review the paper logs from the overnight security guard. It's blank. Probably a slow night. I look to the piles of chip bags in the trash. *Definitely* a slow night.

With it being my second week on the job, I still haven't found my rhythm. Both in the park and in Cedar Cliff.

I'm not sure what I expected to feel after moving back to my hometown. Pride at finally buying a house instead of renting? Excitement with getting a management job at Honeywood? I guess I do.

Isn't all that what sent me packing from Tennessee to begin with?

My hard-as-nails boss at my old warehouse job sat me down one day and asked what I wanted out of life. Why I wasn't instead cooking, like I loved to do, or why I hadn't settled down, or why this, or why that. I finally started wondering all of that myself. By the time he left our company to become a full-time musician in Nashville, I had done my own soul-searching.

I decided, if I was going to do anything, I'd probably pursue culinary school. It was a dream I had as a kid, and now, at thirty, it might be possible. Issue is, I cleared most of my savings just to purchase my house here.

I'm just trying to get my bearings and move into my thirties with some dignity. A house. Friends. Maybe eventually a family.

I've got two out of the three. But that third piece is ... complicated at best.

When I lived in Tennessee, there were a lot of women who laughed at my jokes. Women who flirted with me at the bar. Women who smiled when I walked into a room. And yet, somehow, my heart is only drawn to the one woman who probably wouldn't even tell me if I had spinach in my teeth.

My sister's best friend has held my heart for far too long.

Sometimes, I wonder if my prolonged crush on Quinn Sauer is some form of karmic torture. She's never forgiven me for finding her dropped diary in the hallway of Cedar Cliff High, for having it ripped from my hands by Michael, our football team's captain, and for not getting it back afterward.

Those little *Mrs. Landon Arden*s, written in cursive by my best friend's sister, haunted me for months. Michael and the rest of the team wouldn't let me live it down. They'd pull flowers from my parents' gardens to make a fake wedding bouquet. They'd ask me when the *big day* was.

Quinn and I were never really the same after that and yet ... and yet ...

She was intoxicating to me. She had no fear. She didn't hesitate to flash the middle finger to me and my friends once she learned what the gesture meant. She was a master at the cold shoulder, and my blood pounded when I watched her long blonde hair swish behind her, like it had an attitude all its own.

Even though it was over a decade ago, nothing has changed. I can't seem to fall for anyone who won't scowl in my direction like she does, who doesn't have her confidence, her uniqueness, or her sarcastic wit.

And, yes, I know how it sounds. Feel free to laugh at my boyhood crush, my cruel kink, or whatever it has become. But sometimes, those teenage fantasies have a way of weaving into your being like yarn in a crocheted sweater. Nobody forgets their first love. Or infatuation, I suppose. Heck if I know the truth, and it makes my head hurt to even think about it. All I know is, forming a family seems off my radar until I can get over her. For now, I'll stick with tiny accomplishments, like a house and a job.

I try to distract myself the rest of the morning with Honeywood training videos, watching outdated workplace VHS tapes. I keep looking to my radio, hoping for a call, but there's nothing. After a couple of hours, I finally stand up. I just need some fresh air, maybe to walk a circuit around the park, introduce myself to more people.

But right as I jerk open the door, I tug in a person clutching the handle on the opposite side.

There's a symphony of dinging, clinging, and clattering as I catch them in my arms. There's not much to grab. The person is all featherlight limbs and harsh elbows. I lift them up as they hold a death grip on my forearms. I'm not sure what I expect, but it isn't who I see.

My hands steady up an old woman. Her wrinkled skin shrivels near her lips, as if she were a mother who both loves her child and is simultaneously disappointed by them. Turquoise beads line her neck along with other necklaces of different sizes and material. Her hands are decorated with various eccentric rings—wooden, gold, and some type of spoon?

"Apologies, ma'am," I say, keeping a hand on her forearm. "This is an employee-only area."

"Good, then I will help myself," she says. Her voice is

determined yet accented by the distinct wobble of someone who has spent many years talking.

I can't help but smile at her tenacity and weirdness.

She wears thick black glasses that look almost cartoony in comparison to her frail figure. Her hair is white, to the point of nearly being blue. But then, as I look closer, I realize that it is in fact dyed the fairest of baby blues.

Huh.

"What are you smiling at?" she sneers.

"I can't let you come in here," I say before repeating, "Employees only."

"*Let* me?" she says, her eyes bulging, almost filling the massive black frames of her glasses. "You're funny. A funny man."

She releases herself from me and pats my elbow. The gesture makes me laugh.

"Where am I?"

"This is the security office, ma'am," I clarify.

"Oh good, so you *can* be useful."

I grin. When I do, her face lights up.

"Those dimples, my *God*," she says, reaching up to drag her hands down her own cheeks. "Yes, you're definitely my tour guide today."

"I'm sorry. I feel like I'm missing something here," I say with a laugh. "What's your name?"

"Yuck," she says, shaking her head. "How insulting."

I cross my arms. "Insulting?"

"Echoing me is not becoming of you either."

I squint, and my mind reels through possibilities, but I can't place her.

"Who are you here to see?" I ask.

"You're security," she says. "Shouldn't you know?"

"I'm new," I say. "Admittedly, I don't know much."

"Good heavens, this place ..." The old woman looks up to the ceiling, as if the world were falling down around her.

I chuckle. "You gotta help me out here. Let's start with your name."

She leans in conspiratorially. I have to bend at the waist to meet her.

"I *own* this park," she whispers.

I jolt back, looking her up and down.

"Honey Pleasure," she announces. "At your service. Well, not really. You're at mine."

"Author of *Birds, Bees, and Bears*," I breathe.

"The very one. Now, escort me to the staff area, if you *please*."

The *please* doesn't sound as polite as it should have been, and I think she might have intended it that way. But the directness of it all still makes me laugh.

My walkie scratches on my chest.

"Fred for Landon."

Honey's eyes dart to my walkie, then back to me.

"That's my man," she says, pointing her ring-filled finger at my chest.

"You're here to see Fred?" I ask.

She nods with a solidified, "Mmhmm."

I press the button on my walkie, not breaking eye contact with her as she listens intently.

"Go for Landon," I say.

There's a moment of dead air and then, "We've got a problem at Honey Pleasure Stage."

Honey presses a hand to her chest, creating a symphony from her jewelry knocking together.

"Named after me?" she asks.

I laugh. "You didn't know?"

Her expression drops, and she waves her hand at me.

"I'm being facetious," she says. "*Of course* it's named after me. And you can take me there."

I chuckle, pressing the walkie's button again. "Be there in one minute. Bringing a fire-breathing dragon with me."

Her eyes dart to me. I lift a brow with a grin.

"Oh, I like you," she says.

5

Quinn

I've never quite grown out of playing dress-up.

I love the smiles when people see me dressed as Queen Bee for the first time. I love the stars in children's eyes as they come face-to-face with royalty. I love how kids dress up in miniature versions of my pink ball gown. I love looking out at the line and seeing Buzzy the Bear headbands. I love watching fanny pack–strapped adults try to wrangle children who are too busy waving their autograph books in the air to notice how stressed their parents are.

I love all of it.

Click!

Another photo, another autograph, another royal wave.

I've perfected this character. It's one of the few things I'm truly good at. And normally, it's all sparkles and rainbows and bumblebees. At least, until someone like Handsy Hugh shows up.

Handsy Hugh is your average grandpa from out of town, who takes pictures with Queen Bee so he can also get a handful of my gown in his palm. He's single-handedly—or single-hand-fully—taught me not to trust older people.

They're the ones that lure you into gingerbread houses and prepare you for a stew.

As Queen Bee, handling these types of old men becomes a delicate dance. Little girls are watching. You can't just tell them their grandpa likely has three restraining orders and still laughs at secretary jokes. So, when Hugh walks up, places an arm around my waist, and very slowly drifts his hand downward to the peak of my ball gown, I have to maintain my smile.

He's so predictable.

Under my dress, I apply pressure to his toes with the heel of my sparkling shoe.

His arm jerks backward.

"Oh, pardon me!" I coo.

I can see his face contort, but he's got his kids with him —one of whom wears a Queen Bee crown—so it's not like he can retaliate.

Coward.

He walks away, saving his battle for another day, I'm sure. In his place is a little girl in pigtails, rubbing her eyes with her little balled-up fists.

Now, *this* is why I love my job. Not because of creepy geezers.

I bend down at the waist. "Hi, honey," I say. "You all right?"

Anytime you can insert the word *honey* into your vernacular at Honeywood Fun Park, you're golden. People love that stuff.

"She's just excited to meet you," her mom says.

I stay squatted in front of the Buzzy and Bumble fountain. The sun shimmers between their statues, glistening with water. My crown glitters in the light's beams. The little girl laughs with bright eyes as she hugs me.

We're picture-perfect.

Click!

Memory made.

I start to rise, but the little girl's thumb reaches out to wipe my cheek before I can lean back. Guests aren't supposed to touch me, as evidenced by Hugh, but sometimes, the kids don't know any better. You couldn't pay me enough to swat them away though.

"You're melting," she says.

I let out my most gracious queenly laugh.

"It's a hot day in Honeywood," I answer. "Sometimes, even queens look messy. Did you know that?" I tap her nose with my manicured finger. "And it's okay to look messy."

And with that, I take my cue—my *melting makeup* cue.

I cup my hand to my ear, asking, "Is that my dear Bumble I hear?"

The kids all look around, but there is no sound.

That's because I made it up.

Theater magic, friends.

"I must go," I say, gathering my dress fabric in my hands and dancing off. It's the art of looking like a cartoon without actually looking like a cartoon.

I ballerina my way to the gate behind The Bee-fast Stop, reaching the hidden door through the bushes that leads to the dressing area for staff.

I close the door behind me and lean back the second it clicks shut. Air-conditioning blows on my face.

Bliss.

The dressing room is a tight space, holding racks of yellow Honeywood polos, a stacked washer and dryer, and the mounted whiteboard with schedules and notes. Three different mascot heads of Buzzy are hung along the wall. I always think they look like stuffed hunting trophies.

I walk over to the wall of mirrors, sitting with a cotton ball and makeup remover. Good thing I left when I did. I was five minutes away from my makeup rivaling The Joker.

There's a knock at the door, and I call out, "Nobody's naked!"

The dressing room door opens, and Fred appears behind me in the mirrored reflection.

"Quite a performance out there," he says, waving a hand in front of his face to cool down. He's beet red.

"You might need to reapply," I say. I reach into my makeup bag and toss sunscreen to him.

"Ah, thanks," he says, popping the top off. "I noticed ol' Hugh was here again. He didn't try anything, did he?"

"No," I lie. I don't like to rock Fred's boat. I can handle one irresponsible guest just fine.

"Okay, good," Fred says skeptically. "I actually came here to talk, if you have the time."

"You're the boss," I say, swiveling in my stool to face him with half-done eyeliner. "If you say I get a break, I get a break."

"Good," he says with a laugh. "Let's talk about Ranger Randy."

My stomach drops, and the only thing I can do is comically roll my eyes as hard as I can.

Fred only laughs more.

"What about him?" I ask.

"I have ideas."

"We're not seriously considering bringing him back, are we?"

"Possibly."

"Why?" I hate how my voice sounds like a whine.

"It's a perfect time to try him out again," he says. "The

40

audience reception when he fell on stage was fantastic. And you know numbers have already been low as it is."

"People still come for the fall events, though," I say. "That'll increase numbers plenty."

He snorts. "Buzzy with devil horns has never been a hit. Too demonic for the small-town crowd."

"I think it's cute," I say with a smile, then consider further. "I mean, okay, sure, that's a decent point. Well, we could just ..." I pause. "Never mind."

I don't continue with my thought, even when Fred's eyebrows rise to invite it.

Sure, I have a lot of ideas for our theater department. But it's always a bitter subject when we talk about my role at Honeywood. A college dropout isn't qualified even if I did study literature and theater and have the experience to back it up. My ideas are probably not even that good. How good can I be given I couldn't finish the program?

"Tell me what you have in mind," Fred says.

"Why?" I ask. "You know it can't lead to anything."

He sighs and tilts his head to the side. "You're smart," he says.

I scoff, which only makes him smile more.

"You have good ideas. And lest you forget, I read a lot of your college scripts." He nudges my shoulder. "You're a good writer, Quinn."

"I can't get a full-time job writing or stage managing or anything here, Fred. I need a degree and ..."

"And what if ... I said I had something that might come up?"

I narrow my eyes at him, trying my best impression at reading minds. He squints back, and I laugh.

"Why are you pushing Randy so much?" I ask. "And

what possible *thing* is coming up? Why are you so dead set on change? Nobody likes change."

"You're right," he says with a grin. "Who *actually* likes change?"

I hear the sarcasm in his tone. But as I open my mouth to ask him what he means, the door busts open, and a head pokes in.

It's Lorelei, doe eyes bulging, fingernails tapping on the doorframe.

"Fred, we've got a problem."

It turns out, the guests of Honeywood Fun Park like change very much.

The show at the amphitheater doesn't start for another thirty minutes, yet it's overflowing with guests. You'd think the Pope was about to turn up.

Fred, Lorelei, and I arrive backstage to the loud chants of, "*Rang-er Ran-dy!*"

Chants turn to shouts turn to boos.

The guests have gone wild.

Emily wrings her hands together, looking between us, saying, "How the heck are we supposed to calm them down?"

I glance to Fred right as Emily lets out a small squeak of nervous energy.

"Tell them something," I suggest.

"*I'm* not going out there!" Emily practically wails. I see the shimmer in her eyes.

Good Lord, she's going to cry.

Lorelei pulls her in for a hug. Emily settles her head against her chest like we're in the middle of a war.

I lift an eyebrow in Fred's direction, and he sighs, running a hand over the sparse hair on his head. He might pull out the rest of it.

The crowd gets louder. I think I hear a few thuds.

"Are they *throwing* things?" Emily asks. Her panic is seeping out of her pores.

"Okay," Lorelei says, "let's pull it together."

I finally groan. "This is ridiculous. I'll go out there. It's not a big deal."

"You're dressed as Queen Bee," Fred says. "You can't do that. It'll break the character illusion to talk to guests about the park."

I sigh. "Maybe they'll be a bit nicer to a fictional character rather than someone in a Honeywood polo."

He shakes his head, but I'm already patting out the wrinkles in my skirt and straightening my posture.

This will be fine. It's a performance. I've done this a million times. I hold my head high and step out from the wing.

The crowd quiets the moment my heels hit the stage. I walk to the center, stepping over a syrupy scrap of bumble-bee-shaped pancake.

All right, well, that's just rude.

"Bees and bears of the Honeywood Forest," I start, but I don't get to finish.

A lone voice yells, "Where's Ranger Randy?"

I pause, my hands steadying in front of me, mid-queenly gesture.

I attempt again. "He was visiting Honeywood and—"

"We want him back!"

"We want the shorts!"

It's then that I realize it's not even *kids* here. It's women. Adult women. And a handful of men.

43

"WE WANT THE SHORTS! WE WANT THE SHORTS!"

The script of polite, default Queen Bee responses that I've known for over ten years is stuck in my stunned brain.

I hear Fred say into the walkie backstage, "Fred for Landon. We've got a problem at Honey Pleasure Stage."

My heart stammers in my chest when Landon's low voice replies, "Be there in one minute. Bringing a fire-breathing dragon with me."

6

Landon

I didn't expect to break up a borderline riot today, but so it went.

Fred tells us to meet in his office after we finish clearing out the amphitheater.

Honey grips my arm tighter while he speaks.

"I love a man with a mustache," she says in a whisper that isn't quiet one bit.

"You're impossible," I say with a laugh, then we walk arm in arm to the main offices at the front of the park.

On the outside, the employee offices look like a dilapidated saloon to blend into the country theme. But on the second floor, overlooking the midway, are rows of small offices, closets, and conference rooms.

The offices are outdated, with signs of wear—old hardwoods, threadbare carpets. Everything is used yet immaculately clean and smelling faintly of lavender. One particular conference room has a small vase of fresh yellow tulips. If I had to guess, it's an addition, likely from my sister, in preparation for Honey Pleasure's visit.

Honey pauses to get mineral water from the vending

machine, so I walk ahead and try for Lorelei's office. Someone else lands against my chest at the turn.

My hands balance on Quinn's waist, trying to steady her. She still has that sugary honey scent, yet it's now combined with coffee. A natural mix of sweet yet bitter.

"You're like a brick wall," she comments, hands lingering on my chest before she instantly jerks back.

I'm honestly not sure if it's an insult. But considering this is the second time I've bumped into someone today, I don't have room to talk. Plus, there's the whole *frozen by her biting remarks* thing.

God, she's a firecracker.

Quinn's eyes dart down to my hands. I don't realize I'm still holding her waist, so I let go. Heat courses through me. Her eyes search mine.

Honey's voice breaks us from our moment.

"Is this my Queen Bee?"

When Quinn freezes, Honey continues with a wave of her hand.

"No need to guess who I am," Honey says. "Nobody knows me anyway. I'm Honey."

"Oh," Quinn says, then blinks before her eyes grow wide. "OH. Hi, yes, I'm Queen Bee. Well, Quinn," she says with an extended hand.

She tries to follow up with a smile, but I can already tell it's one of her fake ones. She just had the guests of Honeywood throwing pancakes at her, so I don't exactly blame Quinn if she's not in the schmoozing mood.

Honey assesses her—from the top of her messy blonde bun to her faded Honeywood T-shirt, to her cutoff black shorts.

"Much less ... elegant out of costume," Honey says.

I clear my throat loudly as Quinn flushes a deep red.

"Pardon," Quinn says. It's not a question. Her attempt at a kind facade falls.

Oh boy.

Honey laughs it off, waving her hand. "I'm joking, Queenie. Don't worry. Just an old woman here to make your life miserable."

Quinn sucks in her cheek. "Not *too* miserable, I hope?" Quinn asks.

"Just miserable enough for anyone who dares to cross me," Honey says with a beaming smile.

"What fun," Quinn deadpans with the fakest grin I've ever seen in my life. All teeth. Doesn't reach her eyes.

"*All right*," I quickly interject. "Let's keep the hallway moving."

I usher Quinn onward, and she tenses under my touch.

Honey wraps her hand through the crook of my arm once more.

"She doesn't like me," Honey says.

I don't think she meant for Quinn to hear, but I still see Quinn's fingers twitch by her side.

"Maybe don't pick fights with your leading lady?" I suggest.

Honey *hmms* in response.

When we enter Fred's office, he and Lorelei are already there. He stands behind his desk, hands splayed out over the scattered papers. We're quiet, only serenaded by the muffled sound of guests' laughter outside. It's like enjoyment is just within reach, yet the five of us are inside, looking between each other like we're wondering who the culprit is at a murder mystery dinner.

"Well, that was a train wreck," Fred finally says.

A laugh comes out before I can stop it.

Lorelei's and Quinn's heads swivel over to me.

47

"Come on," I say. "It was kinda funny. They almost rioted over shorts."

"Not funny," Quinn says, sitting in a chair. "Not funny at all actually."

"Well, that settles it then," Honey says. "You're fired, Randy." She winks at me.

I grin to her. "It's Landon."

"Nah, I'm gonna call ya Randy."

Fred exhales, as if remembering that we have too many disasters occurring at once. "Honey, I am so sorry," he says.

"Screaming guests. Pancakes onstage," Honey muses. "Big day."

Lorelei's face falls. "I have muffins," she offers.

"By all means, let's have muffins," Honey says.

I'm not sure Lorelei recognizes the sarcasm because she rushes over to her office.

Fred sighs. "My apologies. I was trying to keep your visit a surprise. I sent an email out to a select few but—"

I raise my hand, trying to help him out the best I can.

"That's on me," I say. "My email didn't load this morning."

"Okay, well ..." Fred starts, pausing when Lorelei returns with the muffins.

I take one, and Honey laughs when I break it in half to share with her.

"Listen," Fred continues. "I think this whole Ranger Randy thing is worth discussing."

Quinn's lips purse, and she shakes her head slowly.

"Let's put it all out on the table," he says. "People want Ranger Randy back. That's a fact."

"It's too late in the season to hire someone for Randy," Quinn says.

Fred's eyes dart to me. "Well, we don't need to, do we?"

"What?" I ask. "Are you talking about me?"

Like most teens in Cedar Cliff, I spent many years working at Honeywood Fun Park. I operated rides, worked the gift shops, and eventually flipped pancakes in The Bee-fast Stop.

But this?

"Acting isn't exactly on my list of skills," I say.

"We'll give you very few lines," Fred responds.

"I don't—"

"I love it," Honey says.

I tense, my head swiveling to her. "You do?"

"You look just like him," she says with a shrug. "Go for it, Randy. Show off those legs."

My face grows hot. "And here I thought, you were cool."

"I *am* cool."

"Something else too," Lorelei interjects, gripping her clipboard tighter against her hip. "And I know we all saw the article ... clearly, it looks like Ranger Randy and Queen Bee are dating."

"Saucy," Honey says, taking a bite of her muffin. Crumbs fall to the floor.

"So?" Quinn's face scrunches up with her nose wrinkled at the top.

I smile. She always gets that look when she's annoyed. A woman driven by defiance.

"They can think whatever they want," Quinn says.

"And what they want is you two together," Honey says with another nonchalant shrug. "Let's throw him in the play." She pumps her eyebrows and takes another defiant bite of the muffin.

I get a feeling she's enjoying this too much.

Quinn twists in her chair. "Why are you here again?"

"Quinn!" Lorelei cries out.

"Stirring trouble," Honey says, bored.

Quinn turns to Fred. I do as well.

"Fred, why *is* Honey here?" I ask.

"You think I can't answer for myself?" Honey asks.

I laugh. "I don't think you'll tell us the truth, you chaos demon."

She sticks out her bottom lip. "Fair."

Fred exhales with a weak smile. "She's thinking of selling the park."

All eyes land on Honey, like she just threatened our democracy or something. She tosses the rest of her muffin in her mouth. Once again, I let out a nervous laugh. Honey laughs with me.

"Sell Honeywood?!" Lorelei sputters.

"Lore, it's a good thing," Fred says, placing a palm on her shoulder.

Her face reddens. It looks like you could pop it like a balloon if you got the right needle.

"Why?" Quinn asks.

"Expansion," Fred says. "Maybe more states. Broader reach."

"And more corporate," Quinn adds.

"More corporate means more opportunities," Fred corrects.

His chin dips down toward her, and she narrows her eyes.

"Why sell now?" I ask Honey.

She shrugs. "Well, I'm gonna die soon, aren't I?"

"Christ," Quinn breathes out.

"You'll get used to my humor," Honey says with a smile.

"This is ... a lot to take in," Lorelei says, the worry apparent in her wobbling tone.

"Then, let's go back to the basics," Fred says. "We need attendance to grow to look good for potential buyers. I think Ranger Randy can do that for us. And Lorelei's right. Ranger Randy potentially dating Queen Bee is a nice touch."

Quinn glances over to me, and I feel my body stiffen as our eyes dance with each other.

"Nice suggestion," she says, turning back to Fred. "But absolutely not."

"Do you want pancakes thrown at you again?" Honey asks. "Heck, Queenie, I might chuck a flapjack myself."

Lorelei murmurs something that might sound like *hostile work environment* under her breath.

I clear my throat to ease the tension.

"What would that entail?" I ask slowly, trying to keep the conversation moving.

"Smiling. Holding hands maybe?" Lorelei says with a small wince to Quinn. "Nothing too crazy though, I promise. Simple show stuff."

Quinn's lips get thinner with each suggestion.

"Okay, and who would be writing that show on such short notice?" she asks.

Fred smiles. "You."

Something tells me that's news to her, just as it is to us. I can feel the shift in the room, the subtle grip Quinn's petite hands have on the arms of the chair. Her nails with pink Queen Bee polish grind like claws into the wood.

"Me?" she asks.

Fred nods. "Well, you and Honey probably."

"Nope, just her actually," Honey says.

Quinn pauses. "Wait, *what?* I don't—"

"Good idea," Fred says, beaming. "Great idea."

"Woah, whoa, whoa." Quinn slashes her arms out.

"Hang on. This is ... going so fast. What about ... I don't know. What about the horny women?" Quinn leans back and crosses her arms, as if she made a valid point. "That's why we got rid of Randy."

I bark out a laugh. She side-eyes me. Sometimes, I don't think Quinn realizes how unintentionally funny she is.

"Horny women don't scare me," I say.

"I bet," Honey mumbles.

"Watch it, you," I joke.

She squeezes my biceps in response. I notice Quinn's eyes darting between Honey's hand and my arm.

"This is ridiculous," Quinn says with a sardonic laugh. "I can't write a whole play ..."

"You can," Fred interjects with a smile.

Quinn continues as if he didn't interrupt, "I can't *pretend* to be in a relationship ..."

"I'm not *that* bad, Barb," I say with a forced chuckle.

"I'd rather fall off the amphitheater stage," she says.

"All right, all right. Quinn, let's reel it in," Fred says. "This is a good opportunity for you. Show off your chops. Think of it like an application."

"An application?"

"With the sale of the park, we could secure something for you. Writing. Stage managing, maybe? Something beyond just Queen Bee."

"I don't ... this is ..." Quinn is stumbling. She looks around the room, as if asking for any form of help.

"This is a lot of new information," I say. "So, let's assume we do this."

"You would?" Quinn says with wide eyes.

"You would?" Lorelei asks hopefully.

"Well, hang on." I hold out my hands, as if to ease our typical Arden family optimism. "Hypothetical here. I already have a full-time job, running security. I can't juggle more."

"I've considered that," Fred says. "We can allocate someone for the few hours you're onstage each day. It's only Friday through Sunday. And of course, we'll give a pay raise for the extra trouble."

I swallow.

Now, *that's* tempting.

I could pad my savings again. Maybe I could actually afford culinary school.

Plus ... well ...

I bite my lip and look to Quinn, whose arms are crossed so tight that I'm surprised she still has circulation in them.

I could also spend more time with her.

Good Lord, I'm hopeless.

"I'm in," I say.

Quinn's head whips around so fast that I wonder if her neck cracked in the process.

"You're *in?*" she asks.

"Why wouldn't I be?"

"Because you're the worst. Heck, *I'm* the worst."

"We wouldn't actually be dating," I say with a grin.

Quinn clenches her fist and unclenches it beside her. Her cheeks grow pink as she bites her lip and looks away from me.

"You're fine with doing this on top of your security duties?" Fred asks me.

I break out of my Quinn-filled trance and shrug. "If it stops me and my boys from breaking up a riot full of moms again, then yes."

Quinn sighs. "So, let me get this straight ... if we add Ranger Randy to the fall play and I write the show *and* it goes well, I might get a full-time job?"

When Fred nods, she exhales and lets out a very biting, "Fine," and the room seems to cool.

At least, it does for two whole seconds until Honey opens her mouth again.

"Wonderful," she says. "Once Queenie fixes her attitude, I think we might have something good here."

7

Quinn

"What the *hell?*" I whisper-hiss to Lorelei. "How does she already hate me?"

Lorelei's head falls to the side with a pleading, "She doesn't."

I lift an eyebrow.

"Okay, it was a rough start," she admits, exhaling. "But you didn't help. It's like you and Honey were two bobcats or something."

I fold over myself where I sit, perched on the queue line railing for The Grizzly. The evening breeze is ruffling my Honeywood T-shirt. The speakers softly play some classic rock song, a serenade for the only two people left in the park.

I'm staying late, waiting for Lorelei, so we can carpool home. It's been a long day, but an even longer afternoon after we met Honey Pleasure.

Honey Pleasure.

What kind of a name is that?

"How am I supposed to write a play for *her* characters?"

I continue, my rant likely going on thirty minutes now. "She doesn't even like me *acting* as one."

"You don't know that," Lorelei says. "Just be your sweet Queen Bee self and write an awesome play that rocks the house every weekend. It'll be fine!"

I sigh with a smile. "How is optimism this easy for you?"

She laughs and shrugs. "I don't know. It's easy to see the silver linings."

Genuine happiness must be fun. I wonder if I should try it once in a while. But one thought of Landon having to hold my hand, and ... yeah, nope. I'll stick with my cynicism.

I kick my legs under the railing. "You don't mind that I'm gonna have to be all close with your evil twin?" I ask.

"Rude," she says, then smiles. "And no. Of course not."

I *hmph*. "I was hoping you'd hate it. Or at least, Honey would want him all to herself or something."

"What even happened with you two?" Lorelei asks.

"Well, Honey is kind of a bit—"

"No," she says with a laugh. "Landon. Why is acting with him such a horrible idea?"

I suck on my teeth and shake my head. "It's nothing. He's just ... him."

Landon wasn't always horrible. Or maybe he just hid it well.

I used to spend every weekend at the Ardens' house throughout my parents' divorce. I'd stay up late after Lorelei went to bed, reading in the hallway. At that point, I'd say Landon and I might have actually been friends.

He'd get up for water and come back, but I'd be so engrossed in my book that I wouldn't realize he was sitting next to me, reading along, until he suddenly said, "Wait, don't turn the page yet," only to follow a minute later with, "Okay, I'm ready."

Those nights, when I still had pink braces and a silly little crush, I would close my eyes and take in everything about him.

I'd admire the hardness in his shoulder when he leaned into mine, cherish the sound of his small breaths throughout the silence of the hallway, and melt into his voice as he whispered, "Wow, so morbid," after every *Grimms' Fairy Tales* ending.

Honestly, I'm just lucky I didn't write fan fiction of us.

But something changed in him between freshman year and sophomore year. We fell into our respective high school social groups. Me into theater. Landon into sports. I was still doodling little *Mrs. Landon Arden*s in my diary, and I didn't stop until it was found.

With life-altering events, you only remember pieces. I couldn't tell you what day of the week it was or even what class I was walking to. But I could tell you that Landon picked up my diary after I dropped it in the hallway. He saw the words written in it. But it was his team captain, Michael, who swiped the book and read it out loud.

"Mrs. Landon Arden?" he said, the words echoing off the lockers. "Are you freaking kidding me?"

Landon looked from it to me, his whole face turning red. But probably not as red as mine.

"Give it back," I said as Michael jerked it away from me.

"Landon, have you seen this?" he asked.

"I ... no, I haven't."

At the time, I think I felt bad for him. My sympathy didn't last long. Every week after that, for months, then years, that football team continued to torment me.

I endured their hushed whispers of, "Mrs. Landon

Arden," or, "Bridezilla." I prepared myself for the letters shoved in my locker with those words scribbled repeatedly.

I'd lift my middle finger, feeling like I bested them, but they'd ignore me, unimpressed by my fight.

Eventually, his mom must have found a note that fell out of my backpack or overheard Landon and his friends talking about me. Mrs. Arden made Landon apologize to me, and he did so with a hung head, barely looking in my direction. I've always wondered if he was ashamed or annoyed.

"You're quiet," Lorelei says, bringing me back. "What are you thinking about?"

She's paused near The Grizzly's track, her clipboard by her side, eyebrows tilted inward.

I sigh. "Just thinking of ways to kill your brother."

Lorelei laughs. It's impossible to stifle her happiness. She's like a shimmer in the dark, a sprinkle of pixie dust. Or a hefty spoonful of blind optimism, but, hey, that's what I love about her.

I'd never tell Lorelei the truth about her brother. It'd ruin him for her.

"Well, if you kill him, make it quick," she says. "I don't want him to suffer."

That makes one of us.

Lorelei goes back to inspecting the track and scribbling on her clipboard as other words cycle in. Like Fred's claim of making me a writer or a stage manager.

God, my mind won't leave me alone tonight.

Could I even do it? I like to think I have the experience, but with it potentially in my reach, I'm not so sure. Who is to say I could do it better than someone who actually finished college, who isn't impaired by the slightest bit of stress?

"You really think I could write that play?" I blurt out.

Lorelei doesn't hesitate to respond. "Of course I do."

"Why did I even ask?" I say with a wave of my hand and smile. "You're biased."

She tilts her head to the side. "Quinn." My name is drawn out and lazy, as if to say, *You silly goose.* "I know you can do it."

"And stage managing?" I ask. "Really? Come on. Nobody will take me seriously."

"You've got authority that people listen to."

I bark out a laugh. "I'm a jerk, you mean."

"You've studied this stuff," she barrels on as if I didn't just insult myself. She doesn't like it when I do that. "You were involved in every play in high school and college."

"Before I dropped out," I toss in.

"No," she says slowly. "Before your life was upended, and it was *not* your fault. Plus, you've got it handled now. You'll be fine."

I smile. "I like to think depression and I are just old friends at this point."

Lorelei laughs.

My dad would have a different opinion on whether dropping out was my fault or not. He'd argue that I was just too much like my mom and it was inevitable. Depression was just an excuse. Part of me—more than I'd like to admit—agrees. Ultimately, I couldn't commit to something, just like her.

"You're smart, Quinn," Lorelei continues. "You've got this. Just try?"

Even though I believe in myself far less than she does, she has a point. I should, at minimum, try.

Except ... there's one remaining problem—the man who haunts my past. The man who still gives that pink-braces girl in my heart some embarrassing type of hope that he won't be a jerk.

The man who paused in the hallway sophomore year of high school, surrounded by his buddies, who saw my notebook full of *Mrs. Landon Arden*s, scrunched his nose, and said, "Not a chance, Barbie."

Not a chance.

The moment that solidified everything. From that day forward, Landon Arden wasn't my friend anymore. And I should have never felt bad for him.

I shake my head. "I don't wanna date him, Lore."

"Who?"

"Landon."

She laughs. "You won't date him. Queen Bee will."

8

Landon

"May peace be with you."

"Oh, come on. It won't be that bad." I laugh.

"Quinn is one hell of a woman."

I tongue the inside of my cheek because *don't I know it*.

Tonight, I have the guys over at my new house. Well, more like guys I've barely stayed in contact with for two years. Thankfully for me, Cedar Cliff is a forgiving town.

Orson—my buddy from high school, who apparently thinks Quinn is *one hell of a woman*—chews on the pepper he just stole from my chopping block.

"I love her," he continues with his mouth full. "But you're going to spend day in and day out with her. All I'm saying is, good luck."

For Orson to say *good luck* is a testament to the months ahead of me even if he said it in a joking manner. Orson exists in a perpetual state of unperturbed. He watches baseball religiously but doesn't dog the opposing team. He's short, but he doesn't make a big deal out of it. He owns and operates the local bar, The Honeycomb, but he doesn't call himself something pretentious, like an entrepreneur. He's not affected by anything. But I guess everyone is affected by Quinn Sauer to some degree.

"Beer?" I ask, changing the subject and reaching into my fridge.

Standing in my living room, with crossed arms and a rare lopsided smile, is my sister's boyfriend, Emory. He shakes his head. Orson, on the other hand, takes out his bottle opener key ring and waves the bottle over to himself.

The front door creaks open.

"Do I have the right house?" Bennett asks.

"Yeah, come on in!" Orson says.

"Why are you just inviting people in?" I say, knocking his arm with a grin. "This isn't your house."

Orson spins his cap backward with a shrug.

Bennett clunks into the kitchen in his work boots, dropping a bottle of whiskey on the counter. "Housewarming gift."

"Is this for you or for me?" I ask with a smirk.

He barks out a full-bodied laugh. "Guess we'll see."

Bennett walks around my house with his tattooed arms crossed. Seeing as he's the head of maintenance at Honeywood, I'm not surprised he's inspecting. He was like this in high school too—always tinkering in shop class or finding projects to work on. He has a keen eye for these things.

"The house is great," he finally says, running a hand through his thick black hair, pulling it up into a bun. "Mrs. Stanley gave you a deal, right?"

"Yeah, real steal," I say.

A very dated, vine-encrusted, fixer-upper kind of steal. My one-bedroom bungalow just a couple of blocks down from Main Street is not much, but it's all I need. Plus, I knew Mrs. Stanley wanted it off her hands.

Bennett turns the light in the bathroom off and on.

"Hey, hey, hey," I say with a laugh. "It's got some sprucing up to do, but the lights *do* work, man."

"You know, if you need to fix stuff around here, we can always help out," he says, tipping his chin toward Emory.

"Yeah, more than happy to," Emory says.

It wouldn't be a horrible idea, having both the maintenance guy and the borderline-genius roller coaster engineer helping with this house. But I fixed up the kitchen just fine. Pans hang over the countertop, cutting boards are propped up from smallest to largest next to the stove, and the knife block is already screwed into the side of the island. The house is perfect as long as the kitchen is; everything outside of that seems trivial.

"Nah! Thanks, but I've got it," I say with a smile. "The house won't fall down around me for a while."

"So, though we're happy you're back," Bennett starts, "why the change?"

"Just figured Cedar Cliff was the next logical step in my life," I say.

"Well, if it means you making me dinner, I'm in," Orson says. "You know, I've been trying to update my menu at the bar. Maybe you could help."

"I don't know if stir-fry would go over well at The Honeycomb," I say with a laugh.

"Nah, but I could use your expertise."

"Expertise," I echo. "I'm just a dude who cooks."

"Don't sell yourself short," Emory says. "Those muffins you dropped off were really good. Better than Lorelei's ... but don't tell her I said that. You could do a bakery or something."

I raise my chopping knife. "If every person who was told they made good pastries opened a bakery, we'd have one on every corner," I say with a grin. I tilt my chin to the onions on the stove. "Orson, you mind moving those around?"

"Well, we're happy you're here," Bennett says. "We need an extra for poker night, so Orson doesn't win all the time." He pours himself a splash of whiskey into a coffee cup after realizing I don't have anything more appropriate.

"I can't help I've got lucky hands," Orson says.

"I think he's cheating to pay for dates."

"Oh, you're on the dating scene?" I ask him.

"Hopping around with the yoga instructors," Emory grunts.

"Meghan and I are sort of dating," Orson says with a smile. "Maybe. I don't know. I'm just having fun."

I laugh. "I wouldn't know what that's like."

"You didn't date up in Tennessee?" he asks.

"Eh, it was off and on," I say. "One-night stands aren't really my deal."

Orson clicks his tongue. "You know, Judy down in my cul-de-sac is single."

"Judy Stilton?" I ask. "The girl who gave me wedgies as a kid?"

"The very one."

"I thought she had a fiancé?"

"Nah, that was Becca."

"Damn."

"But, hey, she's single now too!"

"Y'all are worse than the girls with all this gossip," Bennett says with a laugh.

I grin over at him.

"Y'know, Bennett is settling down," Orson says.

I watch with a smile as they exchange glances. But that smile quickly fades when I see the expressions. Bennett with his jaw clenched. Orson tonguing the inside of his cheek with a grin.

"Get out," I say, pausing mid-chop. "With who?"

"Jolene," Bennett says with a sniff. "You know Jolene. She works at the gym downtown."

"Oh yeah?" I say. "No way, man."

"Yeah," he says. "Two years now."

"Wow. You've never had something serious."

Bennett shrugs, averting his gaze, lightly kicking his boot against the kitchen island. "Yeah, well, times change."

Right.

I stare down at the cutting board, swiping the peppers into the bowl next to it and setting it aside.

Times change.

Maybe a date wouldn't be so bad. Maybe a date would take my mind off Quinn and that mouth of hers. Also, who knows? Maybe Judy wouldn't give me wedgies anymore. One can hope.

"Yeah, times do change," I announce. "You know what? Gimme Judy's number, Orson. I'll give her a call."

"Nice! Judy normally comes to the bar on Wednesdays if you wanna take her there," Orson says.

"Why the bar?" I ask. "You just wanna watch the train wreck unfold, don't you?"

Orson barks out a laugh. "Of course I do."

"I'm down for watching a train wreck," Emory says.

CRACK!

"What the—"

"Christ!"

We watch as a tiny piece of ceiling crumbles down on top of some unpacked boxes. All four of us walk over to the ceiling, peering up into the small hole.

"At least it missed my couch," I say, taking a sip from my beer.

"Doesn't look like there are animals up there," Orson says, crossing his arms and squinting.

"Though I think I see a mummified ..." I start but then grimace. "You know what? I don't even want to think about it."

"I can fix it," Bennett says.

"I'll go home after dinner and get some tools," Emory says.

"This is a metaphor for my life, isn't it?" I ask. "It's all gonna come crashing down."

Orson claps me on the shoulder. "So, when do you start dating Quinn again?"

"Shut up, man."

9

Quinn

The next day at Honeywood wasn't much better.

With more women demanding Ranger Randy—and a limited time pause on pancake sales because they kept ending up onstage—a beer at The Honeycomb is exactly what I need right now.

I would be thankful we're implementing Ranger Randy tomorrow—that way, I don't have to endure raging women—but that only means Landon will be touching my legs again. My face feels hot at the thought.

"Orson, is the air-conditioning even on in here?" I ask.

Orson pauses while extending a beer to our table.

"What? Is the air-conditioning—whoa, hey!"

Theo grabs the beer mid-air. "Claiming this one. Thaaank you."

"Was it even yours?" Orson asks with a chuckle.

"You'll never know," she says, staring into his eyes as she slowly licks the rim. "But I've already claimed it."

Orson inhales sharply. I see his cheeks turn red.

"It was mine, but she can have it," Bennett interjects. "I stole her drink earlier."

I expect Orson to have a sarcastic comeback, but his eyes are too fixed on Theo. He shakes his head and sighs.

"Well, if y'all need anything else, let me know."

I'm assuming my air-conditioning question is now lost to the void.

Ruby waves. "Thanks, Orson!"

"You're a saint!" Lorelei calls after him.

Leave it to Lorelei and Ruby to tame our rowdy herd.

It's trivia night at The Honeycomb, and we're riled up and ready to go. Nothing quite says fun like realizing how little you know about geography while drinking under the soft glow of hanging Edison lights.

Our five-person trivia friend group is a solid unit at this point. We're like those little people paper cutouts, where all their hands connect.

There's me, Lorelei, and Theo at our end of the table. And across from us is Bennett—our locally sourced Viking man with a sleeve of tattoos that change origin stories depending on when you ask him—and Ruby, the only person who probably knows the truth of his tattoo sleeve. She and Bennett have been best friends since elementary school. She laughs more than she talks, but I kinda like that about her.

We're all nearing or just reached thirty, so we couldn't have expected to remain a fivesome forever, given the potential for partners and spouses, which is why Emory is sitting next to Lorelei as our newest addition.

"Gotta say," Bennett says, "it's nice to have another guy in this ... what's the girl version of a sausage fest?"

"Taco fiesta?" Theo suggests.

"Ew," Ruby says with a laugh.

"Cookie coterie?" Lorelei adds in.

"Tamale tango?"

"Enchilada wrap?"

"Flauta bunch?"

"Okay, we're just naming tortilla dishes now," I say.

Ruby whispers, "Quesadilla crew," earning a collective, "Nice!" from the rest of the group and a high five from Bennett. Whenever we can get our quiet Ruby to chime in, it's a win.

"Lorelei, isn't your brother back in town?" Ruby asks. "Should we invite him too?"

"No," I bite out. I don't realize the word came from my mouth until all eyes shoot to me.

My stomach stumbles at the thought of Landon crashing our friend group. No, it topples down the stairs, bumps into a railing, and pokes a hole in the drywall.

"Okay, counterpoint: he's great to look at," Theo says.

"Not a good counterpoint," I say.

"How about the fact that he's my brother?" Lorelei says pointedly.

"Fair," I say, crossing my arms and leaning back in my chair. "Well, if we have to, we have to."

"It's honestly better if he doesn't," Lorelei says. "Imagine if we had to grab more chairs! Even Jolene would put us overboard."

Bennett's smile drops.

"Oh, but we'd love for her to come!" Ruby quickly says.

"Oh!" Lorelei realizes her mistake. "Right. Absolutely!"

"Has she mentioned wanting to come or ..." Theo chimes in.

She's trying to be nice, but we all know Jolene isn't coming to trivia—or anything else we invite her to.

"She's just busy a lot, is all," Bennett says.

Jolene is always busy.

I'm honestly not sure what Bennett and his girlfriend

talk about outside of, *Hey, let's have sex*, or, *Wow, your muscles are super swole*, or whatever two beautiful people who met at the gym talk about. All I know is, she doesn't like to hang out with the group.

"Well, regardless, we invited Emory, and that's more than enough for now," I say.

"Thanks?" Emory says.

"No problem, bud," I say, lightly punching his arm.

I turn to glance at the next trivia question on the television, but then my eyes catch on something different. Some*one* different.

He's here.

Him.

Landon.

"Crap! Did y'all already invite him?" I whisper-hiss to the table.

Everyone turns to look at him at once, a chorus of screeching chairs and table creaks.

"Well, don't be obvious or anything," I mutter.

But it's hard to look away from him. His trimmed beard has an extra tinge of red under the strung bulb lights overhead. An '80s rock ballad plays over the speakers, and it feels like he's walking to me in slow motion, wisps from his hair blowing in the breeze of the fan.

Except the vision is halted when I notice Judy Stilton grabbing the crook of his arm, her chin raised in victory.

Judy Stilton? The girl who gave him wedgies?

"Oh, I forgot. He's on a date," Bennett says.

I slide down in my chair. Unease settles in my gut. It's probably the beer or something.

But still, I ask, "He's only been here two weeks, and he's already on a *date*?"

70

"He's a sweet guy," Ruby says with a shrug. "I'm not surprised."

"Aw, Ruby," Theo says. "We should set y'all up! I bet you would be cute together."

Ruby flushes red when Theo leans forward to put her chin in her palms.

"Like two little puppies hanging out."

"Ruby? Date Landon?" Bennett asks. He lets out a mix between a scoff and a laugh.

"Yeah, it's weird," Ruby says.

"So weird," Bennett agrees, throwing an arm around her shoulders and pulling her in toward him, running his knuckles over her head.

Ruby's face lands right into his chest, and she grins up at him. I watch his hand float to her lower back. Ruby's eyes flash to the group, and when she sees me looking, she tugs out of his grip.

"It'd be weird," she repeats.

She's right. The idea of Ruby and Landon seems ... *wrong*.

I find myself having the same reaction as Bennett. I uncross my arms, then cross them in irritation. After a few more uncomfortable adjustments, I finally settle on resting my elbows on the table.

There. That's perfectly natural.

"Why do you look weird?" Emory mutters next to me.

I give him a side-eye, which makes the edge of his mouth twitch a little, as if he's fighting a smile.

"Ooh, and Landon is super tall!" Theo continues. "God, I bet he could throw you over his shoulder and ..."

"La-la-la!" Lorelei says, pressing her fingers into her ears.

But I've already heard enough. My brain spirals into a fantasy of Landon's boulder biceps pressing against my thigh as he hoists me up. His beard brushing along the outside of my hip. The feel of his heavy palm holding my calves.

He gets closer to us, weaving his way through the crowd as Judy clings to his arm.

It's his second week back, and he is on a date with Judy.

Judy, who I distinctly remember Lorelei telling me was Landon's personal bully. Judy, who doesn't seem like much of a bully now. Judy, who looks like she's doing much better in life than I am.

They reach our table right as Landon says, "Hey!" in the familiar boyish tone.

"Hey, it's Ranger Randy!" Theo says.

"Heyyy!" the rest of the table choruses in.

Both Bennett and Ruby start an intentionally awkward clap, instigating the table to join in as well as the rest of the Cedar Cliff bar patrons, who have no idea why they're clapping.

I snicker when Landon flushes red.

Judy, on the other hand, blinks up at him. "*You're* Ranger Randy?" she asks.

"Oh, yeah, nothing official though," he says, his index finger pressing against his lips with a grin.

"Wow," she breathes.

"Oh, yes," I butt in, "the real *star* of the park is back. Ripped shorts and all."

Landon glances down at me with a lopsided grin. I tilt my beer glass toward him in a *cheers* motion before gulping it down. He doesn't look away, but I refuse to break eye contact first. Heat flows into my chest and settles in my stomach.

"I just can't believe ..." Judy starts, the words floating

off. I don't know if she heard my comment or is just choosing to ignore it. "Well, he's just ... you know."

"Do I know?" he asks her, as if it's a challenge. The words radiate through his smile and right to his dimples. He tilts his chin down to Judy, reaching out to tuck a strand of hair behind her ear.

A fire burns between them that almost makes me feel embarrassed to watch.

I cannot believe he's on a freaking date.

I inhale in, then out, taking another gulp from my drink. When I look away, I see Emory staring me down, lifting his thick eyebrows, as if in a knowing gesture.

I shake my head infinitesimally, as if to say, *What are you lookin' at?*

"Okay, so really," Landon says, "what's the deal with Ranger Randy? I feel like a minor celebrity here."

"He's hot," Judy blurts out with a giggle.

Theo is already nodding in agreement. "Total mom magnet."

"Babe bonanza," Ruby continues.

"Oh, good one," Bennett says. He and Ruby high-five once more.

Lorelei gives a soft, almost-apologetic smile to Landon. "We kind of had to discontinue his character for a bit," she says. "Too many phone numbers."

"The last guy said he got Polaroids from some women," Bennett says with a swig from his beer. "It's not a job for the lighthearted."

Landon shrugs, his bulky shoulders pulling up to his ears. I vaguely notice Judy hold his bicep harder with the motion. I feel like I'm gonna be sick.

"I'm the head of security," Landon says simply. "I'm not afraid to kick out swooning women if I have to."

"Wow, so strong," I say, bored.

Our eyes meet again, and my heart jolts. It's enough fuel to send my body aflame, to have my chest gripped in a tight fist while the extinguisher lies just out of reach. He's looking at me with the same fire as when he looked at Judy. My teeth grind. It's insulting to be second fiddle.

Landon lifts his eyebrows, then says, "Actually, funnily enough, Ranger Randy and Queen Bee are going to be dating this season."

The table goes silent. My face heats more.

"Wow," Judy says, the word dragging out as she looks between us. "You and Quinn. Crazy."

I can feel the sizzle between her and Landon cool slightly, and something in my chest feels triumphant in that knowledge.

"We're trying out the first performance tomorrow," I say. "It's just a makeshift thing until we write a new script for the fall season."

"And I, for one, am looking forward to it," Landon says.

"And I"—I pause for emphasis—"am not."

"It will be great."

"It will be awful."

We stare at each other for a few awkward, silent moments—both of our hands shifting uncomfortably, shallow breaths exchanged—before Lorelei changes the subject. But even when we move on, Queen Bee and Ranger Randy long forgotten, I still steal glances at Landon, only to find that he's already looking back at me.

10

Quinn

We attempt to re-create Landon's first accidental show.

Emily and I place fabric on the ground to simulate his fall. Queen Bee emerges, confused. And then he gets down on one knee, all with one heel in his hand and the other gingerly holding my ankle as the audience watches with bated breath.

His touch is soft as his hand slides over me. His middle finger traces a line up the back of my calf, sending goose bumps over the length of my leg. He probably thinks he's being funny, testing my limits, seeing what will make me break character. At least, I think that until I see his eyebrows stitch in, as if he's in pain by it all. As if *I'm* the one making him suffer.

Puh-lease.

I hate that I can't stop replaying Judy hanging on his arm. I can't stop rewinding the way his eyes heated as he looked at her. How her hands glided across his bicep. I bet he went home with her. I bet I was the last person on his mind.

Landon slides my sparkling heel onto my foot, and you would think we announced world peace by how loud the crowd erupts into applause.

Buzzy the Bear barrels onstage to take over the scene, but by that point, the audience has seen what they needed to see. Buzzy's goofy laugh is drowned out by cheers as Ranger Randy takes his exit.

I try to maintain my cool the rest of the day, taking pictures with the kids wearing their matching Queen Bee dresses and smiling as big as possible. But it's hard to ignore the long line that has slowly transformed into more than just children. With Buzzy the Bear's eyes as my witness, a mom discreetly leans in and asks me when Ranger Randy will be joining me for autographs.

Christ almighty.

I stay in character each time, telling them that Ranger Randy is just a loving steward of Honeywood. I am a queen who needs no man. They aren't satisfied with my response. Somewhere between the first woman asking me and the tenth, I know there is no way we can slow this train.

Our final afternoon show is jam-packed.

And when Landon stares up through hooded eyes and says, "Anything for you, My Queen," it is hard to deny the raucous applause that follows.

I slough off the layers of Queen Bee's outfit backstage. When a piece of tulle catches on my heel, it feels like the final straw for my mental sanity. I let out an irritated whine and slump to the floor.

This whole situation is enough to make me feel like I'm crawling out of my skin.

I pack the ball gown in a garment bag and make my way back to the dressing room. I barrel down the midway, determined to leave as soon as I can. But as I pass the red track of

Bumblebee's Flight, I notice Fred and Honey standing at the railing, watching the roller coaster cycle through.

The last person I want to talk to is Honey Pleasure. She's the reason I'm even in this mess. Suggesting Ranger Randy join the show? What a joke. But unfortunately for me, she catches my eye before I can sneak past.

"Queenie!" she calls. "Come here."

She seems nice, but I don't trust it.

Fred turns and waves me over.

Ugh. Can't walk away now.

I sidle up to them, leaning my forearms on the railing, hanging the garment bag over the side, and watching the roller coaster's train fly by in a roar of wheels and screaming guests.

"How'd today go?" Fred asks.

I want so badly to say it was horrific.

People booed Ranger Randy!

People threw more pancakes at us!

But I can't.

"It went well," I admit with no lick of a lie. "*Too* well."

"The shorts are powerful," Honey says. "We're gonna have to flaunt them more."

"Are you serious?"

"You tell me if you're serious when you're this close to retirement."

Fred laughs, and I shoot him a look.

He pats my forearm, sighing. "Quinn, if attendance isn't any higher, then we'll toss the man out," Fred says. "Promise."

"But for now?"

"For now, he's in it," Fred says. "You said it yourself. It's going well."

"If we're bought out, I'm nixing him."

I notice a side-glance from Honey, a curious type of look, and I inhale.

"Fred, do you really think ... I mean ... well, it kinda feels like you're dangling a carrot over there," I say with a sardonic laugh. "There's a reason I haven't been anything more than Queen Bee up to this point. If we sold the park and if this went well ... would they really allow me to be stage manager?"

"Bigger companies make it easier to hide things from the board," Fred says. "They'll be too concerned with expansion to worry about whether you meet degree requirements."

I snort. "So, now, I'm a dirty little secret?"

"You're qualified from experience," Fred says. "And they don't need to know anything else as far as I'm concerned."

"As far as *you're* concerned," I mutter.

My gut twists at the thought of it all. I do want to stay and take on more responsibility—to write and stage manage like I did in high school and college. I've wanted something *more* for years. But I've also done *more* before—and my entire body crumbled under the pressure. Lorelei might think I won't have a repeat of my junior year breakdown, but I don't believe her.

"I just want to get through this season," I say. "Also, it's ridiculous that my entire career is hinged on Landon freaking Arden," I say, dragging my fingers over my temples and letting the skin pull with it.

"It's not him I'd be worried about," Honey says.

My eyes dart to her.

At this point, I just want to spite the old woman and her cling-clanging rings and necklaces that sound like wind chimes.

If the path to a new future requires playing nice with Landon, then so be it. When I look over at Fred, he's smiling, and it bothers me how kind it truly is. How much he actually believes in me.

"We'll need a new fall show script by next week," Fred says. "Think you can do that?"

"This is so shoestring," I say.

"I can help, if you'd like," Honey chimes in.

The implication makes my chest tighten.

"Do you know how to use a word processor that isn't a typewriter?"

She gives a sly smile. If I didn't know better, I'd say she was proud.

"I like your gumption," she says.

"What gumption?"

"One more thing," Fred interjects. "I think we need Randy signing autographs. Can you train Landon on guest experiences before Saturday?"

"Saturday?!" I squeak. "I feel like you two are trying to watch me die a slow and painful death. That's two days from now."

"Does that work for you?" Honey asks. It feels like a test.

"Sure," I say with an irritated exhale. "Sure, Saturday is perfect, Honey."

"Good."

"But I want rules," I say, turning to Fred, pointing a finger at him. "Solid rules. He isn't gonna be kissing me."

"That's up to you and Landon," Fred says, throwing his hands in the air. "Just keep it family-friendly and in character."

Family-friendly. I guess there goes the idea of flashing him the middle finger in public.

This couldn't get any worse.

My phone buzzes at my side.

I look down and see someone calling me.

Except it's not the usual suspects, like Lorelei or Theo or Ruby ...

It's my mom.

My body stiffens. My face grows hot. Every bit of me suddenly feels like it's on fire. I really need to stop saying things couldn't get worse. Karma, or God, or the universe is having a full-on laughing fit.

I send her call to voice mail.

A low, raspy *hmm* comes from beside me. I look over to see Honey glancing at my phone screen. When I clear my throat and raise an eyebrow, she purses her lips and mirrors my gesture. She doesn't even look ashamed that she was spying on me.

Whatever. Honey doesn't know me or my life. She can't judge my decisions.

I tuck my phone back in my shorts, but my hand is already in a white-knuckled fist.

I throw my gown over my shoulder. "I gotta drop this off," I say.

Fred pats me on the shoulder.

"G'bye, Queenie," Honey says.

"Bye, Honey," I answer through gritted teeth.

My steam doesn't blow off. With each step, I'm angrier and more stressed. First my job. Then Landon. Now my mom. I should have known things were going to get worse. All horrific things come in threes.

The unknown makes my skin itch and my heart pound. And the worst part is, Landon seems to be in the middle of it all.

It's odd how similar hate and infatuation feel. I can't tell if I want to strangle him or if my fourteen-year-old self with pink braces is secretly doodling *Mrs. Landon Arden* in her diary all over again.

"Not a chance."

I groan. It's time to go find Landon. It's time to establish clear boundaries. I couldn't protect the pink-braces girl back then. But this time, she's getting wrapped in armor.

11

Landon

"We need to talk." That's what Quinn says when she comes barreling into my security office.

She doesn't even wait for my answer before she's storming out with extra irritation her step.

The semi-secret trail beside Honeywood's train station is empty, so we walk down the path, crunching over the gravel walkway covered in leaves and branches. The sounds of roller coasters roar nearby. The laughter of guests is muffled by the curtain of trees around us.

I rub the back of my neck, attempting to smile down at Quinn, who hasn't spoken yet. But even her cold shoulder sets my nerves alight. I didn't feel like this on my date with Judy.

Sure, Judy was lovely. She's practically a saint, a cardiologist who fosters dogs. And she didn't give me a wedgie either, so that was a plus. But she wasn't Quinn. She didn't scowl enough, banter enough, or hate me enough.

Yes, I can hear myself.

Yes, I realize I might have problems.

I ultimately didn't ask Judy for a second date. I think I might have even said, "Good date, champ!"

Champ!

I hadn't even meant to say it. It just came out. I dropped her off after trivia and haven't gotten a text since.

"So," I say, tucking my hands in my pockets, "you wanted to talk?"

"Yes," Quinn says. "Yes, let's talk."

"Well, I'm listening, Barb."

Her eyes dart to me, then flick back to the trail ahead of us.

"I've been thinking," she starts.

"Uh-huh."

"And this whole fake dating thing is gonna be weird."

"Mmhmm."

"They want you to sign autographs starting Saturday."

"Wait, autographs?" I ask. "I thought I was just doing the play?"

"Yeah, well ... Saturday, your life changes. Have fun."

My mind is reeling, but she talks so fast now that I don't have time to process.

"But I'm thinking we should discuss stuff."

"Okay."

"I can give you my notes on how to act around a guest."

"Uh-huh."

"The dos and don'ts."

"Mmhmm."

Quinn halts in place, crossing her arms and looking up at me. I forget how short she is until we're side by side. She looks almost pint-sized. Though, that's not to say she's petite. I like that she wears cutoff black shorts that expose more of her curved legs than most people dare. I like how the frays settle on the tops of her thighs. I like that she looks at me with fire.

She rolls her eyes. "Stop making those *uh-huh, mmhmm* noises. It's distracting me."

A slow smile spreads on my face.

"I distract you, Barb?"

"Landon," she says. It sounds like a threat.

I hold my hands up and laugh. "Okay, I'll stop being so agreeable. Go on."

She continues walking.

"Well, aside from *how* you'll act ... the particulars and all ... I've also been *thinking*," she says with emphasis, as if waiting for me to interrupt. I don't. "We need rules."

"Rules?" I ask.

"Fake dating rules."

"Like what?"

"Well, do we only smile at each other?" she asks, kicking her booted foot on the ground. "Do we hold hands? Are you allowed to touch my waist?"

I stop in place. Quinn almost bumps into me, but she catches herself in time by placing a palm against me. I stiffen, feeling her fingers splay against my stomach before jerking away with a flush.

I glance down at her waist. I imagine holding it, and it feels ... forbidden. Like trying to pet a bear. My eyes roam over her arms, her collar, her lips. She's staring at me with wide green eyes.

I laugh to cut the finely woven string of tension between us.

"Do you *want* me to touch your waist?" I ask.

"No," she says, clearing her throat. "I'm just asking what would be suitable, but also make me *not* want to murder you."

"So, touching your waist is fine?" I ask.

"Yes," she answers quickly.

She runs a hand over her shorts. I wonder if she's relieving stress or if her hands are clammy. I stretch my fingers out. I know I'm tense. I feel my heart pounding, just watching her.

Before my brain can stop my hand, I reach out, placing it on her side. She's softer than I thought she'd be. I like the bit of give to her body.

Quinn's pink lips part. She lifts an eyebrow at me but doesn't move.

"So, this doesn't bother you?" I ask.

She looks like she's thinking for a moment before tilting her chin up with all the determination of a soldier on a battlefield.

"No," she says. "And does holding my hand bother *you?*"

She reaches toward my free hand, entwining it with hers, finger by finger until we're looped together.

A slow smile spreads over my face. My heart races.

We've started a game of chicken.

"Doesn't bother me," I answer. "What about this?" I run my thumb over her palm in slow motions, feeling the smoothness of her skin. Smoother than I thought it'd be too.

Christ.

"Doesn't bother me a bit," she answers with a shrug.

I don't believe her for a second, so I grin down at her. This only makes her eyes narrow more.

"What if I did this?" She steps forward, releasing our hands and raising her arms up and around my neck.

My whole body freezes.

"No," I choke out. "I'm fine with that." *Though getting less confident.* "But can you handle this one?"

85

I remove my hand from her hip, hooking my forefinger on her chin. My thumb runs a line down her jaw. Tangling a piece of her blonde hair in my finger, I tuck it behind her ear. My hands feel hot against her. Her ear feels hotter.

"Is this good for you?" I whisper.

We stare at each other, neither one of us breaking eye contact. She shakily exhales. My body feels like it's humming.

"No," she says. "Not that."

"No? That's where we draw the line?"

"No to the *ear thing*."

"*Ear thing*," I echo with a grin. "Okay, no *ear things*. *Waist thing*?"

"Yes."

"And what about the *holding hands thing*?"

"Yes," she says.

"And what about ... well, what about a *neck thing*?" I ask.

"*Neck thing*?" she asks. Her eyes dart between mine. I can see her cheeks flush. "What *neck thing*?"

"Oh, you can't forget the *neck thing*. You know ..."

I plant my large palm against the small of her back. I pull her against me, leaning down and running my nose along her neckline, breathing her in, letting her soft hair fall onto my cheeks.

Quinn exhales into me. Leaning. Melting.

We stay there a moment, letting ourselves settle. And even though my heart is racing, I feel at peace. At home.

I take in a large inhale and lean in further, running the side of my cheek against her neck, my lips skimming across her skin. I wonder if I'm taking it too far, so I reluctantly pull away. But I'm surprised to see her eyes still closed with her free hand now fisted in my shirt.

Quinn blinks her eyes open, and I can see every fleck of color in her eyes. Every shade and tint of green. Even the hints of hazel sprinkled throughout—a color so similar to my own.

Something in her must finally click—some thought or realization—because she twists from my hold, disentangling her hand from my shirt.

"No need to get smug," she says.

I laugh. "I'm not a smug kind of guy."

"No, you're just a *pain in my ass* kind of guy."

I feel my smile falter, but I laugh through it.

"So, no *neck thing*, I guess?" I ask.

"No," she answers, clearing her throat. "The *neck thing* can stay."

We exchange a look. Something I can't decipher.

"The *neck thing* is fine, but not the *ear thing*?" I ask.

"Yes. I have my reasons."

"Keep being vague like that, and I might think you actually like me."

"Keep dreaming," she says with rolled eyes as we continue walking down the trail.

We're silent for a few moments before she blurts out, "And one final rule."

"Okay, shoot."

"No kissing."

My stomach drops at even the thought of that. I didn't consider it as an option until now.

Did she?

"Right," I say. "Good point. You'd like it too much anyway."

I grin down at her. Her face is bright red, and she swallows before shaking her head.

"You wish," she says, almost a whisper.

I chuckle, and we keep walking.

"So, I imagine Fred will ensure *Cedar Cliff Chatter* does its job of spreading the news," she continues. "Easy-peasy."

"And you'll write a new script for us?" I ask.

"Unfortunately," she says.

I laugh. "Don't you want to?"

"I do but ..." she starts, then shakes her head. "Never mind. It doesn't matter."

"What? Come on. What doesn't matter?"

Quinn huffs. "Hey, aren't you getting paid more by playing Ranger Randy? I feel like I should be writing in some acrobatics."

She's changing the subject. I furrow my eyebrows.

"I'm just hoping I don't get punched by Buzzy onstage," I say. "But, hey, so why ..."

"Darn," Quinn interrupts, snapping her fingers. "And that was gonna be the first scene I pitched."

When I smile down at her, I almost expect a smile back based on the lighthearted joke. But her face is still passive. She looks like she's thinking.

I open my mouth to continue the subject she's clearly avoiding, but she talks before I can.

"So, got a date on your second week home, huh?"

The sentence makes me pause, but I end up laughing anyway.

"Jealous?" I joke.

She rolls her eyes. "I'm just not surprised."

"And why's that?"

"Because," she says, "you're you."

My body tenses. "I'm me?"

"Heartthrob of the town. Probably gonna start hanging with your old buddies again too, I bet?"

I sputter out a laugh. "What?"

She laughs, but it's bitter and forced.

"I'm just waiting to be whispered to any day now."

"Whispered?" I ask. "What are you talking about?"

She rolls her eyes. "You know how your friends were."

I halt in place. My gut pinches, like a knife's edge is poking the outside.

"Clearly, I don't," I say.

"Sure, sure," she replies, but it's throwing the subject away, just as she did the previous one.

We reach the end of the trail, emptying out back onto the main walkway.

I don't follow her when she walks on. Instead, I stand there, haunted. Haunted by our past—by the event in the hallway years ago.

I remember when Michael announced to everyone what Quinn had written in her diary.

Mrs. Landon Arden.

I remember how Michael looked at me with his eyebrows raised and jaw ticcing, clutching her notebook in his fist. He had a slight tilt to his head, as if asking me an unspoken question.

Well, are you gonna put up with this? it said.

My whole body froze under the pressure of belonging. I had just made the football team. I had just found a friend that wasn't my own sister. What was I supposed to do?

Not what I ended up doing.

"Not a chance," was what I said to Quinn, and my gut twisted in every way possible as I watched her face fall in betrayal.

I fell into the easy situation just like I took every easy route through life. It was easy to be friends with my teammates. It was easy to choose the college that gave me a football scholarship. It was easy to pretend I didn't care.

The hardest thing I've ever done was confess that event to my mom. She made me apologize to Quinn later, as if I hadn't already been planning on it. I even told my friends it was a funny joke but that we just needed to let it go.

Everything ended right then and there.

My and Quinn's secret friendship.

Our late-night reading together.

But also the bullying. At least, I thought it'd ended.

Unless … unless she is haunted by more bullying I wasn't even aware of.

Good Lord.

Of course Quinn doesn't like me.

I wouldn't like me either.

12

Quinn

Our small-town's newspaper does their job on Friday. In my sixteen years of living in Cedar Cliff, I've never once been featured in this gossip paper. Yet, now, I've been on the front page of the *Cedar Cliff Chatter* two times in under five days. It won't be long until all this fame goes to my head. I'm gonna start demanding more pancakes. More beer. More foot rubs from my nonexistent boyfriend. Maybe I can add that to the list of my and Landon's ridiculous rules.

Ha. Making him rub my feet would be the ultimate revenge for this whole affair.

But not as good as the *neck thing*.

That *neck thing* was ... well, I was saying yes to it before I could even finish processing.

That's on me. I know that. But I can at least get peace in knowing that I made the *ear thing* off-limits. I saw him make the same move on Judy at trivia, and I'm not someone's backup plan. Though maybe he did the *neck thing* to her afterward too ...

I need a pillow to scream in.

"I want to scrapbook all of these!"

I blink back.

"What?"

I'm walking with Lorelei and Emory down the sidewalk to The Honeycomb. She has five extra copies of *Cedar Cliff Chatter* tucked under her arm along with the leftover muffins in a plastic container.

"Come on. Look at y'all!" she says, holding up the newspaper clutched in her hand. "You two actually look kind of happy!"

I glance at the paper and suck in my cheeks to chew on them.

We do. But that's beside the point.

There's a picture of us front and center. Landon's hand is doing the *waist thing* while I stare at him in a dreamy gaze. We look like we were made for a parade float.

I sigh, hearing Emory clear his throat.

"What?" I ask.

"Nothing," he says.

Yet he keeps staring at me, smirking at me with those thick caterpillar eyebrows of his turned in.

"Spit it out."

"You guys look like a proper couple, is all," he says. "It's convincing."

"Oh, what do *you* know?" I bite out, waving my hand.

He chuckles to himself. "I know nothing at all, apparently."

Five minutes later, Lorelei steals scissors from Orson to cut out the newspaper clipping—she's too cute to exist—as we sit in a booth at the bar. The door bangs open, and Theo barrels through. Her feet practically slide over the wooden floor.

"Tell me everything," she demands, out of breath and

clutching the side of the table. Her black curls bounce in every direction.

Emory's eyebrows rise. I'm not surprised Theo showed up as quick as she did, but I forget Emory is new to our crazy, codependent friend group.

"Theo, how cute are they?" Lorelei asks, displaying the picture again.

Theo laughs. "Wait, are you scrapbooking this?"

"It's my *best friend* and my *brother*," she says. "Of course I am."

The front door opens again. Though it's less jerky than Theo's grand entrance. Ruby turns and gently closes it shut behind her.

"Welcome to the party," I say.

Ruby drops down at the end of the table, removing her purse strap over her head and hanging it on the chair.

"Aww, y'all look so cute," Ruby says, pointing at the newspaper.

"Christ, this isn't a wedding," I say.

"It's a big step for you," Ruby says.

But I don't get a chance to consider what she means before my phone buzzes. I expect it to be our last missing piece of the friend group, Bennett, but instead, it's a text from my mom.

Mom: Hi, honey! Thought I'd reach out and ...

It continues from there.

My jaw clenches. I pocket my phone and look around. Nobody notices my discomfort, but I can feel my nerves pull tight, like a rubber band. Pulling, pulling with each added item. Landon. The play. My mom—my mom who hasn't talked to me in six months.

"Where's Bennett?" I ask, ignoring the tension in my chest. "I expected him to be right behind you."

Ruby's face grows almost as red as her hair.

"Uh, he texted me and said Jolene isn't feeling well. He's staying home to take care of her."

It's a lie, and I roll my eyes to make it apparent I think so. Jolene just didn't want him hanging out with us. Even Lorelei's lips tilt to the side in disbelief, but she's polite enough to keep her feelings to herself.

After a few awkward moments, Theo says, "Well, I'll eat muffins on his behalf then." She takes a puffed-up muffin top from Lorelei's box and puts it in her mouth in one bite, saying with stuffed cheeks, "That loser is missing out."

It makes Ruby laugh, which I can tell was the goal. She's always a little off-kilter when Bennett isn't here. Though, in her defense, he's the same way when she's not around.

"Hey, at least take the whole muffin," Ruby says.

Theo swallows her bite. "The muffin top is the best part though."

I snort.

She points a finger at me. "Your mind is only in the gutter because you've entered some super fairy tale."

"What?"

"You and Landon."

I roll my eyes. "Maybe the ones where the Big Bad Wolf eats the little girl or something."

"Are you the Big Bad Wolf or the little girl?" Theo asks.

"I'm the Big Bad Wolf, thank you."

Ruby swoons. "It'll be so dreamy when you kiss onstage!"

Hold the phone. Stop the printers. Cease and desist all activity.

"What?" I ask with a scoffing laugh. "We're not kissing. Who says we're kissing?"

I get furrowed brows from everyone in the room, except Emory. He suddenly looks very interested in something outside the window.

"Why wouldn't Ranger Randy and Queen Bee kiss?" Ruby asks. "It's a fairy-tale play."

I shake my head. "No intimate stuff. It's gotta be family-friendly."

Theo barks out a laugh. "Right. Because cartoons totally don't kiss."

"I'm ignoring your sarcasm and moving on."

"The park guests *would* eat that up though," Lorelei says, tapping her chin.

"Stop pimping out your brother," I say, pointing a finger in her direction.

She curls her bottom lip in with a laugh. "I'm just saying ..."

"Nope!" I say, waving my hands. "I am no longer accepting ideas."

"Were you ever?" Ruby asks with a smile.

But even though I smile back, my mind still reels.

Landon and I already agreed to no kissing. So, why is my heart still racing? It's not that I'm opposed to kissing onstage. I would perform a pole dance in a string bikini if I had to. I couldn't care less about what people see of me. It's that it's *Landon*.

When I think about kissing him, my toes curl. All reason leaves the building, and I have the urge to toss either myself or him out a window. I'm not sure which of us just yet.

The stage play is a problem for Future Quinn. Just like dealing with my mom is a problem for Future Quinn. All I need to do right now is survive signing autographs with Landon as Ranger Randy. If we can do that without killing each other, we can do the play.

But a kiss?

I'd rather call my mom back.

And that's saying something.

13

Landon

My shorts are too tight, but apparently, that's the point. At least now they're lined with stretchy material, so they don't rip.

Our costume mistress, Shauna, pats my back as I walk in front of the mirror, looking Ranger Randy in the eye for the first time. My outfit looks both exactly like the security uniform and completely different, all at once. The shirt is still collared and short-sleeved, but this version is a lighter shade of brown. I wouldn't normally wear a tie, but now, a forest-green one is fastened to the front of my uniform.

I grab my keys and attempt to place them in my utility pocket, but there isn't one.

"Wouldn't a ranger have the same number of pockets as a security guard?" I ask her.

Shauna scoffs. "What gorgeous man wears shorts with tons of pockets?"

"Ah," I respond. "Right."

Then, she mutters more to herself than me, "Might as well have zipper pants that convert to shorts."

I walk down the midway five minutes later, running my

hands through my hair and trying to shake off the last dregs of anxiety. It's the first day we're debuting Ranger Randy as an autographing character. I don't feel prepared. I rewatched the *Honeywood* movie last night to pick up on his mannerisms, and Quinn left me a book worth of notes to read over, but how much can you really prepare for this?

I walk faster, hoping I can cut to the security office before any guests notice me. I make it to the door right before a small hand is placed on my arm.

Caught.

I stiffen, but then I breathe a sigh of relief when I see that it's Honey, frail hand on my arm, mouth twisted to the side.

"And where do you think you're going?" she asks.

"To hide."

"I'm coming with you."

"Why?"

"To ensure you don't run away."

I laugh, and we both shuffle into the security office. I close the door behind us and plop into the swivel chair on the opposite side of the desk.

"Nervous?" she asks.

"Nah," I lie. "Nerves of steel."

Actually, my knee won't stop bouncing, but I hide it under the desk.

I watch as she runs a hand over the cluttered shelves I have yet to organize from my predecessor.

"What do you even do in here?" she asks with an edge.

It's so reminiscent of Quinn that it's startling. I can't help but smile.

"I'm security," I say with a laugh. "I keep people from touching things they shouldn't touch."

Her head swivels to me as her hand hovers over a

control panel. I lean on my desk with my chin in my palm, shaking my head with a grin.

"Like that. Don't touch that."

Her eyes trail down to my costume. "You do look good, kid."

"Are you hitting on me?" I joke.

Honey snorts and chortles out a shaking laugh. "You *wish* I liked younger men." She sniffs, absentmindedly continuing to look around the office. "Not making that mistake again."

I bark out a laugh, but she sighs.

"I've done things I'm not proud of."

I freeze. "Oh, I wasn't ..."

"It's fine. It's all jokes until it's true."

I can practically see Quinn on the floor of that hallway, book in hand, scowling up at me with her pink braces. The sting of betrayal.

Not a chance.

I shift in my chair.

"Yeah," I agree. "We've all done things we're not proud of."

She lifts an eyebrow with a small *hmm*.

The door opens, and Lorelei pokes her head in. With one look at me, her eyes widen.

"Wow, you look just like him," she says.

I glance down, then back up. "I'm never sure if I'm flattered by that or not."

"Are you nervous?" Lorelei asks.

"I'm nervous about how many people think I'm nervous," I say with a grin, shooting a look at Honey.

"It's gonna be great," Lorelei says. "I believe in you."

"Yeah, just don't rip your pants again," Honey says.

"Thanks," I say with a laugh, standing and extending my arm to her. "I'll keep that in mind."

She hooks her hand into the crook of my elbow, and out the door we go.

The three of us walk like a line of defense for the war about to come. When we reach the amphitheater, I see Bennett and then ... Quinn.

My heart halts, sputters, and stops.

That damn dress gets me every time. The way it hugs her waist. The way the sleeves seem to drift like air atop her shoulder freckles. The light, ethereal fabric that almost paints her in vignette. The way the hem of the skirt makes her look like she's floating on air.

I can't take my eyes off her.

She lifts an eyebrow in my direction. "What?" she snaps.

I shake myself from the trance right as she looks away. I instead turn to Bennett. I have to clear my throat before talking.

"Hey, man," I say, nodding my chin toward him.

His eyes look over my costume, and he bites his lower lip with a grin. He's trying not to laugh.

"First few weeks a little rough?" Bennett asks.

"That obvious, huh?"

"And who are you?" Honey asks, shuffling from my arm over to Bennett's instead.

His eyes widen.

I laugh. "I'm so easily replaced."

"Oh, never," she says. "You're my golden retriever."

Quinn's back gets ramrod straight. She looks between me and Honey, her jaw shifting. Her eyes pause at my chest, where the shirt strains against me.

"Don't you have any clothes that actually fit?" she asks.

"Not if costuming can help it."

I chance my hand out to the side, trailing my pinkie along the outside of her palm, coaxing her hand to hold mine.

"What are you doing?" she asks.

"Holding your hand, like Ranger Randy would for his queen," I say.

"Gross."

"If you hate it, then I can stop," I say with a chuckle.

Except she doesn't say anything or move. Instead, her grip tightens in mine, but it isn't sweet or comforting. It's like she's trying to squeeze the life out of my hand.

"Cutting off my circulation, Your Majesty," I say.

She gives another quick squeeze. "Good. Let's get this over with."

14

Quinn

I'm accustomed to running the meet-and-greet sessions. I coordinate the lines, distribute key chains, and sign autographs, all while staying in character as the elegant and poised queen. Sometimes, I have Buzzy the Bear with me, but he's too busy doing cartwheels and passing out to be of any help.

Ranger Randy, however, is—*kill me for saying this*—a nice addition.

While Landon talks with a guest, I'm already signing the autograph book. When we pose for the picture, he's cracking jokes with the parents. When I'm sending them off with a queenly wave, pep talk, and a key chain, he's already schmoozing the next person in line.

It's nice, having the guests' attention dispersed. At least, it would be if I wasn't so distracted by him as well.

Landon is a mouthwatering heartthrob in every sense of the word. He's convincing as Ranger Randy. He gives the image of someone you'd take home to your mama, then would maybe go down on you in a spare bedroom. When he turns around, those shorts hug the curves of his butt. With each step, it makes a nice little flex. I've choked on my own spit a couple of times already. He's walking, talking sex appeal. It's what the people wanted.

I can see in every woman's eyes how they long to touch his chest. The subtle lip bites. The flips of hair. I can't blame them because, if I'm not touching his chest, I'm thinking about it. I feel a weird sense of privilege every time he pulls me in for a photo.

Landon's hand goes to my lower back. I arch into him with a racing heart. We have a significant height difference, but it only makes him seem like that much more of a guardian to his queen. At one point, I peek at one of the pictures someone took on their phone. We look *too good* together. The pink-braces kid inside me is thrilled. I, on the other hand, am irritated.

"Stop being so charming," I mutter after seeing the picture from hell.

"You think I'm charming?" Landon whispers back, sliding his hand along my lower back and to my waist.

My face grows hot. *All* of me feels hot.

It's been so long since someone touched me like this. It's been so long since I've imagined *him* touching me like this. And it's so much better than pink-braces girl imagined it would be.

No. Stop.

Yet when his hand roams down my spine, I can't help but lean in closer. It's easy to get comfortable when I'm looking at him with a beaming smile, saying, "Oh, Ranger, you're silly."

Those are actual words I said this morning.

Gross, I know.

And yet, when I did, he laughed. He clutched his

stomach and let out a booming laugh that was manly and charming and wonderful and *UGH!*

At one point, he held his hand out, palm up. I placed mine in it, and he leaned down, planting a soft kiss against me. His beard tickled my skin, and my breath caught in my throat.

Women swooned. Little girls oohed and aahed. And my own heart exploded into evil little butterflies, only made worse when he glanced up from under hooded eyes with those dimples pressed into his cheeks.

My thighs clenched together with that look. If he didn't pull me in for a photo immediately afterward, I might have fallen over like loose, wiggly Jell-O.

I just need to survive this season. That's all.

Survive.

I force the Queen Bee facade as much as I can, bending down to the little girls in matching dresses to mine.

"Oh, honey, you look lovely," I say.

The little girl smiles at me, but it isn't until she looks up at Landon—the over six-foot-tall hunk of a man—that she lets out a nervous giggle, blushing furiously.

When we take the picture, Landon leans down to my ear, his warm breath against me as he mutters, "I almost thought that 'honey' was for me."

It sends shivers down my spine.

"Don't keep your hopes up," I whisper back.

"No one has to know you like the shorts too, Barb," he says, the words smooth and slow in my ear.

I can feel his beard tickle against me as his soft lips run along my earlobe.

I swallow, inhaling sharply as he clutches my waist tighter.

The little girl drops her key chain, and I bend at the

waist to pick it up. When I do, I lean too far forward. The back of my dress bumps against Landon, and ... oh ... *oh*.

I clear my throat, bolting upright again.

"Down, boy," I whisper.

Landon laughs, but it's shaky.

"Hush, you," he says, his voice breaking.

He steps backward, and the baseball bat–sized bulge goes with him.

Christ almighty.

"I just didn't know you had a weak spot for queens."

"Quinn ..."

My head swivels behind me to look at him, and then something happens. The most annoying thing. Worse than the *waist thing* and the *ear thing* combined. It's a thing where our eyes dance over each other, where I notice the small flecks of green in his otherwise deep brown eyes. Where I get entranced by him, like I'm being put under a spell.

"Are y'all dating?" a kid asks us.

I blink back to the present, looking down to see it's the same kid who yelled it was Ranger Randy at the first performance. I want to narrow my eyes because *all this is totally his fault*. But instead, I smile sweetly and nod.

"Of course we are," I say.

"No, but"—he curls his finger, and both Landon and I bend down—"are *you* and Mr. Randy dating ... in *real life*?"

I blink at him. The kid looks dead serious.

Landon clears his throat and winks. "Shh," he says. "Don't tell anyone, all right?"

The kid grins, gives a swift nod, then runs off to his grandma, a Buzzy the Bear plush clutched to his chest.

"Why'd you do that?" I ask.

Landon shrugs. "Why ruin the magic for him?"

But just before I can open my mouth, Landon whispers in my ear, "Prepare yourself."

"What?"

I freeze as he places a hand on my lower back and leans in.

Panic explodes in me because he is getting closer and not stopping.

Is he going to kiss me?

And then the worst thought of all pops into my head. *Do I want him to?*

Just as I close my eyes, Landon bypasses my lips, and slowly, with warm breath and a soft exhale, he nuzzles his nose into the crook of my neck. The hand on my lower back presses me closer, and I melt into the warmth. Cameras flash, and my eyes flutter closed. His breath is against my neck, shooting nerves through my chest and stomach, down between my thighs.

My body betrays every sense of right I have in this world. Every moment where I knew, without a doubt, that Landon was my real-life evil, cackling villain who made my life miserable. But those butterflies inside me squeal, *No, he's not!* Especially when he lets out a long, exasperated sigh against me that leaves the guests sighing as well. The sigh that has me melting into him too. The sigh that has me needing a cold shower as soon as possible.

"Sorry," he whispers against my ear. "The *neck thing*. Gets them every time."

I let out a small moan, and I can feel him grip my waist tighter, letting out a similar hum against my neck.

This man is going to kill me.

15

Landon

O kay, so maybe I'm enjoying time with Quinn a bit too much. But it's hard to avoid her when my job now requires me to cozy up next to her every day.

I can tell myself I'm acting. That I'm doing this for the money. To save for culinary school. And I am. But that's not the only reason now, and I know that. So, I do the only rational thing a budding addict would do. I employ rehab.

I call Orson, request Becca's number, and plan a date for tonight. I'm lucky that she's free. She seemed nice when we spoke. But the second that thought enters my head, I know I'm doomed. Quinn Sauer ruined *nice* for me a long time ago.

It's because of this that I force myself to make a beeline straight toward the employee exit after my shift. I need to get my head on straight. And to my credit, I almost do. But when I pass by the amphitheater, I see Quinn sitting on the edge of the stage. Her booted feet dangle over the side as she hunches over her laptop.

Somehow, her looking like a gargoyle makes her even more attractive.

God, what is wrong with me?

Nope. Keep walking, keep walking ... aaand I'm walking down the aisle in the theater.

Wonderful.

I take in her blonde hair strung up into a messy ponytail, her T-shirt with the sleeves crudely cut off, the peek of her black bra underneath. It isn't until I'm right next to her that she finally notices me, jumping and pressing a hand to her heart.

I hold my hands up. "Don't shoot."

"What do you want?" she bites out. Her shaken voice is obviously still reeling from being scared. She glances back down to her laptop screen.

I take slow steps toward her with my hands still outstretched until I see a possible hint of a smile on her face.

"What are you doing here?" she asks.

I lean my forearms on the stage. They touch against her thigh, and my heart rate rises.

"Just doing my rounds," I lie.

"For the three people left in the park?" she asks.

A slow smile spreads on my cheeks, and I hate that I can't stop it.

"I'm getting fresh air then," I say.

"It's humid."

"Okay, fine, maybe I'm just getting human interaction."

"Extrovert."

I smile wider. "Why is everything you say to me somehow an insult?"

Her head finally whips up from her computer, and she lifts an eyebrow.

God, that eyebrow.

I suck on my teeth and click my tongue.

"So, what are you working on?" I ask.

"The script for the fall show."

"Dare I ask about Ranger Randy's fate?" I joke.

Her eyes look to the computer, then back to me.

"Oh no. He dies, doesn't he?"

"A girl can dream, but no," she says, leaning a bit closer to me.

I think I see a twitch of a smile, but maybe I'm just looking into it. It's hard to reconcile how close we were earlier—smiling and touching—with how distant we are now.

It was only acting.

"It's almost done," she continues. "I just need final input from Honey."

"Oh yeah? When can I get a final script?"

"What?"

"Well, don't we have to practice lines or something?" I ask with a shrug and smile. "I don't know. I've never done the theater thing."

"God save us all," she says.

She looks to the script, then to me and back again. It's quiet for a minute. Too quiet.

"Actually," she finally says, "yeah, that's not a bad idea."

My stomach plunges down into my feet. I'm stuck where I'm standing, a marble statue frozen in time.

"Wow, did you actually agree to hang out with me?" I ask.

"It's not hanging out," she says quickly.

Is she *flustered?*

"It's work."

"Right," I say. "Work."

"So, when are you free?" she asks, looking back to her screen as she clicks around. All business now. Except I feel her body shift. Her exposed thigh rests against my forearm, almost as if she relaxed into me. Or am I imagining it? "Tonight?"

I open my mouth to say yes, but then my heart sinks.

Becca.

I planned a stupid date because I'm a stupid man.

"Actually, tomorrow works better," I say.

"Why not tonight?"

I don't want to say it. I don't want to admit that I planned another useless date to distract myself from her.

But the fact remains that, "I, uh, well, I have a date."

Quinn pauses mid-keyboard click and swivels her head to me.

"Right." She snaps her laptop shut. "Of course. Okay."

I hate everything.

"Tomorrow though?" I say hopefully.

She clenches her jaw. "Sure. Tomorrow."

I no longer feel as victorious as I did a minute ago.

"Don't dread it too much," I try to joke.

"Already am," she says, hopping off the stage. "Have fun on your date."

I curl my bottom lip in and sigh as she walks off.

So much for a good day.

16

Landon

"Landon?"

Becca tips her head to the side. A strand of her hair falls in her face, and she moves it back behind her ear. It's a cute gesture, but I have a feeling she knows that.

I'm at Chicken and the Egg on my date that is notably *not* with Quinn. It's Cedar Cliff's local all-day breakfast joint. I can't even remember what Becca and I were talking about. I only recall ordering the scrambled egg and steak entrée. I had hoped egg breath would scare her off, but I was too uncomfortable to eat more than a few forkfuls. She didn't seem to notice.

"Sorry," I say. "Busy day."

"That's all right," she says. Her hand covers mine. "You're so easy to talk to, Landon."

I doubt that.

I've zoned out more times than I can count. And every time I look into her green eyes, I only see Quinn.

I'm a mess.

I drive her home after another hour of small talk. Becca's hand tangles in mine as my truck idles outside her house. I don't have the heart to pull away, so I wait until she reaches for her keys to pocket my hands.

"Do you want to come in?" she asks.

"Call me old-fashioned," I say, "but first dates ... you know."

It's not a lie. I don't usually sleep with someone on the first date. But I'm also still picturing the beautiful queen in the pink ball gown, and that's not fair to Becca, who apparently volunteers at homeless shelters in the city on weekends.

"What a gentleman," Becca says.

She leans forward, and I twist at the last minute so that she kisses my beard instead. Her face falls, and I force a smile to ease the blow. Just like Judy, I have a feeling she knows there won't be a second date.

Later, as I key inside my house, my feet echo in the almost-empty living room. I look at the still-unpacked boxes on the floor and toss my keys onto the kitchen counter. I kick open the flap of the cardboard box nearest me. I'll take any excuse to keep my mind busy.

I kneel next to the bookshelf, unpacking book after book. I get into a rhythm until I reach the bottom of the box with high school yearbooks. I crack open the yearbook from senior year. A small piece of paper flutters out—an old movie ticket from my first real date. The football team ended up crashing the theater when they found out.

I shake out the memory but am only taunted further by the front page of the yearbook.

There I am—in my football uniform, surrounded by the rest of the team. The Cedar Cliff Cougars had a perfect season that year. We won the state championship. I was king of that school, and it was the worst thing about me.

I close my eyes, flipping past the page too quick so that it rips a little. I don't fix it.

I keep turning pages until I reach the senior portraits. I tell myself I don't know who I'm searching for, but my finger still lands on the last names starting with S. Quinn Sauer's senior picture has that same raised eyebrow she gives everyone else, as if the photographer was challenging her to a duel rather than aiming a camera at her face.

I flip to the student groups and smile when it's more of the same. Drama club—Quinn's lips pursed together. Yearbook staff—disgusted. The Young Playwrights—mid–eye roll.

I finally flip to a two-page spread about Honeywood Fun Park. They were always credited as the largest employer of CCHS students, and Quinn is smack dab in the middle of the article—right next to my sister in a Honeywood polo. Quinn is mid-laugh. It's the happiest photo of her in this book. I can't help but smile back. It might be the longest moment we've smiled at each other without sustained disgust. I cherish it even if the girl smiling back is twelve years in the past.

I take the movie ticket from the floor and tuck it back into the yearbook, stowing it on the shelf.

I move to the couch, lying down, arm curled under my head, and stare up at the ceiling. When I close my eyes, I see that same green-eyed glare over and over. The pursed lips. The slight lift of the one blonde eyebrow. That bit of playfulness in the gesture.

I find myself with my boxers lowered and my head balanced back against my pillow. My breathing is erratic as I slowly pump myself to that expression. It isn't until I let out an unrestrained moan that I realize what I'm doing.

I stop.

This is the same woman I said, "Not a chance," to. Who I crushed under the heavy words of peer pressure. The woman who bought a cake to celebrate when I moved away two years ago and who glares at everyone, like she gets off on the fact that you've pissed her off.

Then, I wonder how Quinn Sauer does in fact get off. I bet she'd make you work for it. She's the type of woman to dig her hands into your hair and demand more.

No, refocus, Landon!

I remove my hand from my boxers, breathing in and out.

In and out.

The back of my head smashes into the pillow.

Forget it.

Leave it be.

Except I don't.

I grab my phone. I don't know what to say, so my hand hovers for a moment before typing the first thing that comes to mind.

Me: How's the script coming along?

I stare at my phone, waiting and waiting until three dots start to bounce.

Quinn: Aren't you on a date?
Me: Didn't work out.
Quinn: Poor you.

I smile to myself and type again.

Me: Want to practice lines tonight instead?
Quinn: So desperate for company.

Me: Maybe I miss being told how horrible I am.

Quinn: Don't worry. I've got a backlog of insults from the past two years.

Me: I bet you do. Care to share?

Quinn: I don't like making grown men cry.

Me: Liar. You keep a log of your victims.

Quinn: I thought I hid that better.

Me: No, you wear your hatred on your sleeve.

Quinn: It's a fashion statement.

Me: I'll take notes.

Quinn: Tip number one: no pizza underwear.

Me: Ouch. Locked and loaded.

Quinn: Told you.

My head falls back against the throw pillow as I type out, *You are my undoing*, before deleting it from the box. Dots appear, then reappear.

Quinn: Do you seriously want to practice lines tonight?

I pause with my thumbs over the screen, then type again.

Me: Do you?

Quinn: I won't be your backup plan.

Me: You could never be a backup plan.

I wait for the dots to appear on the screen. They appear, then disappear, and reappear once more. Then, finally, a text bubble pops up.

Quinn: Where to?

17

Quinn

I walk into The Honeycomb with my tote bag clenched in my fist.

What. Am. I. Doing?

I can tell myself I'm practicing lines. That I need to test out my script and hear someone else say the lines out loud. But the moment I look around, from the bar top to the long wooden tables, and finally find Landon sitting at one of the high-tops in the corner, his long legs stretched out like a king on a throne, my mind wants to scream, kick, and yell, *Quinn Ophelia Sauer, you are a liar.*

I wanted to see him. And now, here he is, in his white polo that stretches across his chest like some bodybuilder attending a golf tournament. Except knowing him, he'd just offer to be the caddie because he's just that *nice of a guy.*

He looks gorgeous and happy, and I hate it.

His eyebrows rise once he finds me, and a slow, crooked smile spreads over his face, activating those deep dimples like little love dents into his cheeks, which is simply unfair.

I walk over, hang my bag over the chair, and suck in my

cheek. It only makes him smile wider, flashing those white-capped teeth at me.

"What?" he asks.

"I should not be here."

He barks out a laugh. "Wow, we're off to a great start."

Landon stands, his hand curling around my waist. He bends down and places a very small brush of his beard against my jaw. It's not a kiss, but it's also not, *not* a kiss.

I just got here, and I'm about to call the police. Or maybe an emergency vehicle. I'll either kill him or die from arousal. I'm not sure which.

My knees buckle. My fist grabs his thick shoulder.

I jerk my head back. "What are you doing?"

"Would you believe me if I said it wasn't harassment?"

"No."

"Look."

Landon tips his chin, eyes peering behind me, and I turn around.

The kid is there—our regular at the park holding his Buzzy the Bear plush. He's peeking over his grandma's shoulder, staring at us with stars in his eyes.

My head swivels back to Landon, and I whisper-hiss, "I knew you shouldn't have told him we were dating."

"Well, doesn't matter now. We apparently are."

"I'm off the clock."

"Bah, don't be that way."

I roll my eyes.

The things I do for some theme park magic.

This is already going worse than I expected.

I grit my teeth and sit, turning to dig into my bag and hand Landon a printed script. I faintly see his tongue whip across the end of his thumb.

Good God.

He flips through the pages.

"Awful lot of touching in this," he says.

My chest tightens.

"We have to, don't we?" I say.

His eyes flick up even though his head stays tilted down toward the script.

"Says the playwright," he mutters.

I purse my lips, and he laughs, low and husky.

"I'm thinking we run lines a couple of times," I say. "I want to make sure the cadence makes sense before I give it to Fred."

"True," he says. "Don't wanna get you into trouble, now do we?"

Landon's hand slides across the table, and fire shoots through me as he twists his palm and entwines his fingers into mine.

My stomach dips.

"For show," he says. His eyes dart to the boy, then back.

His thumb runs over the back of my hand. I can feel his heartbeat on his wrist.

Is he nervous?

There's no way he's nervous with a smile like that. Flirting is old hat for him, I'm sure.

I grimace. "Let's just read lines, shall we?"

We do exactly that as we order drinks. I thank my lucky stars that Orson isn't working tonight. I'd be mortified if any of our close friends saw me with Landon on our pseudo *date, not date, fake date* thing. But it *is* still a small town, and I see eyes on us from all over.

Frank, our local mechanic, watches when Landon's thumb rubs over the back of my palm. Mrs. Stanley grabs free dog treats from the counter, but I suspect she only does that to look closer when our knees touch under the table—which is unavoidable, given how long his legs are.

The high school coach, Bill, peers over his beer glass when Landon huskily reads the, "*Anything for you, My Queen,*" out loud in this family establishment that doesn't need such sexy live readings.

It's honest-to-God real-life porn.

"Distracted?"

My head jerks up. Our hands are still entwined. His large fingers stroke over my wrist. Everything in me wants to jerk away, but I turn to see the kid still giving us goo-goo eyes. He hugs his Buzzy plush. It squeaks.

Our server—a younger girl, probably still in college—looks between us, lingering on Landon's cheeky grin, before setting down fries.

"Sorry they took so long," she said. "We're getting used to the recipe."

"Nah, they look great," Landon says.

Her face flushes.

"Let me know if you need anything else," she says, her eyes sticking to Landon before walking off with her head to the floor.

When I glance back to him, his gaze hasn't left me. He scoots the fries toward me. I lift an eyebrow.

"God, you're like a wounded animal, Barbie," he says with a chuckle. "Just take the food."

"How do I know you didn't poison it?"

"I would never hurt you."

I blink up at him, my breath caught in my throat. His eyebrows are raised, a crooked smile growing on his face.

"Come on. Let's put the knives down for tonight," he says. "Just enjoy some food."

"I've had Honeycomb's fries before. They're all right."

"Well, try them again."

I look from him to the plate, and the longer I don't try them, the more his face falls. First with his eyebrows, then the downturn of his mouth, and finally his posture, leaning forward in a hunch that seems entirely unnatural for him.

It's like kicking a puppy. I feel awful.

"Fine," I say. "But you're not easing my suspicions by being so pushy about it."

I notice that the fries are less uniform than usual. They're beer-battered and covered in various spices. I pick one up and bite into it. It's crispy, spicy, and salty.

It's amazing.

"Yeah?" Landon asks.

"Yeah, okay," I say. "They're good."

"Orson needed a new menu," he says. "So, I gave him a few recipes."

"You created these?" I ask, eyes wide as I eat another.

He chuckles. "Glad you like them."

My lips purse. I don't like his smugness even though these are potatoes from heaven above.

"Well, they're just fries," I say. "They're not poisoned at least."

Landon leans forward and squints with a grin. "Are they *just fries* though? Maybe I did poison them."

He smells like vanilla and cedar with a hint of malty caramel from the beer.

I feel a small twitch at the edge of my mouth.

"You're joking," I say.

"I'm joking."

I grab another.

"So, you're still friends with Orson," I say, and I can't help but ask, "Any of the rest of them?"

"Who?"

"The old football team," I say.

His face falls. "Ah," he says. Landon leans back in his chair, grabbing a fry along the way. "No, just Orson. Promise."

My body tenses.

"Promise?" I ask, then blow out air through my nose. "You don't owe me anything."

Landon doesn't break eye contact when I say that. My legs cross, then uncross under the table.

"High school was weird, right," he says. But it's not a question. It's a statement.

"Yes ..." I say slowly.

"Yeah," he echoes with a small nod.

"And?"

"Well, I feel like we haven't talked much since then."

"Did we ever?"

"At one point, we did."

The memories come rushing back—the late-night reading, how close we were on the floor of that carpeted hallway —yet neither of us says anything about it. The memories, short-lived, just float.

He swallows and continues. "So, what have you been up to?"

"What do you mean?"

"Life," he says. "What's going on? I feel like I don't know much about you. I mean, we've never discussed college, right? How was that?"

My jaw tenses, and I look back down to my food.

"That was almost ten years ago," I say.

"So? Humor me. Didn't you write a lot? Get involved in theater?"

I shake my head and bite my lip. "Well"—I sit up and

stare him in the face pointedly—"I dropped out junior year. How's that for college talk?"

His face falls. "Oh."

My stomach shifts, so I cross my arms with a wry laugh.

"Wow, is that all it took to get you to stop talking?"

He blinks at me. "Why did you drop out?"

"I guess that's what happens when you don't go to class."

"Why didn't you go?"

"Things happen," I respond with a heavy exhale. I couldn't meet his eyes if I wanted to. I trace my finger over the fry basket. "Couldn't get out of bed."

"Oh," he repeats.

Oh is right.

"It's why I'm still Queen Bee," I say. "Because who wants a dropout, right?"

"That's not true."

"According to a job description, it is."

He shakes his head. "You sell yourself short."

"Maybe."

He chews on the inside of his mouth, sucking on his teeth.

"You want another beer?" he asks. "It's on me."

"Did you make that too?"

He chuckles. "I'm not a brewer. Very different."

"Where'd you learn to make fries anyway?"

"Boredom in high school mostly," he says. "Considered culinary school for a bit. Figured maybe ... I don't know, the extra money from Ranger Randy might give me a second chance at that dream."

"Why didn't you go originally?" I ask.

"Why did you drop out?"

I narrow my eyes. He narrows his and grins. The defiant

look on his face warms my blood too fast for comfort. He's not supposed to do that to me.

"Touché," I say.

"So, beer?" he asks.

I sniff. "No."

"Come on," he says with a laugh. "Let me try to be friends with you."

"We can't be friends."

"Okay," he says slowly. "Then, how about being friends with Ranger Randy?"

"I think I like him less."

"Then, we're truly making progress with you and me," he says.

It's odd, the way his eyes trail over me—from my eyes to my lips, then my chin. His jawline tenses, and even the small flex under his beard is noticeable. My body heats. It's just like how it was years ago. He still has too much power over me, still makes my mind swim with fantasies.

Dang it.

"Come on, Barb," he coaxes.

"That's not my name."

"Oh, right. I forgot we're playing pretend," he says in a low whisper. "*Queen Bee*, would you like another beer?"

I try to fight back the smile, but it doesn't work. And one glance at my badly concealed smile sends his dimples into overdrive.

I roll my eyes. "You're so ridiculous."

Landon tilts his head to the side. "I am, aren't I?"

I feel like I'm forcing myself to breathe, but I'm afraid if I don't, I'll forget how. I must look unnatural, just sitting here, counting my breaths. He's turned me into a robot.

Landon's eyes look behind me. They grow wider.

"Don't turn around," he says.

Julie Olivia

"Why?"

I twist in my seat anyway, and my stomach drops to the ground.

"Crap, crap, crap," I hiss.

Passing the threshold is Bennett with his girlfriend, Jolene.

Landon watches me slump in my chair.

"Wow," he says slowly, dragging out the word. "Way to make a man feel wanted."

"It looks like we're on a date," I say, holding a hand up to shield my face from the door.

"Isn't that the point?"

"Shush."

He looks over me with a lopsided smile. "Well done. Really. All you need now is that glasses and mustache disguise."

I give him the best death glare I can manage.

"I'm gonna say hey to them," he says.

"What?!" My voice cracks. "You can't say hey!"

"Wouldn't it be weird if we didn't acknowledge one of your best friends?"

"It's weirder to be *here with you, alone.*"

"You look cute when you talk through your teeth."

"I'm going to kill you."

"Too late. They see us." Landon's large arm waves in the air with his goofy grin.

"You look too happy," I mutter.

He talks out of the side of his mouth. "Who says I'm not?"

My stomach pitches.

I hear Bennett's telltale sound of work boots on the wooden floor and cringe.

124

"Wow," Bennett says. "Funny seeing ... you two ... here." His voice trails off with each word.

I slowly swivel my head toward him in a close-lipped smile.

"Funny," I deadpan.

Jolene clicks her tongue. "I didn't know y'all were dating."

My eyes dart to her.

I haven't seen Bennett's girlfriend in I don't know how long. I even started telling jokes about how he murdered her—which he did not laugh at—yet here she is, with auburn hair, fire-engine red nails, and winged eyeliner precise as a blade.

I almost feel bad for making those jokes. *Almost.*

"We're not dating," I say.

"Sure," Jolene says dully, like she doesn't believe me.

"Sorry," Bennett says, throwing a thumb over his shoulder. "Landon, have you ever met my girlfriend? Landon, Jolene. Jolene, Landon."

"Oh, wow," Landon says. "Yeah, I've heard so much."

Her eyes narrow. "Hopefully good things." She says it like an accusation.

"So," Bennett says, as if heading off a potentially awkward conversation, *which it totally is now*, "what are you two doing here?"

"Practicing lines," I say at the same time Landon says, "Dinner date."

My following laugh is more nervous than it has any right to be. It's cracked and high-pitched. Both Bennett's and Landon's eyes widen. Jolene leans her head back like I'm a cackling witch about to brew the bones of children.

"Well, a pretend dinner date," Landon says with a laugh.

"But, no, not really a date at all," I answer quickly.

"Kind of."

"Not really."

Jolene's red eyebrows reach the top of her forehead.

"Awful lot of *not reallys* going on," she says.

Bennett laughs, but it's uncomfortable. She shrugs with a bored face.

I clear my throat.

"Well, this is sufficiently awkward," Jolene says. "I'll go get us a table, Ben."

I feel my face scrunch up, and I cut my eyes to Landon.

Ben? Landon mouths to me with an equally put-off expression.

My heart races, and I look away. I will absolutely *not* be sharing a moment with Landon even if it is weird that we've never once heard Bennett called *Ben* in our entire lives.

Jolene pats Bennett's arm, running a line down to his wrist to the pink string bracelet he's worn for as long as I've known him. She gives it a small tug before heading off. When I glance up at him, there's a line going down the center of his brow. He pulls his wrist up, tightening the pink string. I wonder if he realizes he's even doing it.

"She's ... great," I finally say. I hate that I didn't say the last word faster, but he doesn't seem to have noticed.

"Yeah," Bennett says. "Yeah, I wish y'all could see her more."

"I'm sure she feels the same."

His eyes narrow, catching my sarcasm.

"What?" I say with a laugh. "I'm just ... saying, you know. She's the one who doesn't come to trivia or anything." I sip my beer, so I don't shove my foot in my mouth even more.

I catch Landon's brown eyes. They dance between mine. He looks amused by me.

"I know she's a little intense," Bennett mutters. "But I like that about her. Y'all would get along if you got to know each other."

"Sometimes, intensity is good," Landon interjects.

Then, he winks.

Winks.

It's so quick that you might have missed it. But perfect all the same. Some people can't pull off winks. They look like they're stumbling into falling asleep. But Landon is a pro. His wink could ravage pussies.

My heart catches in my throat, and something passes between us. What? I don't know. But I don't want to find out. My stomach is already dead on the floor.

"You know what?" I say, getting up from the chair and grabbing my bag. "We were just finishing up. I think it's time I head out."

Bennett laughs. "Well, now, I definitely think something is going on."

I roll my eyes and joke, "He wishes."

Except Landon doesn't respond, and when I meet his eyes, his eyebrows are tilted in, and he's never looked more intense.

"A-yep," is all I can awkwardly get out of my mouth before I leave The Honeycomb.

I give a passing wave to Jolene on my way out, which she doesn't return.

A-yep.

18

Quinn

The autograph line is long—so long in fact that it starts to wrap around The Bee-fast Stop and blend into the kiddie coaster queue line nearby.

"I haven't seen a line like this in years," I tell Fred. "Maybe ever."

"It's a good sign for the potential play turnout," he says. "How's writing coming along?"

I snort, watching as Landon waves to the moms in the crowd.

"I could write him standing onstage, doing nothing, for thirty minutes, and it'd be good enough."

Fred laughs with me. "But is it going well?"

"It's going," I say, my face falling. *Going awful.*

I spent all last night tweaking the dialogue after Landon and I practiced. I'm not finished yet. But the more I work on it, the more I don't like it, and the less confident I feel, especially with the ending, which feels like it's dropping off into nowhere.

But somewhere deep inside my soul, I know what that ending needs to be.

Any fairy tale needs to end in a kiss.

Sleeping Beauty.

Cinderella.

Snow White.

But I can't bring myself to do it.

From beside me, I see Honey's lips purse. We share a look, and I glance away. I sometimes feel like that old bird can read my mind.

"I'm sure it'll be great," Fred says.

"Don't get in your head," Honey says. Then, she pushes me forward. "Now, go be with your ranger."

"*My* ranger?"

"Off you go."

I narrow my eyes. She waves each frail little finger on her wrinkled hand, like some fairy godmother sending me into the great unknown.

Honey and Fred stand off to the side, holding a front row seat to my misery. To my fake love affair with Landon.

"You two getting along?" Landon mutters to me.

I walk into his outstretched arm with a smile plastered on my face for the line of eager guests. It's Queen Bee that breathes in his vanilla and cedar scent. Totally not me.

"Trying," I say through gritted teeth.

But when Landon grins back to me, my heart sinks into my giant, poofy ball gown.

Something about last night ruined me. Did he actually poison the fries? Am I now sedated around him, brainwashed by his good recipe?

Because when he's Ranger Randy, when his hand snakes over my waist and rests there, as if it's always belonged, we feel different. My face flushes, and I fake smile, but something in it isn't so fake anymore.

What is happening to me? I'm going soft. I'm losing my edge with him.

I fumble into the next guest interaction, trying to laugh louder. Be nicer. Act more elegant than I've ever acted in my life. If I zone out enough, I can pretend Landon and I didn't hang out alone.

I haven't told anyone—not even Lorelei.

Why haven't I told my best friend that I hung out with her brother alone?

It's not like anything happened.

Or that I wanted it to.

My face burns, the possibility of something else happening torching through me, singeing my muscles and bones. And when Landon gently places a hand on the small of my back, I almost melt right there.

It isn't until I'm done talking to a little girl with a matching crown that I come face-to-face with the only thing that could make this day more difficult.

Handsy Hugh.

Ugh.

Not today. *Please* not today.

Landon, none the wiser of the situation, shakes Hugh's hand. They exchange words, but Hugh's eyes don't part from mine. He's like a panther seeking his prey. I glance back at Fred, who is preoccupied and talking to Honey.

Hugh slides beside me and sandwiches my body between him and Landon. I inhale sharply when his grip is not gentle, but heady.

Please don't make me kick you in front of my boss.

My smile falters for a moment, but I try to remember that I'm in character. I plaster a fake grin on my face.

Our photographer counts down, and seconds before, Hugh shifts his arm lower. My teeth grind. I prep my foot, ready to bury the heel in Hugh's shoe, but before I can, something else happens.

His hand lands on someone else's behind me.

"HEY." Landon's voice booms.

The crowd goes quiet. The birds stop chirping. Distantly, there's still the roar of roller coasters, but it's muffled, like we're suddenly in another time and place.

I twist around just in time to see Landon's palm gripping Hugh's wrist, plucking it away from my skirt. His jaw tics under his beard. His body is tense. I've never seen him like this before.

"I don't think that's appropriate, do you, sir?"

I catch a hint of Landon's Southern drawl as his *I* transforms to *ah*. His accent is normally hidden, but now, his voice is so husky, so sharp, so *threatening* that I can feel my heart pounding. My lower stomach clenching. My inner thighs burning with heat.

Landon moves around me, keeping his palm pressed into my lower back as he does. He leans into Hugh's ear. Landon's tone is so low that I can't hear what he's saying.

My eyes dart to Fred and Honey. Our general manager's lips are parted, hands on his hips. Honey's arms are crossed, like she's seconds away from jumping in to solve the problem herself.

Landon breaks away from Hugh and gestures to me with a sudden jerk of his chin.

"My apologies, Your Majesty," Hugh says. "It won't happen again."

I look out at the remaining line of guests, who are staring back at me with awed expressions—guests who look stunned and heated and as if maybe *their* thighs are burning too.

My head swims, my heart paces at double time, and a twitch in my hand longs to reach out to Landon.

Because he defended me.

Me.

"Who's next?" Landon asks, gesturing with his palm up and four fingers waving inward.

About ten women's hands shoot up in the air.

We bring the next guest in, signing their autograph book and taking another picture with us on either side. But it's still quiet. Tense.

When they walk away, I lean into him. "What did you say?" I whisper.

Landon inhales slowly. "I said that if he does that again, I'll break his fingers."

"You said *what*?!" I hiss.

I hear him chuckle, and when I look up, Landon's eyebrows are raised, and he has a lopsided smile and one lone dimple peering down at me.

"I'm kidding," he says. "I said that a queen deserves respect." He leans closer, raspy breath tickling my ear as he finishes, "And respect you will receive, Your Majesty."

19

Landon

Small-town news travels fast. The next day, everyone is talking about my borderline freak-out. I wouldn't exactly call it that, but when I stop by Slow Riser to get coffee, two of the local yoga instructors talk in non-hushed whispers.

"I heard Ranger Randy banned him from the park."

"I heard he punched him."

"I heard his shorts ripped again from the sheer force of his yell."

I dart out of there before they notice me.

When I get to the park, I try to stay out of sight. It's easier with the lower attendance. This is the first Monday we're not open to the general public. The only guests are from a company that rented the park for the day.

I head to the offices.

Fred texted me, saying we needed to talk this morning. My first thought was, *I'm fired.* My second thought was, *How the heck am I going to afford school now?* Not like I haven't had years to prepare for that disappointment, but still.

I just started getting my hopes up for this job, this life, Quinn ...

If that wasn't a sign I've been misguided, I don't know what is.

When I make it to Fred's office doorway, there's a note, saying he's helping at The Grizzly.

I run back down the stairs. When I turn the corner, I bump into someone. I reach out to grab their waist right before they can fall, but I'd recognize that soft waist anywhere.

I look down, and there she is.

Queen Bee herself.

Specks of dust shimmer in the light around Quinn's face. She looks like a blonde angel.

"We've *got* to stop meeting like this," I say.

Her face screws up. "I'm just here to see Fred."

"He's not here," I say. It's then that I realize I'm still holding her.

I gently place her down. Her shirt has shimmied up, and she tugs down the hem. I work my hardest not to look, but the sliver of her stomach I do catch has me nervously putting my hands in my pockets.

"He's at The Grizzly," I say. "Walk with me?"

I see her hesitate before nodding without another word.

We walk down the midway together in uncomfortable silence. Roller coasters are barreling down tracks with half-capacity trains, guest conversations blend together, and various songs blare out of the park's speakers, depending on which part of the park we pass.

I keep looking over at her. She's gorgeous today, but isn't she every day? Frayed black shorts, hair in a messy bun, and her yellow Honeywood T-shirt clinging to her figure.

But she seems distracted. Maybe she got the same text I did. Maybe she's nervous about getting fired too.

"Did you get a text from Fred too?" I ask.

She squints up at me, holding a hand up to her forehead to block out the sun. "Yeah."

"I'm getting fired, aren't I?"

She barks out a laugh. "Probably. Shame too."

A slow smile spreads over my face.

"And why's that?" I ask.

"It was nice to have support for once."

I want to let that wash over me, but something else sticks in my brain instead—something she said the other night.

"Couldn't get out of bed."

Those words repeat again and again, like a curse I wish I could relieve her of. I like Quinn's intensity. It's a pure, precious thing I want to capture in my palms and protect. Knowing there's something else beneath the surface bothers me, like an itch I can't scratch.

What else does she need support for?

We round the corner to The Grizzly, and in the train's station are Honey, Fred, Lorelei, and Theo.

I'm not surprised Lorelei and Fred are hanging out here or that Theo, our Rides supervisor, is taking over the busiest ride in the park.

We climb through the railings and hop over the track in front of the loading train.

Theo is in the operations booth. Her voice carries through the station speakers in an auctioneer-like, "All right, all right, all right. Welcome aboard. To ensure a safe prowl, please keep your paws inside the vehicle at all times. Enjoy your ride aboard The Grizzlyyyy."

The train leaves the station, and Lorelei's shoulders drop, eyebrows stitching in.

"You can't hop over the track like that, guys," she says.

"Emergency," Quinn says.

"What's wrong?" Lorelei asks.

"I can't escape your brother."

"Hey, Lore—" I start, but before I can speak, Quinn twists to face Lorelei, holding out her palm. "See?"

I grin over to Quinn, who, in some miraculous turn of events, gives the smallest of mouth twitches back.

I'll take it.

Honey walks over, rubbing her palms together with a wide grin.

"Think you'll get fired after yesterday?" she asks.

I laugh. "You're a menace."

She pushes my arm. "The best kind." Then, she turns to Quinn. "You look good as Queen Bee. I'll give you that."

Quinn flushes a deep pink.

"Well, I've been doing it for ten years," Quinn says. "I sure hope I look good."

Honey's wrinkled smile widens. "A rose with thorns."

Quinn opens her mouth to retort, but I choke out a laugh and say, "Ignore her."

Honey clicks her tongue and attempts to whack my arm. It's nothing more than a featherlight slap. "Respect your elders."

Lorelei and Fred walk down the line of new passengers, checking their lap bars and seat belts. When they both press their respective buttons, the train exits with Theo's voice heralding their departure. Fred hops over the tracks and walks to us.

"How's it okay when he hops over tracks?" I ask Lorelei.

"He's the general manager," she says. "He can do what he wants."

"Well, I've got good news and bad news," Fred says.

"Bad news first," Quinn says at the same time I say, "Good news, please."

Our eyes dart toward each other and back to Fred.

"Good news first," Fred says. "People loved protective Randy."

"Somehow unsurprising," Quinn says with a bored tone.

"But the bad news," Fred continues, "well, sort of bad news ..."

"Depending on how you look at it," Honey interjects.

"The bad news," Fred continues, "is that Hugh is attempting to press charges."

"What?" I say.

Quinn asks, "Can he?"

"No," Fred says. "Technically, nothing happened."

"Good Lord, we can't avoid lawsuits in this town to save our lives," Quinn mutters.

I hear Lorelei laugh from behind us.

"So, how is this only sort of bad news?" I ask. "Or any news at all?"

"Because"—Fred moves closer so that it's only the four of us in a huddle—"if my daughter has taught me anything about journalism, it's that even bad publicity is good publicity."

"And ..." I press.

"*And*," Honey chimes in, "now, we have a buyer interested in the park."

20

Landon

With official interest in the park from buyers, it seems like everything is ramped into overdrive. We start show practice the very next day, using whatever Quinn has written of the script so far.

I make it to the Honey Pleasure Stage shaking my hands out by my sides. It only takes one look at the stage to make my nerves strike again like lightning in my heart. No amount of shaking will make them disappear.

The lights shine down on the stage like a spotlight. There are some cutouts of bats hanging from the ceiling. A giant cardboard pumpkin is propped next to Queen Bee's honeycomb castle. Fog machines are hidden behind the wings.

It's really happening.

A blonde is at the front of the stage, and it takes me a few moments before I realize it isn't Quinn, but Emily. I've never noticed how similar they look from far away.

I walk onstage, looking out to find Quinn in the audience, head dipped low over her printed script.

"Uh, are you Queen Bee now?" I ask Emily.

"No," she says with a stilted laugh. "I'm standing in while Quinn does the blocking."

"What's blocking?"

Emily giggles. "You're funny."

I wasn't trying to be.

Quinn looks back up and spots me. She doesn't start with hi. Instead, she points the eraser side of her pencil to the left.

"Can you move back a little?" she asks. "Randy is gonna start out in the back."

I point to myself. She nods.

It's mesmerizing, watching Quinn focus, seeing as her lips wrap around the end of the pencil, biting it.

Christ.

"Yep, right there."

"And I just ... stand here?" I ask.

"You got it."

I smile at her. That subtle smile peeks back, and I'm not sure what I did to deserve it. But I still smile back.

She directs either me or Emily or the teenager standing in for Buzzy all morning. I find out *blocking* is setting up where people stand onstage throughout the play. Every time Quinn points, I take a step in the intended direction. When she gives a thumbs-up, the motion is enough to send my nerves on overdrive.

Later, Fred and Honey take a seat on the bleachers. Lorelei is in tow, giving me a goofy wave from the audience. I wave back, feeling a bit more at ease with my sister there. But not by much. I'm still on a stage after all.

We practice the last couple of lines of the play, but it ends abruptly when Quinn says, "All right, from the top, everyone!"

Fred and Honey stir in the audience. While Fred says nothing, it's unsurprisingly Honey who speaks up.

"Is there no ending yet?" she asks.

Quinn twists on her heel, eliciting a small squeak from the stage. Or maybe it's just that loose floorboard near the front.

"Still working on it," Quinn says, but I can feel the tension radiating off her.

Honey's face scrunches up.

"Right. Um, from the top!" Quinn repeats, shaking out her shoulders.

I move to the back of the stage, passing her a smile that she only half-heartedly returns.

When I walk out, script in hand, trying my best to *project my voice*, like Emily told me earlier, I'm less worried about that and more about Quinn. She reads her lines with a shaky voice.

I fall to one knee before her, as instructed in our blocking session. My hand traces over her ankle, running a thumb along the outside edge. She tenses like I just threatened her with a knife at her back. I glance up at her, and she inhales sharply when our gazes catch.

The teen playing Buzzy stares down at his script, trying to find his lines, and I take the chance to whisper to her.

"Everything okay?"

Quinn's back straightens, and she nods. "Yeah. I'm fine."

"What's wrong?" I ask again.

"I just ... I'm distracted," she says, stumbling through the words. But there's an edge to it that tells me she isn't telling the whole truth. "I feel like I'm dropping the ball."

"You're not."

Quinn blinks down at me, swallowing.

"You're not," I repeat.

She slowly pulls her leg from my hands, and when Buzzy's actor finally finds his place in the script, we continue on, as if nothing happened.

21

Quinn

I sit at my laptop, my fingers hovering over the keys.

I type a word.

I erase it.

I type a sentence.

I backspace it into nothingness.

I groan.

I still don't have an ending to this play, and my mind keeps nudging to the obvious. It's a fairy tale. It needs that toe-curling, heart-clutching, weak-kneed ending. It needs true love's kiss. And I can't bring myself to do it.

I slam my laptop shut.

I walk to the kitchen and find Lorelei sitting on Emory's lap in our recliner. They're both looking at his phone. And, God, they're so cute that I could puke. A part of me wants to say, *I need a girls' night, so get lost, buddy*, but I halt mid-step.

I know Lorelei. I'd tell her I'm anxious and she'd immediately be by my side without question. But watching them laugh together, I need to realize that it's not going to always be Lorelei and Quinn. It'll be Lorelei,

Quinn, and Emory. Or sometimes, just Lorelei and Emory.

I try to walk back to my room, but the floorboard squeaks under me.

Lorelei looks up. "Oh, hey! What are you doing?"

I twist on the spot. "I was just seeing if we have frozen pizza or something. We don't."

"We could order some if you'd like!"

"No, no," I say. "I think I'm gonna go out tonight actually."

"Oh, no, stay with us!" she says.

Emory's eyes dart to her with a frown. It's obvious by how his large hands span over her waist and thigh that his mind is elsewhere.

"No," I say. "You two need time together without me third-wheeling for once."

"Aw, but we like our third wheel," she says. "We're the best tricycle around!"

I roll my eyes with a smile.

"Go be a bicycle," I say. "In fact, ride the bicycle. Ride it real good."

"Quinn!" she chastises.

Emory narrows his eyes at me, but I still see a little bit of a smile on his face.

"Don't worry about me!" I say, waving my hand.

"All right," she says, but the tone is skeptical. "As long as you're sure. Pizza this weekend though?"

"Yeah, definitely."

I walk back to my room, scrolling through my phone, looking at our five-person group text. I already know my options are limited. Bennett is probably at home with Jolene, and I know Ruby goes to bed early.

I end up calling Theo. When she answers on the third

ring, the background noise is full of wind. She must be driving with her windows down. My heart sinks.

"Hey, girlie!" she says.

"Hey, what are you doing tonight?" I ask. "Please tell me you're not leaving town."

"Who's that?" another voice says.

I feel like I recognize that boyish, lighthearted voice.

"Is that Orson with you?" I ask.

"No," Theo quickly says. "Ha. Silly. Of course not. Just on a date with some guy. Met him online. You know how it is. You hear one playboy's voice, and you've heard them all."

"Hey!" the voice says.

I snort. "Well, remember that you share your location with me—I hope you can hear me, mystery man!"

Theo laughs. "He wouldn't touch a fly."

"If he does anything, I'll bring a hatchet," I say, then yell so he can hear, "I'll bring my hatchet, man!"

Theo cackles. "I'll keep you updated if I need it."

We hang up, and I'm left on my bed, laptop open next to me. All of my friends have social lives or significant others, and I'm over here with my bad mood.

I don't like feeling this way. Pessimistically hopeless. My friends are the ones who normally pull me out of it. They're always able to look on the bright side of things. Heck, maybe that's why they have a social life, and I ... don't.

I open my phone again. Maybe I'll go to the Ardens' house. Lorelei's mom is like a second parent to me. She probably has a pot roast going or something.

I start to type in *Arden*, but the first name that pops up is Landon's instead.

My finger hovers over the name, and the annoying voice in my head says, *He's a decent distraction.*

I click into our text thread.

The last thing in there is from our plans a couple of days ago. My last response was a middle-finger emoji after he said he was almost at The Honeycomb.

I suck in the side of my cheek.

Wouldn't a good old-fashioned Quinn-Landon sparring match make you feel better? Or better yet, could he help with the script?

It's that thought that has me typing.

Me: Want to practice lines tonight?

I wait, staring at the text thread. My heart is pounding, and I hate myself for it.

You have no right to be nervous, I mentally tell it. But it's hard to ignore the way my nerves sputter like a bad car engine when my phone chimes.

Landon: Thinking of me at night?
Me: Don't flatter yourself. I just need someone to look over this script for me.
Landon: And you thought of me.

I catch the laugh in my throat.

Me: Maybe.
Landon: Then, consider me flattered.
Me: I'll be sure to say very bitter things to make up for it.
Landon: Don't threaten me with a good time.
Me: Down, boy.
Landon: I wish you hadn't sent that.
Me: I fight fire with fire.

Landon: That's a safety hazard. I just bought this house.

Me: I'll leave my matches at home.

Landon: Are you implying you want to come over to my house?

My heart stops.

Me: No.

Landon: Don't be weird. You can come over to my house.

Me: I absolutely do not want to.

Landon: I'm sure hell isn't as bad as you think it is, Barbie.

I freeze, my fingers hovering over the screen. And then I receive another text bubble.

Landon: Also, I'm making homemade pizza. Hope that's okay.

I open the white picket fence into Landon's yard. I don't know what I expected, but it wasn't this.

Landon's small lawn of grass is lush and full—overgrown, yet not overbearing. Vines trail up the side of the house, clinging to the burgundy wood with patches of off-white, where paint has chipped away over the years. A wind chime hangs from the awning over his porch swing, tinkling with the light evening wind.

It's like a cottage from a storybook. Or maybe a house meant to lure in protagonists.

I reach out my fist to knock on his door but quickly pull it back.

This will be the first time Landon and I have truly been alone ... ever? Sure, there were the times when we sat in the Ardens' hallway after midnight as teens, but the rest of the family was still under the same roof. We've never been alone without implied supervision.

I laugh to myself.

This is insane. What do I think will happen? His football team buddies will pop out of the bushes and taunt me again? Call me Bridezilla? Whisper Mrs. Landon Arden in my ear?

Or is it simpler than that? Am I nervous that Landon will touch my waist in the privacy of a home with nowhere for me to go? That his warm breath will soothe over my skin?

No, I'm being ridiculous.

I inhale deeply, roll my neck, then knock on his door three times.

There are footsteps on the other side, and the door swings open.

Oh.

Landon's hair is wet, tossed every which messy way. He's got a simple T-shirt on, loosely hanging around his shoulders, but fitted around his chest like it was meant to be there on his massive build. His hand is still on the door handle, veins sticking out over each finger, wrapping around his forearms. The other hand balances on the opposite side of the doorjamb, displaying his large biceps and their every hill and valley.

I quickly dart my eyes back to his face. Both of his eyebrows are raised, and a dimple is indented into his beard.

I was wrong earlier. In this fairy tale, he's the Big Bad Wolf, and I'm Little Red Riding Hood, preparing to get eaten alive.

"Wanna come in, Barb?" he asks.

Thank God he's great at reminding me why I hate him.

"Not my name," I say, walking under his propped-up arm gating me from the rest of the house.

He chuckles behind me, closing the door with a click.

I peer around the living room. It's so utilitarian. Nothing on the walls, no rugs on the floor. The ceiling has a patched-up hole, and the bookshelves look haphazardly loaded up. A stack of empty boxes litters the corner of the room.

"Does a serial killer live here?" I ask.

He chuckles. "Why? Looking for a partner in crime?"

I bite the inside of my cheek to prevent the twitch at the edge of my mouth.

I turn around, finally noticing his kitchen—a stark contrast to the rest of the house in how used it is. I breathe in the smell of spices, a mix of onion and garlic.

He crosses behind me, placing a hand on the small of my back to shift me forward so he can pass by. I stiffen at his touch, holding my breath until he passes, as if his cologne will cause me to break out in hives.

"So, you wanted me to look over the script?" he asks.

"Oh. Yeah."

I dig it out and plop it on the counter. He pulls it closer and reads.

I step forward, leaning in to look at the script. His face is close to mine, and I can smell his minty breath with each exhalation.

"Am I supposed to be seeing something here?" he asks. "An ending perhaps?"

I hold back a smile. "Shut it."

He laughs again—always entertained with my attitude. I swear he gets off on it.

Nope. Don't think about him getting off.

"You've got writer's block," he says. "Why? Nervous about the park's buyer or something?"

"Oh, we're getting into serious talk already, huh?"

He tilts his head to the side. "It's the only icebreaker I know."

I clear my throat. "Well, I'm not nervous."

"Oh, you're so full of lies," he says with a grin.

"Only with you."

"Quinn," he repeats in a singsong voice. It rumbles in my chest. It feels like he's worming his way into my system, one dimple at a time.

"Fine," I admit. "Yes, I'm worried about it. A little."

"I'd think you were crazy if you weren't."

I scrunch my nose. "I expected you to say I'd be fine. That it'll all work out."

"Nah, pure optimism is my sister's job," he says, then whispers in a raspy tone, "I'm the more realistic twin."

A smile edges at my lips, but I tamp it down by curling them in.

"So, what's making you nervous?" he asks. "Not wanting to leave Queen Bee?"

"What makes you say that?"

He shrugs. "I'm observant."

I cross my arms. "Then, by all means, tell me what else I'm thinking."

"You want to be comfortable. Queen Bee makes you feel secure."

My muscles tense, and I drag in a deep inhale, then let it out.

"Well, I'm not exactly qualified for anything else other than Queen Bee, am I?"

"Ah, there's that again," he says with a laugh, opening the oven.

"What?"

"The lies you tell yourself," he says, pulling the pizza out, placing it on the counter, and steadying his mitts on either side of it. "You've got so many skills. You just don't think you do."

I bark out a laugh. "I don't tell myself lies."

"Then, agree with me when I say you have skills."

"What skills do I have, pray tell?"

"You're authoritative," he says. "Charismatic. Motivated."

"Okay, you're just being an ass now. Those aren't skills."

"No, really. Seeing you with those kids at the park? You've really got something."

"Now, who's lying?"

"I'm being honest," he says. "Isn't that what friends do?"

I blink at him. "Are we friends now?"

He shrugs with a small smile. "We could be."

"I think not."

"Right," he says with a snap of his fingers. "Dating, *then* friendship. How could I be so silly?"

"*Fake* dating," I clarify.

He chuckles. "Where we fake hold hands. And you fake like me."

"You fake like me too," I say.

His eyes dart to me, and he squints with a grin. "Do I though?"

I freeze. He laughs that boyish *all is well* laugh as he drags the slicer over the pizza. His forearms tense with each movement. My mouth gets dryer by the second.

I distract myself with his bookshelf. My fingers play

across the books like piano keys, tracing the spines until I reach something too familiar.

I roll my eyes. *Of course he kept his yearbooks.* Why wouldn't he want to remember the *good ol' days?*

Mine are somewhere. Possibly at my dad's. Maybe my mom's. Though I think she's moved a couple of times since I would have dropped them off, so I bet they're floating around at a Goodwill somewhere.

Good riddance.

I pick one off the shelf that has a bookmark and open it. I don't know what I expected the bookmark to lead to. Probably a highlight of his football career. Him on the shoulders of his teammates. But when I open it, it isn't football.

It's ... me.

Well, me and Lorelei, with our Honeywood T-shirts and grins plastered on our faces. I look so happy. So carefree.

I can feel my face contort, eyebrows furrowing up in concern or something.

Or something.

Why would he bookmark a page with us on it?

I glance over at him, reaching in the cabinet for plates, his hands grasping the stack, the other hand steadying them as they lower to the counter. My stomach clenches tightly when his eyes dart over to me, followed by a smile. He acts like we've been doing this for years—having dinner, exchanging smiles, talking about careers ...

"Whatcha got there?" he asks.

I fumble the book back onto the shelf, as if I just found random porn.

"Nothing. Just being nosy," I answer.

But I can't shake the feeling of seeing my young face staring back with the goofy smile that I feel like I haven't had in years. Was I more optimistic back then? Was I ever that ... smiley?

"Question," I say out loud. "Why was I bookmarked?"

His eyes dart up to mine. "What?"

"In your yearbook. It was turned to me and Lorelei at Honeywood. Why?"

I see his face drop a millimeter and his dimples disappear. Our eyes dance between each other's, as if we're trying to read the other's mind. His boyish smile appears just as quick as it fell.

"I didn't even notice," he says.

I'm calling that a lie.

"I thought we were friends?" I coax.

"Oh, now, you say we are?"

I lift a single eyebrow. He inhales sharply, standing taller.

"What?" he asks. "Are you worried I might have liked you at some point?"

"I didn't even consider that."

His, *"Not a chance,"* rings through my head, an echo of a memory.

"I don't see why you wouldn't," he says. "You're very likable. You might even say I *real* like you instead of fake like you."

He's playing with me. Trying to get me to break. Landon is the only person, aside from my friend group, who isn't scared of me. Part of me wonders if I'm starting to be scared of him though. Especially with how my heart races when he implies he might like me.

"Don't be an ass," I bite out.

He shrugs. "I'm not. Pizza?"

I keep staring at him as he arranges my plate on the bar top. He stands on the opposite side, lifting a slice and biting into it. When I don't move, he tilts his head toward my plate.

"You coming?" he asks. "Or have I finally beaten the mighty Quinn?"

"Shut up," I say, walking with heavy feet over to the stool.

He stares at me when I sit down and watches as I take the first bite.

Holy God.

I try not to moan, but he can see my eyes roll back.

"Taste good?" he asks.

"Christ, where'd you learn how to cook like this?"

He laughs. "Practice. I had to earn the right to wear pizza underwear."

I snort. "You really could do this for a living."

"Maybe," he says. "I'd like to, but we'll see."

"Now, who is doubting their skills?"

I expect him to laugh with me, but when I finally meet his gaze, he's nodding.

"What?" I ask.

"Something's been bugging me," he says. "And feel free not to answer. But ... you mentioned something the other night."

"I mention a lot of things."

"You mentioned not getting out of bed years ago," he says. "In college. What happened?"

My stomach drops, and I immediately shake my head, but I can't stop the memories that come rushing back in. The loneliness. The self-loathing. The feeling of my mind being both empty and full at the same time, like it'd burst from the seams, only to turn out as cotton balls.

I don't want to relive junior year of college. And I definitely don't want to do it with Landon.

"You're right," I say. "I don't want to answer that."

He nods slowly. For a second, I wonder if he's going to push it further.

Instead, he says, "I also make killer milkshakes, y'know."

I blink. "Okay ..."

"I can make us some," he says. "We can sit on the back porch. I have a hammock too."

Is he serious?

I look out the back of his house—a wall that is windows from floor to ceiling. His backyard is more maintained than the front. There's cute, low grass with a walkway, leading to a rope-spun hammock, illuminated in the setting sun. It's idyllic and unreal.

"You're going to make us milkshakes," I deadpan.

"Yes," he says. "Would you like one?"

"Are you trying to bribe me to stay?"

"No, I'm being a gracious host," he says. "For my friend."

"Gross."

"Okay, you caught me. Yes, I'm trying to bribe you."

I consider turning him down, but the tug at his lips has me slowly nodding my head without realizing it.

"Fine," I say, throwing my napkin at him. "But nobody can know you called me your friend. And I'm only staying because your kitchen skills are so good."

He lets out a small, almost-inaudible groan from his throat. "Don't try to give me compliments. It's weird."

"You don't like weird?"

He pauses and leans against the fridge door with his arms crossed. "No. I actually think I like weird a bit too much."

I give a mocking laugh, and his smile deepens.

"So, what is"—he flings open his fridge door with a flourish—"your favorite flavor of milkshake?"

"Strawberry."

He smiles. "Strawberry it is."

"Yours?"

"I'm a good ol' classic vanilla kinda guy."

I laugh. "Who in the world loves a *vanilla* milkshake?"

"People who like milk."

"The '90s really had us in a chokehold with the Got Milk campaigns, huh?"

"Sure sold the Arden household."

He sidesteps past me in the small space to reach under the counter for the blender. When he does, his chest brushes mine. I suck in a breath.

Nope. Nope, nope, nope.

"I'm gonna go ... check out your yard," I say, cringing.

"Yeah," he says with a laugh. "You go do that, weirdo."

I slide open the back door, stepping out into the yard. Small garden lights line the path to the hammock. I walk over and fall into it. He comes out with both milkshakes five minutes later, handing me mine and leaning against the tree trunk, hand in pocket. We drink in silence as fireflies blink around us.

"So, do we make small talk now or later?" he asks.

I sputter into my drink.

He sighs. "Love it when you laugh at my jokes."

"I can try small talk."

"Go for it."

"What else is on your bookshelves, outside of creepy yearbooks?"

"Yikes. Stab to the heart immediately," he says. "Well, I don't know. Fiction. Why? What have you been reading lately?"

I take a long sip of my drink.

"I'm actually rereading some fairy tales," I say.

At least, I was as of this afternoon. And to my lack of surprise, there was kiss after kiss after kiss. I flipped through pages like a madman, trying to find another solution. There wasn't one.

Sleeping Beauty? Kiss.

Snow White? Kiss.

Cinderella? Shoe, then marriage, then kiss.

It was never-ending.

"I always liked when you read those," Landon says, breaking me from my thoughts.

I pause. It's like getting transported back in time. Me in his parents' hallway. Him sitting next to me, peering over my shoulder, asking me to wait before I turned the page. Following along in horror as we read the original versions of cartoon movies. *Grimms' Fairy Tales* were indeed grim.

I shift in my hammock uncomfortably.

"Did you really enjoy reading over my shoulder?" I ask.

"Lived for it," he says with a laugh. "So, what fairy tales you reading now?"

My stomach drops.

"Wait, wait, wait," I say, holding out a hand. "We can't just bypass what you said."

"What'd I say?" he asks. Boyish. Innocent.

He knows what he's doing.

"Landon," I say.

"Quinn."

And my name on his lips—my real name, not Queen Bee or Barbie—sends a chill down my spine. But I hold his gaze, staring him down as the night breeze washes over us.

He tongues his cheek. "Fine," he says. "Yeah. I thought you were cool. But that isn't news, is it?"

I pause. "You thought I was cool?"

He chuckles. "Yeah, Barb. The coolest."

I think that line short-circuited my thoughts because for ten minutes after that, we circumvent every conversation deeper than *here's the book I'm reading* and *how's the weather* and *here are some ideas for the play*.

For some reason, that line is what sticks with me the rest of the night.

Landon Arden thought pink-braces girl was cool.

22

Quinn

I have every intention of giving Landon the cold shoulder this morning because *how dare he trick me into having fun with him last night,* but I don't have to. Landon says hi, throws me a casual side-smile, then continues talking to Lorelei and Honey. It's like we're strictly coworkers instead of newly formed secret hang-out frenemies.

He acts like nothing changed at all. Yet it feels like everything has changed.

I feel like *I've* changed.

When we hold hands, nerves zip up my arm. When he laughs, tingles rise through my chest. And when he traces his thumb over the back of my elbow, I am two seconds away from melting into the floorboards.

It's like he performed hypnosis of the wickedest kind, and I was gullible enough to watch the pendulum swing.

We wrap up in the morning, and I hang behind after we're done. I don't see Landon anywhere and hate how that deflates me. I went from wishing he weren't here to wondering when he'd left.

I fall back on the stage, staring up at the ceiling.

I'm losing my mind.

My phone buzzes beside me, and I glance over.

My stomach churns with how badly I wanted to the see the letters *L* and *A*.

Instead, I see M-O-M.

Today is not the day for this. And yet part of me—the part that feels lost in this moment—unlocks my phone and views the text thread.

Mom: I'd like to talk if you have time.

I slide the phone away from me like it's on fire. It catches on the loose floorboard and halts not even a foot away.

Another complication in my life.

This is always how it starts with my mom. She texts me, wanting a relationship. I text back, and then I receive one or two replies before it fizzles out again. It's like Sisyphus trying to push that boulder up the hill, only to have his efforts fall back on him for eternity.

I spent so many of my teen years trying to get her attention, to get her to make me a priority. She was too busy, being caught up in herself. I know, rationally now, that she was just a kid in an adult's body. That she wasn't ready for me. But that doesn't change the fact that I needed her.

My dad isn't much better. He only contacts me on my birthday, living in bliss on the beach with a martini and whichever woman of the week will keep him company. I now prefer our limited communication, as does he. Dad has made it too clear over the years that he doesn't want me to end up like Mom—especially after junior year of college. I think he's terrified of it. For him, ignorance is bliss.

I know I'm nothing like her. If I had a kid, I would make

sure to go to their plays, or their parent-teacher conferences, or, hell, even their graduation. My mom and I have gone years without talking before. I'm not above doing it now.

I give her another day. She'll forget about me, as she always does. And I'll move on with my life.

"You look like you're holding a grudge."

I sit up. At the end of the aisle, I see Honey.

She shuffles down, her turquoise flats kicking around pebbles over the gravel. Even from here, I can hear her jewelry clanking around.

"Why do you say that?" I ask.

"Your eyebrows. They're all scrunchy," she clarifies, her voice shaky as she pauses next to my dangling feet. The hunch on her back barely reaches the stage. "You look like you've got an issue with someone. A chip on your shoulder."

"I don't know if I'd call it that."

"Maybe not, but I know that look."

"How?" I ask. "Do you have a chip on your shoulder?"

"Oh, yes. A big one, Queenie," she says with wide eyes. "A big one."

I narrow my eyes. "Why are you here?"

"Ah," she says. "Well, don't we have a park to sell? Last I checked, you have no ending."

I grunt, pulling my legs up to sit crisscross onstage.

"I'm working on it," I say.

"Ah, the elusive ending," Honey muses. "Which is actually"—she smacks her lips—"not that elusive."

My body shifts. My stomach tightens.

"I feel like you know what I'm going to say," Honey says. "But for some reason, you don't want me to say it. Curious."

I swallow, but it doesn't quell the dryness in my throat.

"It's a kiss," I say. "True love's kiss is what we need."

She taps my knee. "That's correct."

"I can't," I say. "That's not in the cards."

Honey lets out a laugh, but it's more like a pop of air and a scoff. An engine backfiring.

"I'd take any excuse to kiss Randy," she says. "Are you kidding me?"

I shake my head, but images fly through my brain faster than I can stop them. His warm breath against my ear. His hand on my waist. The *ear thing*. The *neck thing*.

"No," I repeat. "Not happening."

"Ah, so you have history," she says. It's not a question.

"No, we don't," I say. "Stop prying."

"I'm incapable of *not* being nosy," Honey says with a shrug. "So, you'll just have to tell me, or I'll bug you about it till the end of time."

"I can outrun you," I say.

She grins. "You can try. I'll haunt you as a ghost."

I shift on the stage, looking out at the empty theater, the rows of seats that will be filled in only a week.

I'm sure Lorelei is doing her part in marketing to draw people in, but word of mouth is better than anything else. And a play where the hot Ranger Randy kisses someone? Anyone? *Me*? It's admittedly the best solution. It's the only thing that might get me to a stage manager role. A writing role. Something that is more than what I have now.

But at what cost? And could I even handle it?

"Listen," I finally say. "Landon was an ass in high school, and he's probably an ass now. That's the history. And that's all the reason I need not to kiss him."

Honey nods slowly and lets out a small *hmm* before saying, "You said *probably*."

"What?"

"You said he's *probably* an ass now."

"Definitely," I clarify.

"Uh-huh, and what did he even do?"

"He's ... it's complicated."

"That puppy dog hurt you?"

"Believe it or not, he wasn't always so nice," I say. "He let things happen."

Honey *hmms* again, a low, contemplative noise.

"Well," she says, "he sure didn't stand there and let things happen the other day, did he? Hugh got a mouthful."

I dart my eyes to her. "That was different."

"Was it?" she asks. "People do change, you know."

They do. Some, like my mom and dad, grow more self-ish. They get distant; they curl inward.

But Landon also *feels* different. And not in a *his chest is massive and hard as a rock* way, but in a *I can't put my finger on it, but I'm suddenly comfortable around him* way.

Why did last night feel like our relationship upgraded to something more?

Why do I feel like we're friends?

I glance back to Honey, who looks like the cat that ate the canary. Wide smile and sparkling eyes.

And why do I feel like she's plotting my demise?

I make a mental note to never let her know where I sleep.

"Y'know," she says, "I'm actually glad we talked, Quee-nie. I think you know what needs to be done."

I narrow my eyes. "No, I don't."

She leans in with a wink. "That's the *chip* talking."

23

Landon

"Well, look at you. What brings you here?"

I sigh. "A desire to not go home."

Orson winces. "Yikes. That's not a good sign. Beer?"

"Yes, please."

I sit at the bar in The Honeycomb, an hour or two after my day at Honeywood ended. My mind is still a mess, and it's not getting any better.

I wanted to be casual today, trying not to draw attention to the fact that Quinn and I weren't fighting as much anymore. Trying not to scare her off. I'm not even sure it was a good decision. Attempting to be friends with Quinn is like trying to pet a stray cat. It's a lottery on whether you get the claws or not.

Orson pulls down the handle over the glass and slides it across the bar top.

"So, how is it?" he asks. "Being back in town?"

"The same," I say, taking a swig. "And different."

"That's not cryptic at all," Orson says.

I chuckle at the same time that he smiles. He twists his

ball cap backward and leans forward on the bar. His eyebrows rise expectantly.

"Question for you," he says.

"Answer for you."

"Why don't you want to go home?"

Memories. Restlessness. The fear that I might cave and ask Quinn to come over.

"Eh, it's boring," I lie.

"Uh-huh," Orson says with a slow nod. "Yeah, and what's the real reason?"

I take another drink and place it down on the bar top.

"Fine," I say. "You wanna get into it? Let's get into it. What are your thoughts on Quinn Sauer?"

He barks out a laugh. "Why? Interested in your sister's best friend?"

He pauses and one look at me seems to signal the truth. Maybe it's my tired face, or maybe he can hear my heartbeat in my chest.

Either way: "Oh, whoa. You are."

"It's ..." I want to say *not like that*, but it absolutely is. "Complicated."

"I'll say. Doesn't she hate you? And—don't take this the wrong way—I kinda thought you didn't like her that much in high school either."

My stomach drops.

"Why?" I ask. "What makes you say that?"

"You ... well, you ran with the crowd that had a problem with most people," he says. I can tell he's softening the blow.

"It was just the football team," I say. "You were on there too."

"I didn't hang out with them after practices," he says with a shrug. "I couldn't handle them like you could."

"Handle them?" I ask. "What did they do?"

"You don't know?"

"Should I?"

"They were awful to Quinn," Orson says. "She's told me over the years what happened ..."

"What happened?"

The front door roars open. Bennett eyes us at the bar and gives a raise of his chin in acknowledgment.

I bite the inside of my cheek and give Orson a *don't you dare say anything about Quinn* look. He nods.

"Hey," Bennett says to me, elbowing my arm resting on the counter. "What are you doing here?"

"Thinking," I say with a shrug.

Orson bites his lip and snickers. Bennett doesn't seem to notice.

"Yeah, me too," he says.

"Hard day?" I ask.

"Hard week," he grunts.

"Wanna talk about it?"

Bennett's face falls. "Do y'all think I'm irrational?" he asks.

Both Orson and I glance at Bennett, lips parted, eyes wide.

"I mean, aren't we all a little irrational?" I say.

Bennett swivels his eyes to mine without shifting his head away from his beer. "Yeah?"

"Oh, yeah, definitely. I mean, here I am, back in my hometown, and I'm playing some fictional children's book character. In a job where I'm *supposed* to be security," I say with a lighthearted laugh. "What rational guy would do that?"

What rational guy would continue pining for a woman who doesn't like him?

It coaxes a chuckle out of Bennett, a low, rumbling kind of thing that would instead come from a snoring bear.

"Good point," Orson says, tilting his head to the side. "What rational guy *would* do that?"

I shoot him a glare that says *don't you dare.*

Orson leaves and comes back with three shot glasses, pouring them to the brim with something that I don't recognize or care about. We simultaneously clink our shots together and swing them back.

"Okay, no more talking," Bennett says.

I nod, hissing as the liquid sizzles down my throat. "Fair enough."

Orson flicks the television to a game. I pull out my phone to check the time and am surprised to find a text waiting for me. My already-upset stomach wraps around me more, tying all sense of reason into the tightest death knot imaginable.

Quinn: What's for dinner?

I stare at the text for a solid ten seconds, my mouth twitching into a slow yet heart-racing smile.

Me: That's presumptuous of you.
Quinn: Or maybe I'm just trying to be nice and ask about your night.
Me: You're right. Because you sound so nice.
Quinn: You like that, don't you?

I bite my lip and glance away. *This woman, my God.*

Me: I'm at The Honeycomb with Bennett and Orson. Might make grilled chicken later. If you're into that.

Quinn: I'm very much into that.

Me: Why do I feel like I'm being used for my cooking?

Quinn: I'm a simple gal. I come for cooking and a good fight.

Me: Showing all your cards tonight, aren't you?

Quinn: Some people might say those requests are unreasonable.

Me: Only the reasonable people would.

Quinn: And which are you?

Me: The most egregiously unreasonable.

Quinn: So, we'll have dinner at seven and a fight at eight?

Me: Try seven thirty.

Quinn: I'll pencil it in.

24

Quinn

I shouldn't be flirting with Landon over text, yet I did.

I shouldn't be itching for more of him, yet I am.

I shouldn't be at Landon's house again, yet my car door shuts behind me and—*whoops*—I'm pulling the latch for his white fence open.

Present Quinn feels like Past Quinn would be sorely disappointed. Or maybe proud. I'm not sure. Am I experiencing growth? Or am I slowly ruining my life? It's a toss-up.

I open his front door without knocking, and I'm greeted with him in the kitchen, paused with his hands holding a chicken breast.

"Hello there," he says. "Why, yes, come on in."

"I figured we were at that point."

"I didn't know that."

"Now, you do."

A slow smile spreads over his face. His dimples press deeper into his cheeks. My heart picks up at the sight of them.

I take my script out of my tote bag, sliding it across the counter.

"Are we practicing lines?" he asks, washing his hands in the sink.

"Why else would I be here?" I ask. "Friendship?"

He smiles. "Of course not."

Landon flips through with slightly damp fingers. I watch his deft hands move over the pages, admiring the defined fingers and bony wrists.

"Gonna mess up the entire script or just part of it?" I ask when a couple of wet drops sprinkle the page from his hand.

He smiles, ignoring my comment. "Ready?"

I feel the corner of my mouth tip up, and I start on the first line.

We cycle through the script as he cooks, pausing so he can flip the chicken in the skillet and fry the vegetables in the one beside it. It smells unreal, and yet I can still pick out his cologne through all of it.

"Smells great," I say out loud. "The chicken, I mean."

Landon looks around the room, as if searching to see if there are hidden cameras.

His eyes narrow with a smile. "Are you trying to be nice to me?"

"Psht, no," I say, forcing a laugh.

"Kind of seems like you are."

"Get your head out of your ass."

"Ah, there she is," he says with a nod.

"Who?"

"Feisty Quinn."

My muscles tense at the word *feisty*. How he said it with a purr in his throat.

169

We keep reading, and even once we finish and dinner is eaten, I find myself staying in my chair. Unmoving. Not wanting to leave his house. Instead, I watch him walk through the kitchen, tilting my head to see his body flex with every movement. I'm trying to guard myself from emotions, and yet here Landon is, being Landon. I'm fourteen all over again.

He meets my eyes.

Crap.

He walks to the fridge and edges it open.

"Milkshake?" he asks.

Without skipping a beat, I say, "Yeah."

Yep, I'm doomed.

A grin breaks across his face, and he nods, pulling out the ingredients. I grab our dishes from dinner and put them in the sink. I turn on the water, and he gives me a side-eye.

"What are you doing?" he asks.

"What?" I ask. My face heats. "Let me do the dishes. You cooked."

"Yeah, and you're my guest."

"And I don't want to be a useless guest."

He inhales sharply, then lets out a weak laugh that ends in a small groan, as if I pained him physically.

"You are ... so interesting, Quinn Sauer," he says with a sigh. "Just go outside."

When I turn back to the sink, his palms land on my waist from behind. I stiffen like a board beneath his touch as he guides me from the sink to the edge of the kitchen.

"Go," he says.

"I'm not Old Yeller."

"And I'm not shooting you."

Debatable. I'm getting shot right to the heart.

I walk outside anyway, sitting in the hammock, swinging myself back and forth, feeling the evening breeze.

Chill, Quinn. Chill.

A minute later—or maybe an hour, but I don't know because time is irrelevant at this point—Landon walks into the yard. It's so hard not to admire him with every step. How tall he is. How built he is. How a smile dances on his face.

He leans against the tree trunk, like he did last time, handing me my drink. His eyes glance over me, scanning from my head to my stomach, then my toes.

I curl in on myself. "What?"

"Nothing," he says. "Well ... I mean, you're here. Hanging out with me. Again."

"Yes, and?"

"I would have never seen the day."

"Too embarrassing for you?" I ask.

His face falls, and then he forces out a laugh. At least, it sounds forced.

"Come on," he says. "You were my sister's mysterious best friend. And there I was, just being an idiot with my equally stupid friends." He sighs. Wistful, almost dreamy. "Embarrassing? No. Humbled maybe."

My chest drops. Suddenly, my drink feels unsettling in my stomach. My knees weak. My toes curling inside my boots.

I blink, trying to take everything in.

"You're joking," I say. "Tell me you're joking."

"Why would I be?"

"Because you ... your friends ..." My words fade off.

The yard turns silent at that. He stares at me, and his free hand tightens by his side.

"My friends what?" he asks.

I scoff. "Okay, you're not allowed to defend them."

"Defend them? No, that's not what's happening here. I

171

want to know what they did to you. Because, apparently, I'm missing something."

I look at him, trying to see if he's joking, but his expression doesn't change.

"What are you talking about?" I ask. "You *found* my diary!"

He stiffens. "Yeah," he says. "I remember that. I remember ... that ... I didn't handle it well. At all."

"No shit," I mutter.

I sink into the hammock. There was venom in those words. It settles in my chest like a disease, a death sentence for any good I might have had in me.

Honey was right.

I *do* have a chip on my shoulder.

"I'm sorry about that," he finally says. "I am. Please ..." He closes his eyes. "Please tell me what happened after that."

His plea is odd.

Does he really not know?

"You and your friends wouldn't let me live it down," I say.

"That," he says, pointing a finger at me, "that I don't remember. They bugged *me* about it for a while, but ... I don't remember ..."

"Whispers in the hallway?" I ask. "Notes in my locker? Bridezilla?"

"Bride—"

"It's a stupid nickname," I rush to say. "But you already know that."

"I don't." His face is steel. "Quinn, I promise I don't."

"You didn't leave the notes?"

"I didn't *know* there were notes. And I can't ... I can't imagine how horrible that must have been for you."

I blink as his eyebrows stitch in. As he transforms from anger to sadness to desperation. To hurt.

He's serious.

He wasn't involved at all, was he?

I feel like my world, my beliefs, everything I thought up to this point is crumbling down. For years, I thought he was part of their jokes, and ... he wasn't?

"I'm sorry," he says. "I cannot apologize enough. For how unbelievably out of touch I was."

"You really didn't know," I say, but it's not a question.

His jaw tenses. "I didn't."

We look at each other for what feels like minutes, hours, weeks.

"I'd redo it all if I could," he finally says. "In a heartbeat."

I feel like the world is pressing me deeper in the hammock, the ropes burning into the places they touch. My thighs, my arms, my neck. If gravity had any conscience, it would release me from its prison. But I can't move.

"I'm sorry my friends made your life a living hell for however long they did," he continues. "I won't ask you to forgive me because that's not my place to ask. But ... I am so sorry."

I don't say anything. I'm not sure what to say. Something in me wants to say, *You're forgiven*, but it would be cheap if I didn't fully mean it, so I don't say it.

The energy around us is now awkward, stuffy with humidity and sour memories.

I let out a sarcastic laugh to break the tension. "Might be easier to forgive you if you got on your knees."

His eyebrows rise. I thought he'd laugh with me, but he doesn't.

Julie Olivia

"Quinn," he says, his tone raspy and low, "if you want me on my knees, I can get on my knees."

My face burns. My heart stammers.

I quickly jerk my head away. "Don't be ridiculous."

I awkwardly sip on my milkshake. The slurping sound echoes through the yard. It feels inappropriate.

Landon lifts his arm to rest on the tree, hooking his fingers onto a branch. His scent almost matches the fallen brown leaves, like the comforting smell of autumn lingers on his skin.

I don't know what else to say. And yet his face is still drawn. Still stoic.

I think he might actually be sorry.

"It's good tonight," I say, breaking the silence. "The shake."

A slow smile tips at the edge of his lips. "Yeah?"

"Mmhmm."

"Wanna try mine?" he asks. "You might like vanilla."

"And drink after you?"

"Don't knock it till you try it."

I can't tell if he's talking about the taste of vanilla or the taste of him. His sly smile doesn't give me a clear answer.

I take his cup, like an olive branch extended between us, wrap my lips around the straw, and take a long draw. And it turns out, he's right. The vanilla is kinda nice. Plain but simple. Not overpowering.

"You like it?" he asks.

I hand it back to him.

"You do, don't you?"

Evil little butterflies erupt in my chest.

So, so evil.

"It's not horrible," I say with a smile.

"So ..." He kicks his shoe on the ground, rustling the

grass. "Just curious ... why'd you come over tonight?"

"To practice lines," I say without skipping a beat.

With a downward turn of his chin and a subtle smile, he adds, "Be honest."

I roll my eyes, but I can't help the way my heart skips at those words. It's the way they were said, low and intimate. As if we have a secret just between us. As if he trusts me to tell him the truth.

I did want to hang out with him. For some inexplicable reason, I didn't like that we'd barely talked today. And I can't reconcile that in my mind—especially after what just happened. But the look on his face makes my lips curl in.

"Friends hang out together, don't they?"

It's like I can see a light spark in his eyes.

"Yes," he says, "I suppose they do."

But the vulnerability makes me instantly feel, well, *vulnerable*, so I can't help the additional, "And I had nothing else to do," that leaves my mouth.

"Ouch," he says, placing a palm over his chest with a *thump*. "Right to the heart. What, no Lorelei?" he asks. "Everyone else is busy?"

I mix my straw in my cup.

"I told her she should hang out with Emory instead of me," I say.

"Oh, Emory," he muses. "Sometimes, I wonder if my sister is just blinded by the fact that the guy designs roller coasters."

I laugh. I can't help it.

"I like Emory," I admit. "Plus, he gets me."

"Someone *gets* you?" Landon asks. "What is his secret?"

I shrug. "He's surly. I'm surly. What can I say?"

"So, I should be surlier," he says. "Is what you're trying to tell me?"

175

"Why?" I ask. "Do you want me to like you?"

He gives a small shrug as he tips his head to the side. "Wouldn't be so bad, would it?"

For a moment—a single, solitary moment—I glance down to his lips and wonder what it'd be like to kiss him.

What if Honey was right? What if this grudge is holding me back? Could I let it go? But just how heavy is that chip on my shoulder?

"You don't need to be surlier," I say.

"What a relief," he says. "I'd suck at it."

I let out a small breath of light laughter.

"You know what we've never talked about?" I ask.

"Hmm?"

"Your pizza underwear."

He spits out part of his drink, and I can't hide the laugh that breaks out on my face too.

"My lucky underwear?" he asks.

"Not so much now, is it?"

After a moment of staring off, he finally shrugs.

"Nah," he says. "I think they're still lucky. I'm hanging out with you, aren't I?"

My breath hitches in my chest.

"Don't get used to it," I say.

"Too late."

I still smell his vanilla and cedar scent on my pillow that night. It's in my hair. On my skin. Around my soul. Like a freaking wizard casting his silly little spell. I try to imagine Landon in a bright blue wizard costume, patterned stars and all, and somehow, my mind still sees his muscle busting out of the robes.

Sigh.

After lying in bed for an hour, I roll over and grab my laptop.

I read my script as is. Ranger Randy on his knees. Ranger Randy sliding on Queen Bee's shoe. Ranger Randy saying things like, "Your Majesty," and, "Anything for you, My Queen." Swoonworthy lines that will drive the audience wild. That drive *me* wild.

I shift my legs underneath my laptop, curling my toes. I feel guilty with each key I press. Guilty for thinking of Landon like that. For enjoying every sentence of the script. For feeling the heat between my thighs spark like lightning. For ultimately accepting his apology tonight with jokes and unspoken words.

And when I finally get to the end of the script, I consider the impossible.

What if Ranger Randy and Queen Bee kissed?

If we were at any other theme park with queens, princesses, and princes, it would be business as usual. No big deal.

But it's also *Landon.*

I stare at my computer screen, the cursor blinking over and over on the script.

My mind wrestles with the possibilities of what I could write instead. But I know what I have to do. It's the only thing to move the needle toward selling the park, toward my future as a stage manager, and toward staying at Honeywood—a place that has been my home for so many years.

I type the final words and send it off to Fred and Honey for final approval.

But once the deed is done, I still spend far too long staring at the final line.

Queen Bee and Ranger Randy kiss.

25

Landon

I arrive at the amphitheater the next day, driven by the energy coursing through me at the thought of seeing Quinn. It feels like I'm a teenager again, except with far less ignorance.

I'm still reeling over what she told me. How she was bullied and I had no idea. I feel like an idiot. But mostly, I feel like I want to do anything I can to make it up to her.

I grip the edge of the stage and jump up, scooting to the left when I feel the creak of a floorboard beneath me.

Honey, Fred, and Lorelei are already in the audience. They all lean into a huddle, looking at a laptop. Honey has her arms crossed, her thick glasses dipping down to her nose. There's a slight downturn to Honey's mouth, like she's disappointed in what the screen deigns to show her. The expression reminds me of Quinn.

I chuckle at Honey, and her eyes dart to me. I can see the slow tilt at the edge of her mouth.

"What are you laughing at, Randy?" she asks.

I grin. "Nothing. Nothing."

She snorts. "You're gonna give a woman a complex."

Then, as if realizing something, she sighs, and her face falls. I feel my own expression falter. I open my mouth to ask what's wrong but am interrupted before I can.

"All right," Quinn says. "Final scripts, everyone!"

At the top of the amphitheater, Quinn waves papers in the air. Something as simple as her ponytail bouncing behind her makes my whole body light up.

Emily takes the stack from Quinn and passes them around.

I take one stapled copy, flipping through until I read the end.

My body freezes.

I swallow, my eyes darting up to Quinn. She's not looking at me. I look down and reread it again.

Queen Bee and Ranger Randy kiss.

"Any questions?" Quinn asks.

Lorelei exchanges a glance with Quinn that I can't decipher. Raised eyebrows. A lip bite. A half-smile.

Everyone says something like, "Looks great," and, "Let's do this."

I just nod and mutter, "Mmhmm. Yeah."

What else is there to say?

My blood is pumping, and my head feels heavy.

"Then, let's get going!" Quinn says, clapping her hands together.

I watch as she climbs the stairs backstage. Her lips are pursed in concentration. The same lips I'll be guaranteed to kiss at some point in the future.

I lift myself from the stage and walk back to Quinn. I look around, and nobody else is nearby, so I quickly tilt my head down to her.

"So, we kiss?" I whisper.

Stiffly, she nods. "We kiss. Made the most sense for the ending."

She side-eyes me. Her expression is muted.

I raise an eyebrow in challenge. "Nervous?"

She mirrors my raised eyebrow, lifting her lips into a smirk.

"Am I nervous?" she echoes with a scoff. "No. Are you?"

I smile. "Terrified."

Emily bursts through the backstage door, and I give a final look to Quinn—her lips are parted in disbelief—before walking to the opposite side of the stage.

26

Quinn

It's been three days since I wrote the ending to the script. Three days of practice.

Two days of lighting tests.

One final day of throwing on our costumes and performing the entire thing from start to finish. All without the kiss.

Except, as each day passes, I swear our glances linger even longer after that final line. And a million questions cross my mind each time.

How will we kiss? Will it be fast? Lingering? Tongue? No tongue? A full-on lipstick-smearing make-out with one leg mounted on his hip?

Is Landon even *good* at kissing?

I stop myself before I get too far down that rabbit hole.

I haven't hung out with him since the script was revealed. No dinners. No milkshakes. Part of me wonders if we're avoiding each other, and it puts me on edge, especially after our last conversation. Does he feel guilty?

I'm not proud of the fact that I break our text abstinence first.

Me: Got any strawberries?

Landon: If I didn't know better, I'd say you want to be around me.

Me: *Your kitchen. I'd like to be around your kitchen.

When Lorelei walks by, I shove my shameful evidence between the couch cushions. But then my phone buzzes, and I scramble for it. Scramble. Like a freaking fish to Landon's water.

Landon: If you had a choice between me and Fred, who would you kiss?

Me: Fred. It's the mustache.

Landon: I knew it.

Me: You?

Landon: Always Fred.

Me: I'm screenshotting this conversation to show Fred later.

Landon: Is it blackmail if I want it to happen?

Me: Be sure to pack your pizza underwear tomorrow.

Landon: Of course. I'll need all the luck I can get.

I don't respond. I won't let myself. Because that would mean I wanted to talk to him more.

Instead, I go for a walk to clear my mind.

After thirty minutes, I find myself in historic downtown, strolling by the brick buildings, walking under the cloth awnings, passing the fogged windows of the gym, looking into Slow Riser. I can't believe I'll start working there again in a couple of months, but even my looming winter work schedule at that coffee shop can't puncture my whirling thoughts.

Queen Bee and Ranger Randy kiss.

I should be more focused on what this play will lead to. The opportunities for a future at Honeywood or how I plan to navigate that future. But the thumping of my heart to the beat of *Landon, Landon, Landon* isn't letting me think too clearly.

When I pass the yoga studio downtown, I see Theo inside, holding herself up against the wall, mid-handstand. I push the door open. The smell of patchouli hits my nose. It's quiet, save for the dribbling fountain at the front desk.

"Oh, hey, you!" Theo says, upside down. "What are you doing?"

"Hating myself," I say.

She laughs, lowering herself down with a partial cartwheel. She takes a drink of water from her cup on the desk. She holds it out to me as an offering, and I shake my head. It only reminds me of sharing the milkshake with Landon. With him. Capital H *him*.

We've already swapped spit, right? Easy-peasy. We can do it again. Just like sharing a milkshake. Except with heady breaths and desperate groans.

Yep. Totally the same.

"Quinn?" Theo asks.

"Hmm?"

She smirks. "Are you thinking about kissing Landon tomorrow?"

My stomach drops, and I laugh. But it's my typical nervous laugh that sounds like a witch cackle or a killer clown.

I really have to work on that.

Theo's eyes widen. "Are you planning on kissing him or killing him?"

"Still up in the air."

"Are you gonna tell Lorelei when you like it?"

"No," I say. "I'm not gonna tell anybody." Then, I sputter out, "And I'm not gonna like it!"

"Aye, aye," Theo says with a weak salute and wink. "You almost forgot to add that addendum though."

She pumps her eyebrows at me, taking a triumphant, empty slurp from her cup. I grab it from her hands and toss it in the trash for her.

"Stop looking so smug!"

Theo laughs. "Listen, I know y'all don't get along. But whatever history y'all have is so old," she says. "Like, that beef is probably old enough to drive or buy alcohol, you know?"

"Maybe a learner's permit at best."

"Doesn't matter," she says. "He's not the same as he was years ago. Cut him some slack. Enjoy kissing a hot, bearded dude who you trust."

Do I trust him? It's hard to think he could be so different from who he was. But, God, how hypocritical of me. Aren't I different? Haven't I changed? After junior year of college, I am arguably *not* the same person. So, if I feel changed, why wouldn't he?

Maybe he has changed.

Theo's phone buzzes at the same time mine does.

I fumble in my pocket but am disappointed to find not Landon's name on my screen, but *Mom*. I look at Theo's phone and see *Orson*.

Her face reddens, and her lips curl in with a smile.

I lift an eyebrow and grin. "Theo? Got something to share with the class?"

My phone buzzes again. This time, it is Landon's name.

Theo's smile grows wider, and she angles her head toward me. "Do *you*, Quinn?"

184

"No."

She giggles. "If you like him, I promise not to tell."

"I won't tell either." I nod at the waiting text on her phone from Orson.

She sets her phone aside. "It's nothing. Really."

"And neither is mine," I respond. But it feels like a lie. I feel like I'm walking into the great unknown.

Is this how Rapunzel felt before descending her tower? Is this what Red Riding Hood thought before journeying into the woods?

"Well, even if you don't like him," Theo says, "there's no backing out now."

She's right.

No backing out now.

27

Landon

Backstage is ten times more nerve-racking when there's an actual audience. I can hear the loud hum of conversation. I catch words here and there, like *Ranger Randy, beard, tight shorts.*

I rub a hand over my face.

"No!" Emily hisses. "Don't do that! You'll smear the makeup."

I pull my hand away. I had to put on a layer to ensure I wasn't "washed out," according to Emily. Some theater thing. I instead opt for pacing back and forth.

Quinn is on the opposite side of the stage. I catch glimpses of her massive pink dress between the curtains. She seems to be pacing too. I pause. I raise my hand in a small wave. She blinks back at me before waving too.

She points to my shorts and slowly mouths the words, *Pizza butt?*

I laugh and nod back to her.

I did in fact wear my pizza underwear.

The music swells on stage, and both our expressions drop. The lights backstage click off.

This is it.

I feel a tiny tap at my shoulder.

"Ready?" Emily whispers, dropping two sparkling heels into my palms.

I nod, inhaling deeply. The narration over the speakers starts. The orchestral music grows. And I take my first step on the lit stage.

I squint out at the audience. The light from the sun scatters through the canopy above. Emily said on enclosed theaters, you normally can't see the audience. But with this being an outside venue, I'm not as lucky.

I see every staring face. And it is dead quiet. Right as I forget my first line.

No. No, no, no.

Think, think, think!

What do you need to say?!

I'm frozen in place. I hear Emily whisper, "Crap!" behind the curtain, but then I breathe in, close my eyes, and speak.

"Queen Bee!" I call. "Oh, Queen Bee!"

Quinn emerges from the wings. Her hands are raised. Her mouth is open in awe. Her bright doe eyes are now as wide as saucers. A beautiful vision in pink.

"Ranger Randy!" she calls. "What are you doing in my Honeywood Forest on this lovely autumn day?"

Something in me shifts. The moment I see her, all my lines come rushing back. I feel relaxed. I feel like I might actually be able to do this.

And then we're off. Two racehorses barreling down the track. Two cars zooming at top speeds. Two roller coasters launching from the station. Quinn and I have practiced our lines enough to where we're no longer actors on a stage, but Ranger Randy and Queen Bee in Honeywood.

We're in the forest.

We're talking with Buzzy the Bear.

We're awkwardly avoiding the wobbly floorboard, which, to its credit, almost trips me.

I'm entranced by it all, no longer thinking, but living. I almost forget the inevitable end.

Almost.

But I know what's coming as soon as Buzzy takes his exit. My heart suddenly picks up speed, and it's just me and Quinn, apart yet together, across the stage yet seconds away from joining in the middle.

We pause for a moment, like one of us is daring the other to move first.

I step forward. Then, she does. We walk toward each other, two souls attracted like magnets, and we stop once we're toe to toe.

Quinn says her final line, and then it's time to deliver mine.

I reach out, holding her waist, pulling her against my chest, staring down at her green eyes and scattered freckles. Her pink lips. Her angelic blonde hair. How she's *always* looked like an angel to me.

Quinn raises her eyebrows. Her lips part.

I say my final line. "Anything for you, My Queen."

Then, I lean down right as she rises to her toes, and our lips meet.

Quinn Sauer tastes like honey and berries and heaven.

Our lips move together. Slow at first, feeling for each other. Then more. Desperate. Harder. Faster. Wanting. It isn't my tongue, but hers that flicks against my lips. Then, it's both of us tasting each other, fighting for more.

I inhale against her, gripping the fabric of her dress in

my fist right as she curls her fingers around my tie. I take a step closer, tugging her closer to me, trailing my palm over her spine. She whimpers a small moan, pulling me by the tie to deepen our embrace.

I hook my hand under her knee and tug her leg up to my side. With one hand on her lower back and the crook of her elbow now slung around my neck, I dip her as low as we can go until I'm sure her hair cascades onto the stage. I exhale into her. She runs a heavy palm over my beard.

Our kisses finally slow down. They change from deep desperations to little pecks, like promises—each one feeling like the inevitable last. And when we finally pull apart, her eyes are still closed. Fluttering. Dazed.

I slowly lift her back up from the dip until both her feet land on the stage.

The curtain drops, and the crowd erupts into massive applause.

My heart is pounding. My ears ringing. Quinn opens her eyes and stares up at me. Her arm is still wrapped around my neck. My hand is still on her waist. Our chests are heaving against each other.

"Holy crap," Emily says, running onto the stage. "Holy crap!"

The world comes rushing back in. Quinn and I jerk apart at the same time. I already miss her warmth.

"What?" Quinn asks, running her hands over the full skirt.

I straighten my tie.

Fred appears in the doorway backstage. Lorelei is behind him, giving me a mix between a cringe and a smile. But Honey flies in behind her with an exaggerated wink, mouth open and thumb in the air.

"That was ..." Emily starts, her sentence breaking through her lips in half-words, half-laughs. She looks around, as if begging for assistance.

Finally, it's the teenager in the corner—the one in the Buzzy suit with his head removed—who says, "It was hot."

"Yeah, *super* hot," Emily breathes.

"Absolutely spectacular," Honey finishes with another inappropriate wink.

"Maybe more family-friendly next time?" Fred asks, wincing.

"More family-friendly next time," Quinn repeats. "Got it." Then, she cuts her gaze to me and adds, "Right?"

Next time.

I can't tell if it's a promise or a threat, so I nod, a slow smile breaking onto my face. The feeling of happiness finally allowing itself to burst in my chest.

"Right," I agree.

The comments continue to bounce back and forth between the staff. But Quinn keeps standing there in silence. I can practically see the gears turning in her brain. I nudge her elbow with mine.

She looks up, blinking at me through her massive eyelashes, her pink face, her pouty lips.

"Wanna come over for dinner tonight?" I ask.

She wrinkles her nose in disgust, but it seems half-hearted. Forced.

"And do what?" she asks.

"Practice lines, of course," I say, the smile on my face growing by the second.

Her eyes dart between mine, glancing to my mouth and back up. Her tongue whips out over her lips, and I swallow.

"With milkshakes," she says. It's not a question; it's a demand.

"Of course with milkshakes," I say. "Who am I, Satan?"

"I'm no longer sure."

28

Quinn

I slam my head against the wheel of my car, honking the horn into the dead of night.

I'm in Landon's driveway. About to go into his house, and all I can keep telling myself is, *I do not want to kiss him again.*

What.

A.

Lie.

I knew the moment our lips touched that I was a goner. I knew the moment his hand swept up my spine, the instant I gripped his tie in my fist—not sure if I wanted to pull him closer or clock him to the ground.

It was fight or flight, and normally, I'd pride myself on the fact that I am an *all fight, fists up* kinda gal. But Landon's lips melted me into the stage, a puddle of lust and regret.

I groan to myself.

There's too much going on for me to deal with this. Honeywood's sale, my mom, and the uncertainty of my future.

But there's also *his kiss*.

"Go inside, you coward," I whisper. I get out and shut my car door behind me.

Landon, already in the kitchen, pauses with blinking eyes when I waltz into his house without knocking.

"Did you honk your horn?" he asks.

"I scared off a possum in your driveway," I lie. "You're welcome."

His eyes dart to my arms.

"Wow. Is all that for me?" he asks.

I look down. I brought stupid little cupcakes because I figured he was making me dinner, so maybe I should contribute something other than my bad attitude. Now, it just feels ridiculous.

I hold it out to him.

He grabs the Tupperware from me with a chuckle. I've never realized how low his laugh is. Okay, I have, but I've never really registered how the sound steeps like a tea bag into the water of your soul, letting loose leaves of comfort.

That's exactly what it is. Comforting. Enough to have me waxing poetic about it.

I'm losing my mind.

But when his large hand grazes over mine, sending a shiver down my spine, part of me knows—no, a huge part of me knows—that I'm not losing my mind. I'm just lusting after yet another kiss from this man.

"Making spaghetti and meatballs tonight," he says. "That cool?"

I wonder if I'll be having *his* meatballs too.

Wait. No. Stop. Gross, Quinn.

I feel my heart trying to beat its way out of my chest. I wonder if he can hear it.

I give him a copy of the script. He eyes it, then me.

"Running lines?" he asks.

"Isn't that why I'm here?"

"Yes," he says with a grin. A knowing grin. An *I'm making meatballs for you* grin.

We run lines, as if we don't already know them by heart. It's a ruse. A silly little game we're playing as we try to avoid the unavoidable.

I swallow once we reach the ending and drop the script. I practically toss it, as if it were on fire in my fingertips. Landon gives me a cursory glance, his lips upturned in a curious lopsided smile, but he doesn't move, and neither do I.

What if I just leaped across the kitchen island and pounced on him? What if I just knocked over the food, crawled to him on hands and knees, and begged for him to touch me? What if I put myself on a silver platter for dinner?

Here you go, buddy! Eat up!

But I don't.

We ultimately eat his delicious spaghetti and meatballs —literally—only talking about work stuff. Stupid little work stuff.

He starts making our milkshakes without asking if I want one. I don't complain.

When I grab mine, I walk outside and sit on the hammock. And when he looks down at the space beside me, his eyebrows pulled in together, I make an infinitesimal scoot to the side. And for the first time, he sits next to me. My body is on fire where our arms meet. The outside of our thighs rubs together as his long legs start to push us back and forth.

"So," he says.

I glance to him. "So?"

He chuckles, and my heart aches.

"We just gonna swing here?" he asks.

"Yes," I respond, taking a long sip from my straw.

"Fine, then I'll just enjoy the sound of your obnoxious slurps."

I do it again, and he laughs again.

"So defiant," he mutters, the words a whisper on his lips. It sends a zip of nerves down to my stomach.

I let us swing in silence, closing my eyes at the sound of his breaths. Feeling how his body presses into mine with each inhale and relaxes with each exhale.

"All right, Quinn," he finally says. "Let's do it."

My eyes pop open, and my stomach drops.

"Excuse you?"

He grins. "Let's talk about the kiss. What did you think I meant?"

I shove his arm, and he laughs.

"See? It doesn't have to be awkward between us."

"It's not awkward," I counter.

"It is very obviously awkward now," he says.

A half-laugh exhales through my nose as I groan.

"How was the kiss for you?" he asks.

My body tenses immediately by how forward the question is.

"It was a kiss," I say bluntly.

"Was it everything you'd hoped it would be?"

"Pass."

"Did you think I'd be good at it?" he asks.

"That's stupid."

"Why?"

And that feeling—the impulse to shield myself from him, to lie for my own self-preservation—is what spurs the next sentence from my mouth.

"Because that would require me thinking about you at all."

I hear something leave his throat. A small groan? An irritating growl? Do people actually growl?

My stomach shifts. Goose bumps erupt over my arms and chest. I watch his large, veined hands clutch the drink harder. And then I look into those brown eyes. This close, I can see the flecks of green in there. It's a color similar to my own. Just pieces of something we share together.

I pull my knees up to my chest, resting my feet at the bottom curve of the hammock. I clutch my cup close to my chest. Anything to keep myself grounded.

"It wasn't bad," I finally admit.

"Nah. I didn't think so either."

I notice the dip in tone. Raspy. Rough. Filled with something that wasn't there a few seconds ago.

His raises his arm around the top of the hammock, his hand so close to my shoulder, and my heart starts to pound. I want to kiss him again. So bad. So bad that it almost hurts my chest.

I raise an eyebrow at him. I see his body stiffen in response. His palm grips the outside of the ropes. His fingers brush my shoulder.

Kiss me.

"You gonna stare at me all day?" I challenge.

The side of his mouth twitches up at the edge at my statement.

"You gonna tell me what to do?" he counters, almost a whisper.

But before I can come back with anything, Landon leans forward. The hammock creaks below him. My body sinks into the ropes as he moves closer. His hands reach down, taking my legs into his palms and placing them on his lap. He steadies himself with one hand as the other rests beside my hip, centimeters from where my own hand rests. Our fingertips touch, and neither of us shifts away.

Instinctually, my head moves back, taking in his figure almost hovering over me. My eyes look from his jaw down to his neck, to his broad chest. I can smell the autumn scent on him. The crispness of it. The hints of bonfire and fallen leaves.

I don't move as he leans in and lingers his lips on my cheek. He moves closer toward my lips, placing another kiss to the corner of my mouth.

My eyes flutter closed. I can barely breathe. I reach up to clutch his shirt, gripping the fabric into my hand. It is the only thing that will keep me in this moment, the only thing preventing me from flying away from him in fear.

The hammock shifts, and I feel his hand on my waist. His palm spans over my ribs, down to my stomach, halting at the outside of my thigh, the place where the ripped hem of my shorts ends and my skin begins. One of his fingers toys with the strands of fabric, and every wisp of his skin against mine is a cruel touch that sends shivering goose bumps down my spine.

This backyard couldn't be more tense if we tried. And we're trying damn hard.

I feel him pull away from me, and I hesitate to open my eyes, but when they open, I look at his face as he gazes upon my own. His eyes dart down to my lips and back again.

"Your Highness, you look flushed," he whispers.

My mouth feels dry, and I can't find any words to respond.

I inhale sharply when his hand shifts along my thigh, splaying out over my skin, warmth radiating through his palm, a single finger long enough to skim just under the hem of my shorts.

I can feel my jaw tense, imagining him against me, a shaking breath exhaling into him. His lips tip to the side, inching up to a boyish smile.

I'm too nailed to the hammock to move an inch. I can't bring myself to smile back. I'm terrified by this moment. I'm terrified by how much I want this and how, with each passing second, I'm dying a little more inside as I wait for our eventuality.

Then, suddenly, he pulls away.

The whole moment changes. The cicadas buzz back into my ears, a whir of an air-conditioning unit hums nearby, and the awkwardness comes rushing back into my chest.

My heart sinks down to my stomach. My arms shake. And my knees pull up to my chest quicker than I can blink.

"What?" I ask. "What happened?"

He looks at me, running a hand over the back of his neck.

And my whole body shuts down.

"Not a chance," echoes in my brain.

I'm just a game to him. And I lost.

"Why would you do that," I whisper. It's not a question. It's a statement of fact. An accusation. A knife into his heart that I ripped out of my own back.

His face falls. "Wait ... wait a second."

I crawl out from under him, almost falling when my feet hit the grass. He reaches out for me, but I ensure my knee sidewipes his wrists.

I'm such an idiot.

I slam open his sliding door, snatching my tote bag off

the floor, throwing it over my arm. All in one swift motion, as if it were a dance I'd practiced.

"Wait, hang on," he says from behind me. "Wait, Quinn!"

I snatch the cupcakes from the kitchen island.

It's high school all over again.

Mrs. Landon Arden.

"Quinn!"

I slam the front door behind me.

29

Landon

I wanted her. I wanted her so bad that I could barely breathe. But when Quinn didn't make any moves forward and when she looked at me with terror in her eyes, I assumed she didn't want to kiss me.

I played it off.

Ha-ha. Funny Landon. Kissing? Blegh. Totally not us.

But then I saw her face contort into anger, and I knew I'd made a mistake.

She wanted to kiss me.

I run a hand over my face, only to have my elbow grabbed and jerked away.

"What's wrong?" Lorelei asks.

I'm in my full Ranger Randy getup, staring at my security office door, seconds away from going out there and pretending Queen Bee and I are in love. I don't know how we'll do it.

"Nothing," I say. "Nothing is wrong."

"Landon," she says, "my twin senses are tingling. I can tell something is up."

I sigh. "Let's not do the twin thing today."

Her lips twist to the side, and she nods.

Quinn is already at the fountain when I arrive, looking as gorgeous as ever in her pink ball gown. I run a hand through my hair and walk over, placing a hand on her waist. She stiffens under my touch, but she doesn't turn toward me.

"I'm sorry about last night," I whisper in her ear.

"I don't want to talk about it."

My jaw tightens, and I shake my head. "No. I'm not playing that game. We're talking about it."

Her head jerks up to mine. "*No,* we're signing autographs."

I inhale sharply, looking out as the line starts to form. We look like a zombie couple rather than a fairy-tale one.

Okay, so she has a point.

"After," I insist.

"No," she bites back.

And that's the last honest thing we say to each other for one hour. The rest of the time, Ranger Randy and Queen Bee talk with fake smiles and forced laughs. For a moment, I almost forget we're fighting, that she not-so-secretly wants to strangle me. Like maybe she might want to kiss me.

I can remember my first kiss in high school. How rushed it felt at some party where I just wanted to check the boxes of firsts. But most of all, I remember coming home that night, and the first person I saw was Quinn—sitting in our family's hallway, a book in hand, hunched over with her knees pulled up to her chin.

"Hey," she said.

"Hi."

I sat down next to her and leaned in. She was reading *Sleeping Beauty* again, a princess woken by true love's first kiss. That night, I only pretended to read with her. I was just enjoying her company, trying to forget my own first kiss. I remember wishing she could have been the one to take it instead.

I had my chance to rewrite history last night, and I ruined it.

The moment we announce our exit, Quinn power-walks toward the dressing room. Her arms pumping by her sides.

"Quinn," I call.

"No."

"You can't get far in that dress."

"Shut up."

"Quinn!"

"NO."

I sigh.

This woman will be the death of me.

But I'm not stopping this time. I'm not spending the next sixteen years trying to get her to like me again. I'm nipping this in the bud right here, right now.

I follow her all the way to the dressing room. She throws the door open. I close it shut behind us.

"What the hell are you doing?" she finally asks.

"Something I should have done a long time ago."

Then, I cup her jaw in my hands, bend down, and kiss the ever-loving hell out of her.

30

Quinn

My heart is a predictable piece of crap. I know this because I fall into Landon without a single fight.

His hands grip my jaw closer. My lips wrestle his. He walks us backward. I push him forward again. He spins us so that my back hits the door to the dressing room. I bite his lip in response.

Landon bends and grips under my thighs. Without thinking, I hop up. My legs wrap around his waist. The skirt of my ball gown rustles between us. The tulle bubbles around me, allowing a modest foot of distance for Jesus.

Not that it would do any good.

I hook my heels into his back. There's a rumble in the back of his throat as he turns to walk us to the makeup counter. Landon sweeps one hand behind me, scattering brushes and compacts before placing me on the countertop.

He cups my cheeks in his large palms before burying them in my hair. I feel my crown get knocked off my head, sliding down my hair, clinging for life in my curls. I arch into him. He moves his hands down to my waist, then lower to my skirt. He fumbles around my fabric, probably trying to find a break in it before letting out a frustrated groan.

I reach for his tie, tearing it from its hold, throwing it to the side. My fingers tangle in his buttons, undoing the first, then the second. He pushes my hips back. The cold mirror stings my shoulders. I grip the folds of his opened shirt, pulling him closer.

His kisses are desperate on my mouth. Again and again and again. When he pulls away, I let out a whining moan. But he keeps kissing along my jaw, my neck, and groans into my collarbone.

"Wait," he growls.

And then we pause.

I drag in deep breaths and swallow.

Landon leans back, looking me in the eye as he grips the fabric of my dress in his fists. It's almost as if he's steadying himself.

"We ... need to ... talk," he says through heavy breaths.

"I don't want to," I say.

"I don't care," he says with a playful smile and a shake of his head. "Talk to me. Last night. You left. Tell me why."

Last night hasn't left my mind for a second, so I say exactly what I remember.

"You didn't want to kiss me," I say. "But you pretended you did."

His breathing is heavy. His chest rising and falling as his heady eyes search mine.

Landon shakes his head, slowly at first, then quick. "No. I didn't think *you* wanted me to kiss you."

"So, you played the role of the gentleman?"

"Damn right I did," he says, leaning down to my level, taking my chin in his palm.

How can a movement be both rough and polite, all at once?

He strokes my jaw, searching my eyes. He looks the same as when he snapped at Hugh. Angry. Passionate. Heated.

"I will never make you do something you don't want to do."

"Except talk."

"It's normal communication, Quinn. I won't apologize for that."

"I swear you get off on talking about your feelings."

"I get off on a lot of things. Your scowl. Your bad attitude."

I blink at him. "Come again?"

"I wanted to kiss you," he says. "I wanted to do more, if I'm being perfectly honest. But I didn't want you to feel like you had to. Because of some obligation to the play or some other stupid reason. And I didn't know what else to do. So, I panicked."

"You *panicked*?"

"Yeah," he says with a slow nod. "You make me panic. How are you surprised? I'm a mess for you."

I gulp, the words spearing my heart, all the way down to my weak knees.

"We shouldn't do this," I say.

"And why not?"

"Because I'm me," I say. "And you're you. And you piss me off."

He lets out a breathy laugh. "You know, I think you just like being pissed off at me."

"And I think you like pissing me off."

He lets go of my jaw. He doesn't say anything. But his eyes, blinking down at me as he towers above, say this isn't over. Far from it. His hand traces along the tulle of my dress. He inhales, exhales, slower and slower until he finally lets out a long, exasperated sigh.

"What if I said I like pissing you off?" he asks. "That I like the little line between your eyebrows. Your glares. Your crossed arms. Your combat boots that could probably kick my ass."

"Masochist."

He chuckles. "When it comes to you? Yes, I just might be."

My heart sinks. We stare at each other for what feels like forever, and I can't stop admiring the way his eyes flick between mine. Like he's trying to see inside my soul.

"Last night," he finally says, "did you want me to kiss you?"

I look to the floor and kick my heels beneath the counter.

"What kind of stupid question is that?" I ask.

His thumb and forefinger turn my face to his. He brushes down the center of my chin before releasing me. And my chest is filled with something. Butterflies? Moths? Flesh-eating bacteria?

"Did you want me to kiss you?" he repeats.

"Maybe."

"Maybe," he breathes with a small smile. "Of course *maybe* with you." And it feels like admiration, like a weird sense of pride.

This only makes me straighten my spine more, tilt my head to the side, and inhale with him. Both of us finally breathing in tandem.

He places a hand on the mirror behind my head, caging me in.

"You ..." His mouth lowers until it's hovering over mine. "If only you knew how much you drive me insane."

"So dramatic."

His eyes are like fire as they stare at me. My pulse pounds harder. He dips his head down to my neck. I can't help the gasp that escapes as he plants a single kiss on my shoulder.

He whispers into my ear, strained and gritty, "I would do anything for you, if you'd let me."

My whole body tenses. For once in my life, I struggle to find the perfect comeback. I don't know if it's his warm breath on my neck or simply the fact that, in this moment, I want nothing more than to have his lips pressed against mine. He kisses just below my ear, nuzzling his nose into my hair as my eyes flutter shut.

The heat between us is unbearable.

I let out a small whimper as he kisses the edge of my mouth, just as he did last night. His beard wisps over my skin, his lips a moment away from meeting mine.

"I was into it," I finally say. "I wanted you to kiss me last night. And I want you to kiss me now."

He leans in, but right before our mouths touch, his walkie scratches, and a familiar voice comes through.

"Lorelei for Landon."

We both hesitate. Our mouths hovering over each other.

The walkie scratches again. "Lorelei for Landon."

I'm gonna kill *my best friend later.*

Keeping the other hand on my hip, he smashes the button on the walkie.

"Go for Landon," he says.

"We've got a straggler who won't leave The Grizzly's restricted area. Security would be nice, if you've got time."

"Copy that. Be there in five."

He straightens up, looks down at me, his chin to his chest. He leans back, as if taking in my full figure.

"Come over tonight," he says.

The word *yes* is on the tip of my tongue, but I shake my head.

"I can't," I say.

"Why?" he breathes, the word almost a desperate whine. It melts me almost as much as heady Landon did.

"I told Lorelei we'd have a girls' night once she finishes with the contractors."

He sucks in one side of his cheek.

"Sneak out," he says.

I smirk. "You gonna throw rocks at my window?"

"That, or hold a boom box."

"How about tomorrow?" I suggest.

He grips my skirt in a fist and groans. I laugh. He lets out a weak laugh in return.

"Can't wait?" I tease.

That reliable dimple indents into his beard. His forehead presses against mine before he plants a single, hard kiss against it. I let out a sigh, louder than I would have liked.

"I would wait forever for you," he says.

When he pulls away, he blinks down at me.

"Do me a favor."

I shrug. "Depends on what it is."

He smiles at my insolence. "Tell me you like me."

"That's ridiculous," I say.

He laughs, and his hands grip the back of my neck, pulling me up to him.

Our mouths meet again.

It's hard. It's soft. It's everything in between.

I clutch his shirt in my fist, pulling him closer. He lets

out a low whimper, a thing that ignites me further, opening my mouth right as he opens his. Our tongues intertwine, fighting for power over the other. Yet, for once, we're equally matched.

I pull away first, looking up at his face. His cheeks are red. I can feel that mine probably are too. He runs a hand through my hair, looping his finger through my curls. He tucks a strand behind my ear.

He doesn't say anything. Neither do I. All he does is lean his forehead against mine one last time, button his shirt back, and leave without another word.

31

Landon

I'm wondering just how much of my life is a big karmic joke from the universe. I finally kissed the woman I want, but then I'm stuck in the security office the rest of the day, organizing paperwork. When I look at the clock, it's well past closing time.

I groan to myself, twisting my security hat backward and wiggling my mouse for the umpteenth time to wake up my monitor. Across my screen is a display of camera footage in the park.

We have a security camera at every main point in Honeywood. I see Lorelei at The Grizzly with Emory, Bennett, Quinn, and some contractors. There's Theo in the main lobby of the employee offices, texting on her phone. And another camera near the Bumblebee Greenhouse, where Fred and Honey stand a few feet apart. The computer's sound is tuned to that zone.

"No. I won't do that," Fred says.

Honey's arms are crossed. "It's the best offer we have."

Fred shakes his head, almost grunting in the process as his hands fly up in the air.

"I won't do that to my kid," Fred says. "I made a promise to her."

"She needs to be kicked out of the nest eventually," Honey says.

"Not like this, she doesn't."

I minimize that screen and mute the volume. My chest feels tight at what I might have overheard. My mind reeling from possibilities.

Kid? It could be his daughter, Jaymee, the gossip columnist for the *Cedar Cliff Chatter*. Though that's less likely. How would Honey even know her? The more likely answer is that it's someone at Honeywood. Fred refers to almost all the longtimers as his kids. Could he mean Lorelei? Or possibly even Quinn?

I wish I hadn't heard the little that I did. You spend enough years in security, and you know not to eavesdrop. Especially on your own boss. You'll never like what you hear even if it's just a snippet.

I maximize the camera window again. Fred and Honey are gone now. But I still see Lorelei and Emory with the contractors. I don't, however, see Quinn.

She must have left. Some part of me hoped Quinn would come see me before then. I wonder if she doesn't want anyone to know about us. I wonder if it's her own personal hell. I wonder if she's fighting to make room in her heart for the guy she resented for so long.

I should leave. It's already getting late. Maybe Orson will be at work. The Honeycomb would be a decent distraction from what I'd rather be doing with Quinn.

I shut off the lights and close the security door, locking it behind me. But when I turn around, Quinn is on the other side of the walkway, lips parted, toying with the frays on her shorts.

My heart explodes in my chest at the sight of her.

"Hey, you," I finally say.

"I was just coming to say bye," she says.

"How sweet of you."

She flashes me the middle finger.

I chuckle, walking toward her, absentmindedly grazing the back of my knuckles against her shoulder once I reach her. I don't think about what I'm doing or how it's so blatantly in public. It just feels natural, touching her.

"Wanna make out?" I whisper.

She laughs. "What are we, fourteen?"

"Is that a yes?"

She looks left, then right and entwines her fingers in mine. I take a step toward the security office door, but she shakes her head.

"Come on," she says. "If we're gonna do this, let's be a bit more adventurous."

"I'm security," I say. "The last thing I am is adventurous."

She rolls her eyes and pulls my hand. "Just follow me."

Quinn guides me down the trail beside the offices. I follow, letting her hand tug me until we go past the tree line, down to the edge of the woods. It's right next to where the train rolls by and the maintenance tunnel empties. Unless someone were aboard the train—the one that isn't currently operating—our small square of the seclusion is not visible from the main path.

"So, Mr. Security, are there cameras out here?"

I grin and shake my head. "No. But how'd you know that?"

"I'm sneaky," she says, lifting an eyebrow. "Also, I was seventeen before."

"You were sneaking around at that age?"

She shrugs. "No, but I always thought that *if* I did, I wanted to know where."

I squint. "Are we living out some teenage fantasy of yours?"

"I don't know. Are we?"

I shake my head with a smile, running my thumb along her bottom lip. "Come here, you."

She rises to her toes, and our mouths meet. In an instant, immediate fire sparks through my chest. It's only been a few hours, but I missed the way she tasted. How she breathed into me, like sending life into my soul.

I walk forward, and Quinn backs herself against a tree. She reaches between us, palming below my belt. I let out a breathy laugh against her lips.

"You are ..."

"Amazing?" she asks. "Wonderful?"

"Intoxicating." I cradle her cheek and press us together once more.

She's more than intoxicating. She's fire licking across my nerves, a venom in my heart, a glass shard stuck in the depths of me that I'll never be able to dig out.

Quinn bites down on my lip as she strokes over me outside of my pants. I moan against her.

She might be glass, but I want to see how easily she breaks.

With my free hand, I undo the button on her shorts blindly. The zipper hisses down, and I flatten my palm against her stomach to dip beneath her underwear. She's already slick in my fingers.

"Good God," I mutter against her mouth. I circle along the outside, eliciting a breathy moan from her. "I want you so bad."

"So needy."

"Oh, hush."

Her hand runs up my neck and over my cheek. I break our kiss, angling my face to place my lips against the inside of her palm.

"Didn't I say you'd get the respect you deserved?" I whisper.

"Landon," she breathes, and my name is a dream on her tongue. A mist in the air. A wish to the night.

I dip a finger inside her. Quinn's head falls back against the tree with a whine. I pull out, then in, finding the sensitive spot inside and circling it as she clenches around me.

"Is that good?" I ask.

She nods, her eyebrows cinching in. I add another finger, eliciting a low moan from her. I pump faster, rubbing the palm of my hand over the outside, trying to find all the spots that make her already-stilted breath even more broken.

"More," she whispers.

"Now, who is needy?"

But before she can answer, I bury my two fingers in her fully. She trembles beneath me as I curl in, then out, and with each exhalation of her breath into my ear, it spurs me forward. Thrusting, curling, kissing along the exposed column of her neck. I dip fingers inside until she's letting out inexcusable moans that echo through the forest. But I only get to savor them for a few more moments.

I watch as Quinn's head falls to the side. Her eyebrows stitch in, and she pulls in a sharp inhale.

"I'm gonna—"

I don't need to hear Quinn say she's about to finish to know that she does. I can feel her on my fingers, see her body shake against me, and hear her final whining moans.

It's brilliant and beautiful and more than I could have hoped for.

Her head falls back against the tree, eyes closed, breathing winded. I kiss her collar and pull her underwear back in place. Slowly, I lift my fingers into my mouth and lick off her pleasure from them. She watches as I do so and lets out an exasperated laugh. It's so vixenish that I could die. I laugh with her.

But I'm broken from her spell when someone exits the maintenance tunnel.

We both freeze, turn to our right, and see Bennett.

"Oh," Quinn and I say at the same time.

Bennett's eyebrows rise. It's only then that I realize my palm is still spread over her pelvis. I step in front of her. I hear her fumble her zipper back up.

"It's not ..." Quinn starts, but he levels a look at her. She levels it back. "Bennett, if you say one word ..."

He tosses his hands up. "No words at all. The forest though? Really?"

"Bennett ..." she warns.

The maintenance tunnel opens again, and Emory and Lorelei come out.

Dear God.

"Oh, party in the forest?" Lorelei asks.

Thankfully, my sweet sister doesn't seem to notice anything awry. She's all smiles.

However, Emory's eyes dart from Quinn to me. He's far less oblivious.

But before any of us can talk, the silence is broken by Quinn's phone going off. She grabs it instantly, as if determined to do literally anything but stand here in awkward silence.

We all watch as her face falls.

"You all right?" I ask.

"It's my mom," she says.

"Has she been calling a lot recently?" Lorelei asks.

Quinn nods, looking to me, then averting eye contact.

"More than usual," she admits.

Quinn walks over and hands her phone to Lorelei.

I want to ask so many questions.

What's wrong with your mom texting? Did something happen? Why don't you talk to her?

"You know what?" Lorelei says after reading the text. "Let's all have dinner at Mom and Dad's house tomorrow, huh? Come on." Lorelei gives her signature sunshine smile and shakes Quinn by the shoulders with a laugh. "Family dinner?"

I don't really like that Lorelei is emphasizing a *family dinner* to the woman I would like to do very un-family-like things with, but one glance at Quinn says she's seconds away from saying yes.

Because we *are* her family.

"Yeah," Quinn says. "Yeah, that would help."

32

Quinn

U p until recently, I hadn't heard from my mom in six months. Admittedly, they'd been a very decent six months. Yet, now, out of all times—when I'm trying to balance this new play, and Honeywood potentially selling, and my whatever it is with Landon—that's when she reaches back out again.

I keep glancing at her text as Lorelei's car rumbles down the unpaved path to the Arden household. Lorelei's parents are the ones who took me in during my parents' divorce, and if anyone can make me feel better, it's them.

Mama Arden is the type of mother who calls you on a weekday with nothing to say, except, "I was thinking about you." She's the woman who stays in the doorway as you leave, coaxing you back in for another cup of coffee. She will mail you a card on your birthday and underline every word she feels is special, resulting in a card with mostly scribbles because, "I meant it all."

I walk into their home like it's my own, taking off my shoes in the mudroom with Emory and Lorelei.

I breathe in the pot roast and melted butter. Louise is

over the stove, looking so similar to Landon when he cooks that it's almost funny. Her messy red hair is curled into a bun, held in place with a daisy. Her patchwork capris are somehow stylish yet also out of fashion.

When she sees us, she instantly holds her arms out for a hug. I barrel in.

"How are you, honey?" she asks into my hair.

"I'm fine," I answer.

I'm home.

But just as I'm breaking away from her, I catch him from the corner of my eye.

Landon. Leaning against the doorjamb, like he always does, with his hands in his pockets, looking at me with a crooked smile and a dimple pushed into his chestnut beard.

I don't know how to act now. This is the man who taunted my teenage years, but also the same man who has given me the best orgasm of my life.

"Hey, Barbie," he says to me. It's just as he always says it. Happy. Teasing. And yet there's an undercurrent of something different. Something *implied*.

Or maybe I'm just too horny for my own good.

"Mom, you need help?" he asks.

"No, no!" Louise chimes in, taking off the lid of the Crock-Pot.

My head swivels back over to him, tilting to the side. Landon's eyebrows rise, and he grins.

Yeah. I definitely can't handle this tension. I want to jump his bones in the kitchen with everyone and God as our witnesses.

I need air.

I leave the heat of the kitchen and go upstairs to the hall bathroom. I close the door behind me, leaning against the sink, staring at myself in the mirror. My messy bun. My blotchy pink cheeks. The heat in my eyes for that evil twin downstairs.

"Pull it together," I whisper to myself.

I splash my face with water and leave, walking down the hall until a light peeks out from a bedroom. I follow the source and take in Landon's childhood bedroom.

The room is a memorial to a former life. Football jerseys, championship trophies, old stacks of paper that might be essays or graded tests or textbooks. There's an old book bag. A video game console. An alarm clock. And just below the bay window overlooking the gardens outside are low wooden bookshelves.

I don't remember him being a huge reader in high school. The most reading he did was beside me in that hallway. Just silly fairy tales. So, when I walk over to his books and glance at the titles, I'm stopped in my tracks.

They're the same fables.

Aesop's, Grimms' ...

"I didn't peg you for a snoop."

I turn on the spot and see Landon in the doorway.

"Did you read all these?" I ask, pointing a thumb at them.

Landon chuckles. "Yes, Barbie, I am in fact capable of reading," he says in a low tone.

But I don't miss how he avoided the question.

He slowly closes the door behind him, leaning against it as it quietly clicks shut.

"Should we be in here alone?" I ask.

"You tell me."

I bite the inside of my cheek before releasing it, looking back at the bookshelves.

"These are the books I used to read," I say. "I didn't know you had them too."

"I didn't," he says, taking steps toward me. "I bought them after."

I consider this. I consider how we stopped reading together after freshman year. I consider that, over the course of fifteen years, we've been like ships passing in the night.

"How long have you liked me?" I ask.

He sighs. "Don't embarrass me."

I grin. "Oh, I definitely need to embarrass you."

Landon smiles, dipping his head down. "Since I was fourteen."

"*Fourteen?*"

He bites his lip and winces. When I don't say anything, he laughs again. That's so Landon, using laughter to scare away the awkwardness. I smile back, reaching out to intertwine our fingers.

He exhales, and I hear him swallow once our hands touch. His eyes roam over me. My nerves go haywire at the motion, but I say nothing. He reaches forward, taking a strand of my hair and tucking it behind my ear.

"You promised not to do the *ear thing*," I say.

"Objectively, I think the *neck thing* is far worse," he says, bending down, nuzzling his nose into my hair, kissing the dip in my neck.

I let out a small, barely audible moan.

His palm brushes down my shoulder to my forearm, then down my hand. He walks us over to the bed. Landon lies down first as I stand beside the mattress, watching him in awe. I can see the ridges of his muscles through his shirt. A sliver of stomach peeks between his shirt and his boxers. The small line of reddish-brown hair trails underneath. My heartbeat races.

"Are you trying to seduce me, Landon?" I joke with a lift of my eyebrow.

He chuckles, his hand absentmindedly reaching out, tracing along my exposed thigh.

"Caught me red-handed," he says. "You know, I barely got the chance to enjoy you yesterday. We should fix that."

My breath catches in my throat. "Right now?"

His eyes flicker up to me.

"Yes," he says. Then, he licks his lips, tips his chin, and says, "Sit on my face."

My whole body is rigid as I try to register the words.

All I successfully get out is, "*Christ*, Landon."

"Yeah," he continues, the dimples in his beard deepening. His eyes crinkling at the sides as he grins. His white teeth on full display. "Pop your cute ass up here."

"We're in your parents' house," I say.

"Didn't you ask me to be a little more adventurous?"

"Ha-ha. Very cute, but they'll hear us."

"Then, I guess you'd better be quiet, huh?"

I can feel my face heat. My ears feel hot, and I'm not even sure how I'm still standing upright with how much my mind swims.

"Please," he says. His tone is low and gravelly as his palm clutches my thigh in a grasp.

My heart pounds, but my heartbeat spirals down my body and into my stomach. And then even lower.

"Stop being so desperate," I choke out with a laugh.

But that only causes him to pull me closer. I see the fire in his eyes, the same one that ignited when I told him he annoyed me. It's almost a determination. A carnal desire.

"Oh, but I am desperate," he says.

The front of my thighs hit the mattress. His large hand rises higher, grabbing a handful of my ass in his palm.

Before I can think, I lift my knee onto the bed, letting it

land on the mattress on the opposite side of his waist, straddling his chest.

"You're begging me now?" I ask.

He lets out a low groan, a rumble that echoes into my chest. Both of his hands smooth their way up the length of my legs, over my pelvis, to the dip in my waist.

"I can beg some more, if you'd like," he whispers, sitting up a little to kiss the area just above the waistline of my shorts.

I inhale sharply as he unbuttons them with one hand, letting the zipper slide down.

"*Please* take your shorts off, Quinn."

The sound of my name on his lips is like an aphrodisiac. The crack of the Q in his throat. The way it settles on his lips and groans in his chest.

"You're serious?" I ask.

"*So* serious."

Well, who am I to say no?

I roll my eyes, moving to the side of him, jerking down my shorts and underwear and kicking them off my ankles. I'm not even fully on top of him before he picks me up—*holy crap, he picks me up*—by my waist, gripping my thighs and dragging me up to straddle his chin. My legs are spread on either side of him, and instantly, I feel his beard dragging against my inner thigh.

His warm breath against me is wild. His soft lips kissing inward sends my nerves on alight. Landon's eyes flicker up to mine as he rolls his tongue against me.

My head falls back with an exhale.

And then he does it again. And again.

I shiver with the slow lap of his tongue and the brush of his beard against my thighs. I don't realize I'm breathing heavy until he laughs, the sound echoing up to my chest.

"God, you taste so good," he says, louder than he should be.

"Shh," I hiss.

I twist my head over to the door. It's closed, but not locked. I still hear the clinking of plates downstairs and the flow of conversation from his family. I don't know how much time we have or what we can even get away with. But the idea of being in Landon's room, on his bed, sitting on his bearded face with the risk of someone walking in ... it does more to me than it should.

"Quinn," he groans.

"Yes?" I hear myself say.

A slow smile edges over his face, and those dang dimples shine through.

"Relax," he says. "And let me show you just how desperate I can be."

Landon's arms grip the back of my waist, and he pulls me down. His face buries between my legs, and I'm overwhelmed by so much. His tongue. His beard. His warm breaths. How deft he is. How quick he is. How easily he finds the exact spot he was looking for.

My head falls back in ecstasy as every movement of his tongue drives me higher and higher. From zero to one hundred. Like a man finding water after being lost in a desert. I have trouble finding my breath, but when I do, it releases in a moan. I cover my own mouth with my hand.

"I wish I could hear that voice," he whispers, continuing to lap me up like I'm not his appetizer, but all the dang courses.

I'm getting so close. I can feel a bundle of nerves building in my lower stomach, the rise of it spreading everywhere.

"Landon—" I start.

Landon growls against me, dipping his tongue inside. And that's what sends me over. The final lash of his tongue against me, the grip of his palms against the back of my thighs, the grunt of his efforts against my pelvis.

I'm lost to my orgasm. My fingers dig in his hair. My black-painted nails are such a contrast to his copper locks, like I'm the witch possessing the prince. And when my breathing returns to normal, he kisses the inside of my thigh.

"You liked it," he says. He almost sounds ... relieved?

He lifts me off him and places me down next to my shorts. I slide my clothes back on as he stands, adjusting himself in his own shorts.

My eyes dart down to that bulge, then back up to him. He runs a hand over his beard before bending down to kiss me. And it strikes me that we haven't even kissed until now.

"Thank you," I whisper against his lips. "Again."

He chuckles. "Pleasure was all mine, I promise."

I reach down to feel him through his shorts. But when I stroke along the length, his hand grips my wrist. He glances toward the door. I can see the worry in his eyes.

"Oh, so you can, and I can't?" I joke.

"We've already been gone too long, haven't we?"

"Unfair."

"Sorry," he says, planting a kiss on my forehead. "Definitely later though."

"I'm holding you to it."

He pauses, swallows, then says, "You are my undoing, Quinn Sauer."

"And you are full of shit, Landon Arden."

He laughs, kisses me again, then swings open the door. And even though I'm not sure what to make of this or us, I have never felt safer or more wanted than I do in that moment.

33

Landon

Here's a fun role-play activity: dress up like a fictional character and call your partner by a different name.

Saying, "Hello, Your Majesty," to Quinn while onstage is enough to make her face turn ten shades darker than her pink powder blush.

I live for it.

When we kiss in front of the audience, my hand on the small of her back, my neck bent to reach her lips, it feels like a privilege—a lioness allowing me to finally pet her.

"That was *great!*" Emily says backstage, moving from foot to foot in excitement. "Much more family-friendly. You guys are really getting the hang of it!"

"You're ridiculous," Quinn says, but I see the smile twitch at the edge of her mouth.

She looks up at me, and I swear I see stars in her eyes. Though I can't tell if it's admiration or just the illumination of the stage lights. With Quinn, I never know.

"I bet the security office is empty," I whisper.

She elbows me and grins. "You dog."

I pump my eyebrows at her. "Woof."

The tiniest of smiles tips the edge of her lips. "I swear you're the devil."

I lean down, curling my finger so she leans in too. "Yes, but don't you think I sin really well?"

She grins and leans in closer. "I sin better."

I reach out for her hand, but the second I do, Lorelei appears backstage. I jerk my hand back as she practically tackles Quinn, talking so fast that I can barely process their words. *Great* and *beautiful* and *elegant* are some that I catch, but the next thing I know Lorelei is dragging her out the exit in a blur of stage talk I don't understand.

Quinn's eyes turn to find mine as I mouth, *Later*.

She flushes, then leaves with my cockblocking sister.

I inhale and stand there, my hands at the sides of my tight shorts I need to change out of. Regardless of the flexibility built in, I'm pretty sure my circulation is getting cut off.

I go to the security office, check my emails, and see that my paycheck was deposited overnight. I notice the additional bonus for costuming as Ranger Randy is added, but when I see the breakdown of income, my face falls.

It's not a lot. Granted, it's not like I expected a ton anyway, but this, combined with my base salary, will result in a slow build to save for culinary school. I might make decent money as head of security, but I want the majority of that to go toward emergency savings.

The bonus will be enough. But it'll take more time.

I smile to myself.

But as long as I'm with Quinn, I'll spend all the time in the world as Ranger Randy.

I run a hand through my hair right as the door bursts open.

"Jesus!"

I turn to find Bennett standing with a tape measure, nails, and a hammer. He looks like a picture-perfect home improvement guy, save for the bright yellow Honeywood polo that contrasts with his tattoos and bun.

"So, you and Quinn," he says.

"Why didn't you knock?"

"Was I supposed to?"

I dip my chin toward the hammer. "You plan to hit me with that?"

"Why? Need to be?"

"Possibly."

He grunts with a smile.

"What are you doing?" I ask.

He looks to his hammer. "Oh. I was taking a look at the stage. That floorboard is ... anyway, so you and Quinn."

I grin, folding my arms over my chest and narrowing my eyes.

"Bennett, since when are you into Cedar Cliff gossip?" I ask.

"I just want a little perspective, is all."

"Why?"

He shrugs. Slow. Deliberate. "I like Quinn. She's like a sister to me. I'm just ..."

"Wanting to know my intentions?"

He barks out a laugh. "No. Not exactly. I'm confused."

I shrug. "Quinn is Quinn. She's always been Quinn. She's sarcastic. Honest. And it's refreshing."

"Hmm," he grunts. "Sure you don't want another happy-go-lucky kind of girl?"

I laugh. "Nah. I've tried that. I need that sarcastic wit in my life. I think everyone needs a bit of a push like that."

"Need?" he asks.

"Maybe not in a *food, clothing, and shelter* way," I say.

"But in a way where she gives me an extra push that nobody else gives me, you know?"

I don't realize how much I mean it until the words leave my mouth.

I grew up with my sunshine-filled family. But sometimes, I need a little harshness in my life. I need the barked words of Quinn, the sarcasm that rips me from my comfortable reality into the real world. I need the intensity.

I realize we've been quiet for too long, and Bennett looks lost in thought.

"You all right, man?" I ask.

"Oh," he says, as if I snapped him out of a trance. "Yeah. Yeah, I'll be fine."

I'll be fine. As if he isn't fine now.

I narrow my eyes. "You sure?"

"Yeah," he says with a deep inhale. "You're right. We need the women who push us in life."

"So, do I get your blessing?" I joke.

He barks out a laugh. "It's not mine you'll need."

"Whose then?"

"The only blessing you need is Quinn's," he says with a laugh. "If she wants something, we can't stop her. And if she doesn't, then that's even worse."

34

Quinn

Landon is the Prince Charming I don't need.

I don't need him dipping me so low in the show. I don't need him smiling at me with those gorgeous dimples. And I definitely don't need the sweep of his lips over mine, making me melt right down to the creaking stage.

Why? Because I feel like Sleeping Beauty rising from the depths of a dark slumber. I notice everything about him now. I notice how he waves at every kid in the park. I see when he helps Honey, arm in arm, back to the offices. I even daydream about his booming laugh when he tells a joke, making sure to include everyone in the conversation.

Every memory fills me in a Landon-filled stupor, and all I can do is walk down the midway and hope he stops invading my thoughts soon.

There's a light breeze this evening. Autumn in Georgia is starting to rear its head, burying the midway in rustic leaves. The sun goes down earlier, leaving the park lit by only the glow of lamps and the track lights from roller coasters.

I walk to The Bee-fast Stop, intending to grab a honey

iced tea to go, but I lean on the railing at The Beesting's queue line, watching the riders yell as it shoots down the massive drop.

I close my eyes and take it in. Who knew bloodcurdling screams could be peaceful? But my Zen is broken by the feel of my phone buzzing in my shorts pocket. I tug it out.

Mom: Call me?

I told myself I wouldn't respond. I swore to myself I wouldn't. But I find my fingers hovering over the screen.

I wonder if I should. If Landon can change, who is to say my mom can't? But I don't know what I'd even say. We've gone down this road before. We exchange a few texts, then say nothing for months. I can't endure that again. Your parents aren't supposed to break your heart as much as she does mine.

"And here I thought, you'd left already."

I recognize the voice as Honey's. The wobbly yet somehow still harsh voice that has me closing my eyes. I inhale deeply, pocketing my phone.

"Hey, Honey," I say.

She shuffles forward, the jangle of her bracelets heralding her arrival.

"How's that whole *chip on your shoulder* thing going?" she asks.

"Way to start a conversation," I say.

"So, not going well?"

"I added in the kiss to the play," I say. "Isn't that all you wanted from me?"

"Bah," she says, waving her hand. "Only sort of. How's it going with my golden retriever?"

I shift from foot to foot uncomfortably. The idea of

Landon being *her* golden retriever feels odd in my stomach. But it's not like he's *mine* either, is he?

"He's not in the doghouse," I say.

She lets out her usual low rumble of *hmm* in her throat as we both watch The Beesting rise, then fall with screaming riders once more.

My phone buzzes in my pocket. I close my eyes. It buzzes immediately after.

"Answering that?" Honey asks.

"It's probably just my mom," I say.

"Not on good terms with your family?"

I dart my eyes to her. Her eyebrows are turned in.

"It's complicated."

"You know," she says with a sigh, "I've made a lot of mistakes in my life."

"You seem like you're doing well for yourself."

"Now, maybe. Sort of," Honey says, her face scrunching up, consumed by lines. "But I neglected a lot of people I should have in life. Did you know I got a divorce?"

"I heard three."

She grunts. "Rumors. Just one husband. The divorce was my fault, you know. My career was great. My books were selling. Who was he to hold me back?" She sighs. "He never forgave me, and I don't blame him. Well, I dated a younger man after that. He *only* wanted me for my money." Her wrinkled lips purse. "Ended up cheating on me with someone his own age. I didn't want anything to do with anyone after that. And I can see you doing the same."

"Okay, except I don't have a husband or ... gold-digger boyfriend, I guess."

"No, but you've got the same chip that I do. I can see that you're stuck."

"How'd you get out of your rut?"

"I created a theme park."

I laugh. "I don't think our situations are exactly apples to apples then. I can't just *make* a theme park."

"You can do a lot to change your life."

"Like what?"

"Well, is your mama included in the chip on your shoulder?"

"Honey," I say, almost as a warning.

"Fine. Then, where do you see yourself next year?" she continues.

I open my mouth and shut it.

"What do you mean?" I ask. "In life?"

"Sure."

The question feels odd. Unnerving. And when I look at her, she blinks back.

"I'll be Queen Bee," I say tentatively.

She does her little *hmm* thing again, and I narrow my eyes.

"Hopefully stage managing, but I don't know."

"Have you ever considered getting a degree?"

"What?" I ask. "I ... I tried. I just ... no. Maybe. I don't know. I don't think I could."

"Says who?"

I'm suddenly uncomfortable, tightening my grip on the railing. My phone buzzes in my pocket, and I white-knuckle the railing harder.

"I don't want to think about it," I say.

I don't like how Honey's eyes narrow, as if there's an agenda I'm not aware of. Conversations happening without me present.

"What do you know, Honey?" I ask.

She side-eyes me and purses her lips.

Then, another voice comes from behind me, and I

recognize the happiness, the gruffness, the lilt of light-hearted sarcasm before I see him.

"Am I walking into a storm, or is it safe?" Landon asks.

I turn to see him approach with his hands raised, as if he were taming two dragons.

"Welcome to the party," Honey says, hooking her hand into the crook of his arm.

I side-eye the gesture. It looks automatic, like it's a rhythm for the two of them. I wonder just how close they are. And why does my heart feel wrapped in a fist at the thought?

My phone buzzes again, and I groan.

"Wow, that poor person texting you." Landon laughs. "You haven't even looked."

"I don't need to," I say. "It's probably my mom."

Honey forcefully sighs, an edge to it.

"What's wrong with your mom?" Landon asks, frowning.

"You don't know?" Honey asks.

I roll my eyes. "*You* don't even know, Honey."

"Well, I wanna know," she says.

"Me too," Landon chimes in.

"You sound like you got left out of tag in kindergarten."

He grins. "I did actually."

My phone buzzes again. And again.

Landon looks down to my pocket, then back up.

"Come on," he says. "Answer if it's her."

"It's not that easy to just answer my mom."

"Of course it is."

"Says the man with the perfect family," I say.

"You're in our family too."

I look from Honey and back to him.

"That a kink I don't know about?" I ask. "Family love or something?"

He tongues the inside of his cheek right as Honey barks out a laugh.

"Funny," he says, shaking a finger at me. "You're very funny, Quinn Sauer."

I knock his shoulder with mine. I don't know why I did it, but he exhales into it, leaning down and kissing the top of my shoulder in one smooth motion, angled away from Honey. My heart flutters.

My phone buzzes once more, and he glances down.

"You're sure you're not gonna check?"

I reach into my pocket, lifting an eyebrow right as he lifts one in return. I look down and see the texts are not from my mom, but from the group chat.

Bennett: Dinner at Chicken and the Egg tomorrow night? I rented a party room.
Lorelei: What's the big occasion?
Bennett: Friendship?
Lorelei: Wow, I'm so honored.
Theo: And I'm suspicious.
Ruby: I'll be there!

"What's going on?" Landon asks.

"I don't know," I say. "Bennett is inviting us to dinner or something."

"I see that little scrunch in your nose," he says. "Is Bennett inviting y'all to dinner odd?"

My hand darts to my nose. "You know I'm confused due to a scrunch?"

A smile breaks out over his face.

234

I narrow my eyes and continue, "Yes. We normally just meet at The Honeycomb."

"Maybe he's switching things up."

"We never switch things up," I say.

I type out a quick text, saying I'll be there or be square, but when I'm done, I realize Landon is still looking down at me.

"What?" I ask.

"Well, are you gonna ask me to be your dinner date?"

"No," I say. "You'd like that too much."

A little smirk pops onto his face, and I feel it soothe every crack in my dark, bitter bones. Every worry about my mom or whatever cryptic conversation I just had with Honey feels like it doesn't matter.

Honey lets out a short cackle. I almost forgot she was here.

"Shush," I say, which only makes her laugh harder.

Landon dips his chin down to his chest. "I'll pick you up at seven tomorrow."

"You don't even know what time the party is."

He smiles. "Then, I hope we aren't late."

35

Quinn

Landon opens the side door to his truck.

"What a gentleman," I say.

He rolls his eyes with a grin. "Your sarcasm doesn't scare me. Don't pretend to be unimpressed."

"What are you talking about?" I ask, batting my eyes. "I am on a date with *Ranger Randy*."

"All right, all right, Barb. Very funny. In the car you go."

I hop in right as he pats my butt with his palm.

We rumble the five minutes down the road to downtown, parking on a side street and walking down the alley toward Chicken and the Egg.

The back door, more akin to a speakeasy—only there if you know it—opens to a cramped hallway. The walls are lined in various knickknacks—porcelain chicken statues, brown egg cartons, multicolored eggs. It's like a museum for poultry. It's my favorite part of this restaurant.

"This is my favorite space here," Landon says, echoing my thoughts.

I blink up at him.

He chuckles. "What?"

I smile and shake my head. "Nothing."

Landon places a hand on my lower back, and we follow the familiar voices down the hall. Ducking under a turquoise linen curtain, we enter the low-ceilinged party room.

Theo leans against the empty cloth-covered buffet table, likely reserved for other parties. She rips off a cherry from its stem with her teeth. Emory is standing with his arms crossed, watching the clock on the wall, while Lorelei rests her head on his shoulder. The only sounds are the distant hum of the restaurant and some '80s ballad echoing from the lobby.

"Why is everyone so quiet?" I ask, announcing our presence.

Theo's eyes widen. "Oh my God, right?!" She rushes toward us. "This is weird. This feels weird."

"Why are we in a party room?" I lean back to peer out the curtain. "They're not even busy."

Theo and Lorelei answer in a chorus of, "Absolutely," and, "He's acting *off*."

The group settles into silence, as if we're all trying to crack the case. After a moment, Lorelei's eyes swivel to mine. Then Landon's. Then the space between us, which is not as wide as it should be. Her eyes slowly narrow.

"Did you two carpool?" she asks.

I blurt out, "My car broke down," at the same time Landon says, "Thought it could be fun."

Our heads jerk to each other. He's smiling. I'm not.

Lorelei slowly says, "Thought *what* could be fun?"

Before we can provide another half-baked answer, I hear a sarcastic, "Wow. Hey," from behind us.

I twist on my heel—notably *away* from my too-clever best friend—and see Bennett paused in the hall next to Jolene.

"Wow. Hey," I mimic unintentionally.

I don't have to look at Lorelei and Theo to know they're just as surprised as I am. Jolene never comes to group events. Is it her birthday or something? Is that why we're in a party room?

Bennett grins. "All my favorite people!"

"Quesadilla crew!" Theo whoops from the corner.

"What fun, Ben," Jolene murmurs. Her smile is so flat that an iron would be out of a job.

"So much fun," Landon says, except his voice sounds genuine.

Either he's oblivious to how odd this is or he's really good at acting. Though, after performing side by side with him, I'd say it's the former. I smile a little at his cute innocence.

"Oh!" Ruby says. She stops short at the curtained archway, her hand settled on the strap of her purse. She seems just as surprised as the rest of us. Her face is flushed. "Hey, Jolene."

Bennett nudges Ruby and grins to her.

"Swanky," she whispers.

"Yeah," he says. "Well, Honeycomb gets old sometimes."

I notice Jolene's eyes dart over to their conversation. She purses her lips.

"Uh, anyone order yet?" Bennett asks, walking over to the long table in the corner.

We all look at each other after he walks past.

I silently mouth to Lorelei, *What the heck?*

She shrugs.

We follow, almost single file, to the table. Landon takes my hand, rotating them behind us so that nobody can see. His palm slips into mine as if it's as natural as breathing.

He leans down, and in the lowest, softest, *I almost don't hear him* whisper, he asks, "So, we don't like Jolene, do we?"

I can't help the smile that creeps onto my face at his observation.

"We're ambivalent," I whisper.

"Cool."

He looks down at our hands, as if admiring them together, then gives my palm one extra squeeze before pulling away.

We order a round of beers and mingle—if you want to call it mingling. Ruby asks Jolene how her job hunt is going, but Jolene only answers in clipped tones. Theo tries to joke with Emory, who keeps looking at the clock on the wall, as if in pain. And Lorelei stares at me and Landon with narrowed eyes.

I flash her a look that says, *What?*

And she responds with raised eyebrows, as if saying, *You know what.*

A couple of minutes later, Orson appears in the doorway, apologizing for being late. I see Theo tense and grab another cherry to pop in her mouth.

"Great," Jolene huffs, tossing her napkin on the table. "I knew we didn't get enough chairs." She gets up to grab another before Bennett can fully stand, looking baffled.

Under the table, Landon's hand skims over my knee and up my thigh. My face heats, and I give him a pointed look. He grins and tosses me a wink. I shake my head with a grimace as my soul sinks into the floor below me. He could kill a woman with that wink.

Jolene comes back, manhandling the back of a chair.

We scoot to make room, Orson taking the seat next to Theo, right as a large basket of biscuits is dropped off.

"Ordered for the table," Bennett says.

"Mmm," I hum sarcastically. "Biscuits and beer. Perfect combo, *Ben*."

Bennett flashes me a look, and I give him a wide-eyed *what* look.

Landon chuckles at my sarcasm even though nobody else does. His large hand widens over my thigh, trailing a line up, up, up. Shivers roll over me. He angles his hand to cup me, running the pad of his thumb on the outside of my shorts.

I slap his hand. He removes his hand with a grin.

"Good boy," I whisper.

He pinches my side in retaliation, and I smack it away.

If I could crawl out of my body and look down at us from above, I wonder how we would appear. We're at a dinner with friends, acting playful, like we're an actual couple or something. There's nothing that says we're coworkers, pretending our fictional characters are in love. There's nothing that says he's my best friend's brother, who I've grown to hate, then tolerate, and now want to devour in a locked restroom of this restaurant. We're not pretending at all.

I look across the table and see Lorelei spreading butter on a biscuit. Her stare is concentrated on us. She narrows her eyes. I narrow mine.

I'm onto you, her look says.

I don't know what you're talking about, mine responds.

We break from our battle of mental wills when Bennett clinks a spoon against his glass. We all turn to face him. He's standing—when did he stand? And he's holding champagne

—when did he get champagne? This big man with tattoos and a band T-shirt is holding a tiny glass of bubbly.

"Um, hey," he says.

"Hi," we all chorus at the same time.

"Ha." Bennett looks down to the floor, then back up. "Right. Well, uh, I wanted to thank everyone for coming."

"Speech!" Orson says.

Theo elbows him.

"Getting there," Bennett says with a grin. "Um, well, I like to have my close friends around for all the big things in my life. For all the moments that mean the most to me. And today is a big moment. Tonight, I mean. Right now. Uh ..."

Bennett is stumbling, and I can feel myself tensing because something in my gut twists. The mood shifts. The room grows quiet.

And then it happens. It's so fast that I can barely blink.

Bennett tugs Jolene out of her chair. He pulls something from his pocket and lowers to one knee.

"Jolene," he asks, "will you marry me?"

Jolene covers her mouth with her hands, her eyes tearing up, and she nods. "Yes!"

I inhale sharply.

Is this real? It doesn't seem real.

There's no fluff. No *you make me a better man* or *this is everything I hoped for*. Just the question. Even the way Bennett gives a half-smile seems off. It's an expression I've seen on my parents countless times, growing up, a look they'd wear if they thought I couldn't see. A slip of the mask.

I look around. My friends' faces are also shocked. But most of all, Bennett's best friend, Ruby, is stiff in her chair.

I look to Landon, and he claps. And when his eyes meet

mine, there's a kind of sparkle to them. He's genuinely happy, and I wonder if he could make me just as happy one day.

36

Landon

Too much happens all at once.

Bennett gets on one knee and proposes.

Lorelei chokes on her water with a tear-filled, "Oh my God!"

Ruby's fork clatters to her plate.

I start clapping once Jolene says yes and begins to cry.

Orson joins in with a loud, "Oh yeah!" Why he decided to go with the Kool-Aid Man noise, I'll never know.

I stand up to give Bennett one of those *this is totally fine that we're hugging because it's a special occasion* kind of hugs. Lorelei takes Jolene's hand and gawks at the diamond. Theo pulls Bennett into an exaggerated bear hug, mocking the one I gave, which gets a laugh from Orson. But when I look around, I don't see Quinn or Ruby anymore.

After a couple of minutes and after a quick toast to Bennett, I notice the drinks are already getting low.

I clap Bennett on the back. "You know what? I'll go get a bottle of wine for the table. On me."

"Thanks, man!" But when I twist to go, he grabs the

crook of my arm and leans in. "Hey, can you ..." He looks from side to side, as if he's whispering a secret. "Can you check on Ruby? I haven't seen her in a bit."

I blink. "Uh, yeah. Sure, man."

I exit the room. But I barely make it down the hall to the bar before I see Quinn standing outside the restroom, back pressed against the wall.

I grin. "There you are."

Quinn's head turns to me, and she gives a weak smile.

"What's wrong?"

"Nothing, nothing. Ruby just felt sick," she says. "I think it was the biscuits or something."

"Does she have a gluten allergy or ..."

"She's got allergies," Quinn says vaguely with a shrug.

"Uh-huh."

We're silent next to each other until we hear a gasp. At the end of the narrow passage, right at the turn before the restrooms and the kitchen, is the little kid from the park, mouth gaping open, arms clutching his Buzzy the Bear stuffed animal.

"You've gotta be kidding," Quinn mutters.

I give him a happy wave, and Quinn reaches out with her pinkie, tracing along outside of my palm. She intertwines her fingers with mine.

He squeaks as if he saw a ghost and runs off.

I look down at our hands, then back up.

"You just made his day," I say. "And mine."

"Oh, I know I did."

I can't help my next action. I'm a man possessed. I run a hand into her hair while my other hand tilts her chin up. I place my lips against hers. She pulls in a sharp inhale, winding her hands up to my chest and tracing along my bearded jaw. I only let it linger for a moment before we both pull away.

Quinn's face is flushed a light pink. Her eyelashes flutter, as if blinking back from a dream.

"What was that for?" she asks.

"For being you."

She smirks. "You're so full of feelings."

"Tons of 'em."

She bites her lip and looks away. "So, you've liked me since you were fourteen, huh?"

"Aaand we're done with me trying to be sweet," I say with a laugh. I plant a hard kiss on her forehead. "I'm getting more wine for the table. Come with me?"

Quinn laughs. "Let me check on Ruby, and I'll meet you at the bar."

"Sounds good. And, hey, Quinn?"

"Yeah?"

"Feelings are fine to have."

A slow smile spreads across her face. "Go away."

I walk backward and pump my eyebrows. "Yes, ma'am."

At the bar, I rap my knuckles on the counter as I request two of the nicest bottles of wine they have. I'll likely spend all of the Ranger Randy bonus I just earned, but that's all right. Bennett is worth it. Plus, things are going so well with Honeywood's buyout, Quinn, and everything else that being one pay period behind on my goal isn't so bad.

"Ranger Randy," a voice breathes behind me.

I turn and see the same kid from earlier.

"Uh, hey, buddy," I say. "Very cool bear you have there."

The kid leans back and holds his stuffed toy at arm's length, as if he forgot who he was holding.

"It's Buzzy," he says, hugging it back to him.

"You know, I'm friends with Buzzy."

He gasps. "Wow."

"Yeah, so, uh, where are your parents? Do you need help finding them or—"

"Mike!" a voice calls. "Good Lord, there you are, Mike!"

The kid turns at the sound of his name.

"You need to come on back, bud."

I look up and see a familiar face. Familiar but lined with twelve years of age. He has a beard that he didn't have before—though I guess I do too, but his is speckled with gray. For second, I wonder if it is who I think it is, but I could place that smirk anywhere.

"Michael?" I ask.

"Landon! Wow, hey!"

I hold out my hand, and my old football team's captain claps his hand into it.

"I didn't know you still lived in Cedar Cliff," I say.

"No," he says, throwing a thumb over his shoulder. "I'm just visiting the kid's mom." He ruffles his son, I guess Michael Jr.'s, hair. "I've been in New York for a few years now."

It's like everything comes rushing back at once. High school. Him stealing Quinn's notebook from my hands. Him asking me when the big day was. And then the things I've only just realized. The bullying that went on without me even knowing.

My fists clench at my sides.

"So, what about you?" he asks when I'm too quiet. "You still here?"

"Just moved back," I answer.

"No kidding! Man, I followed you through your college years. Always put you on my fantasy football team. It was more to tell people I knew who you were than anything else, but ..."

Then, I hear a soft, "Landon?" from behind us.

We both turn. Quinn stands there, her lips parted, her face blank. My stomach sinks. I watch Michael's eyes rove over her lips, down to her chest, then up again.

"Daddy," his kid says, tugging at the sleeve of his shirt, "they're *together*!"

Michael continues to blink at her, then back to me.

"Wow. Mrs. Landon Arden," he says. "Manifested that one, huh?"

Quinn's mouth closes, and her jaw tightens.

"What a blast from the past," Michael muses. "Weird."

"Yeah," she says, her voice as faint as wind. "Really weird."

"What did we used to call you back then?" he says, snapping his fingers. "What was it?"

"Bridezilla," she says dully.

My heart rate rises.

"Yes! That's the one." He barks out a laugh.

I don't think Quinn finds it as funny. Neither do I.

"Sorry for that. I was a little shit. Oops, don't repeat that, bud. But I hope you're doing good. I mean, wow, you two." He holds out a hand and gestures between us. "Woulda never thought. Could say it's a bit weird."

"Could," I say. I reach out to intertwine my fingers with Quinn's. "But you shouldn't."

Quinn clutches my fingers tighter. I rub my thumb over hers.

He slowly nods. "Huh. Well, hey, nice to see you guys again."

Quinn only *hmms*.

247

I ignore him and instead hold my hand out to his kid. "High-five," I say.

He jumps and slaps my hand with his.

When they both leave, I look over at Quinn. Her jaw is still grinding, but her palm cups mine tightly.

37

Quinn

You never forget your first love, and you never forget your high school bully. You just kind of hope they were never friends. I'm not so lucky.

All the feelings from high school came rushing back the moment Michael looked me over from head to toe. I felt scanned, like some alien intruder. Like I shouldn't have been standing next to Landon. Like we didn't fit.

I sit next to Ruby in the party room as she downs another glass of wine. After the proposal, she told me some things in the restroom that I'm having a hard time forgetting. I wonder if, because of those memories, Ruby also feels like an alien intruder tonight, haunted by the hope that she and Bennett would have been the ones engaged instead of him and Jolene.

But that's just how things go, I guess. You plan for one thing, and if life doesn't agree, you're done for. I thought I'd learned that lesson by now.

I try to forget it and instead smile when Landon sits next to us. He cracks jokes about Bennett's awful speech skills and makes Ruby laugh. In that moment, I'm thankful he's my friend—or, well, my *something*.

Landon isn't the only one who buys more wine for the table. By the end of the night, we've gone through a few bottles too many. And when we leave, I'm good and tipsy, walking back down the alley, holding Landon's hand. I trip along the sidewalk. He laughs.

"Ha-ha," I mock.

He chuckles. "I'm a few blocks from here if we just wanna walk to my house. I can pick up my truck in the morning."

But the thought makes my chest twinge.

When I shake my head, he says, "Quinn, I'm not gonna try anything. You're all bubbly drunk and cute. I plan to take the couch."

But something still settles in me weird.

I do think I trust Landon, but ... seeing him with Michael again tilted my world a little. It's the association—the way they almost seemed like they were smiling together when I walked up.

No, you're being ridiculous. He's not friends with Michael anymore.

Landon kisses my head when I don't respond.

"All right, drunkie, I'll take ya home," he says. "But let's at least walk it off a bit."

I steady myself with a half-smile and a nod. He shifts me to the other side of the sidewalk, taking my place on the outside as a car passes by.

We cross to the small park in the center of downtown. It's just enough room for a fountain, various wooden benches, and a white gazebo—the location of so many Cedar Cliff High School prom pictures. The sprinklers spray across the grass. Slow piano music courses through the speakers.

Landon pauses, reaching out for my hand.

I halt. "What?"

He pulls his shoulders up to his ears, letting them fall again with a smile. "Dance with me, Queen Bee."

My heart races, and I let out a laughing scoff. But he still tugs on my hand so that I walk into him. My free hand rests on his chest. When I meet his gaze, his brown eyes seem filled with hope, maybe happiness. I roll my eyes as his palm rests on my lower back.

We sway together in the park. I don't know how much time passes. A song. Maybe two. He starts to hum the familiar tune. I lay my cheek against his chest, letting the low rumble of his hums vibrate into me. He rests his chin on the top of my head.

It feels nice, just being with him.

"Not so bad, is it?" he asks. "Dancing with me?"

"Terrible," I joke.

He chuckles, extending out his hand and curling it so that I twirl out, then back in. It's peaceful. It's flawless. It's like we're in a fairy tale. I close my eyes and breathe in his vanilla and cedar scent.

It's in that moment that I realize Landon might have been Michael's friend in high school, but he's my friend now.

I almost wish we'd had more time. That neither of us had been so dumb in high school. That he had just told me he liked me when he saw my ridiculous diary.

"What's going on in that head of yours?" Landon asks.

"How dumb you are," I say.

He barks out a laugh.

But another part of me, the one still seeing that smirk

from my high school bully, feels like I've been duped. Like I fell for the guy who hadn't stood up for me. Like I'm dancing with the same guy who told me, "Not a chance," and let me live with that moment for years.

"And what about now?" he asks. "I can practically hear the gears turning."

I sigh. "I'm thinking about us."

"Oh yeah? And what have you come up with?"

"I'm still thinking. Parsing through it all."

"Like one of those machines?"

I laugh and pull back. "What machines?"

"I just imagine the little bank machines. You know, one of those like"—he rolls a finger around—"the money counters at the bank that whirs."

"It *whirs?*"

He chuckles, and the longer we stare at each other, the more I find myself smiling. I can't deny those dimples of his.

"Yeah, Barb, it *whirs.*"

He leans down, and we both inhale as he kisses me. He seems to like doing that. I like it too. My breath feels stolen by him, just like every other part of me. He cups my cheek, pressing his thumb under my jaw so that my neck tilts up and our kiss deepens. I let out a moan against him.

"That sound is so beautiful," he murmurs against my mouth.

"And you're so full of it."

"Full of *you,*" he whispers back.

I move my hand to his chest, pushing him back until we hit the park's gazebo. We both let out a groan in response. I bite his lower lip, eliciting a small whimper from him. His fingers grip into my side right as my phone buzzes in my purse pocket.

I pull away and look down to see the all-too-familiar name shining back at me.

"Your mom again?" Landon asks.

I swallow.

Well, if that isn't a bucket of cold water, I don't know what is.

Here I am, dancing in a park with sprinklers and piano music, while my fate stares back at me—a reminder that I'm not meant for happiness. My mom didn't know how to handle it, and I'm not sure I do either.

"It's nothing," I say, pocketing my phone.

He laughs. I don't laugh with him. His face falls, and he tips my chin up with a curled forefinger.

"Quinn, you can tell me."

I blink up at him.

What will Landon think when he finds out the truth?

I can't guarantee I won't be like my mom. I can't promise that, even though I take medication for my depression, I will never be *perfectly fine*.

What will he think when he finds out I'm just a ticking time bomb?

"No," I say, then add, "It's personal."

"I'd like to be involved with your personal life, if you'd let me."

I shake my head. "No."

"Why?"

"Because that's too real," I say. "All of this is too real."

He chews the inside of his cheek. "It was Michael, wasn't it?"

"It's been everything," I admit. "The sale of Honeywood, my mom, you, me ... and now, yeah, I guess Michael didn't help either."

"Dick."

I breathe out a laugh through my nose, and then my face falls again.

"Anytime things go well, it always kinda shifts into something bad," I admit. "I'm just waiting for the other shoe to drop."

"But what if it's not that loud of a drop?"

"There's that trusty optimism." I pat his bicep. "Let's call it a night, Ranger. I'm about to turn into a pumpkin."

"I like pumpkins though."

I lean forward, resting my head on his chest. He rubs my back.

"You're right," he says. "Let's go, Barb."

We walk to his car, and when we settle inside, I look out the window. I watch the telephone poles fly past, the bright streetlamps flaring and then disappearing as we pass under them. We drive past our neighbors' front yards—both cut and uncut—and the sidewalks slowly end until we reach my house.

"Thanks," I say. "For being my date."

He shrugs with a smile. "That's what friends do, right?"

I sigh.

Yes. And maybe that's all we should be.

38

Landon

The following Saturday feels uneasy.

I make my way from the security office to the amphitheater, decked out in my Ranger Randy gear. Quinn is already on the other side of the stage, pacing back and forth. A wash of worry in pink.

She had the last four days off, given that the park wasn't open due to our fall schedule. She texted me occasionally, but not as much as I'd thought she might. I invited her over yesterday, and she said she was busy with Ruby. I didn't question it. Except now, she won't look at me.

Maybe it's just the weather, I reason.

Maybe it's her mom.

And then I consider, *Maybe it's* me.

We walk through our performance with less gusto than usual. When I touch her waist, she's stiff. When we tell jokes, her laugh is stilted. And when we kiss, when I finally have her in my arms after so many days, my heart sinks, as the kiss feels forced. It feels too much like an obligation, like it's our job.

The crowd claps as the curtain falls. She pulls away.

My whole body feels cold.

"Did I do something?" I ask.

Quinn pauses. Emily, who was walking toward us with a large smile, slowly starts to backstep into the wing. A moonwalk of trepidation.

"I'm fine, Landon," Quinn says.

I don't like the way she says my name. Harsh. Professional. Pointed.

"You don't seem fine," I say.

"It's all good."

I try to talk to her more, but Emily takes the moment of silence to rush to us before I can speak.

Dang it.

I decide I'll just talk to her during our signings. No big deal.

Except when I get there, she's already in character. She's greeting guests early, starting autographs before the allotted time. The guests are overjoyed, but something in my gut tells me that was on purpose.

She's avoiding me.

With every signed autograph, every fake smile, and every loss of eye contact, my heart dips deeper and deeper into the pit of my stomach.

Then, a kid gets on his toes and whispers, "My friend said you two are dating."

"Why, we are!" Quinn says, lighthearted in her queenly voice.

The kid's face scrunches. "In *real life*," he whispers.

I chuckle. "Was, by chance, your friend's name Mike?" I ask.

His face brightens up. "Yes, sir!"

I grin down at him and wink, but I don't confirm or deny.

But from beside me, Quinn shakes her head. "No," she says. "No, we're not."

The kid's face falls.

My head jerks to her. "What the heck, Quinn? Err ... Queen Bee?"

The line is frozen.

She swallows. "Well, we aren't. Are we?"

I blink. She's lost it. She's completely lost her mind.

She closes her eyes and shakes her head. "I should ... I should go."

"Wait, uh ..." I try to tell the crowd that we'll be back, but something tells me we won't.

I run after Quinn to the dressing room, chasing behind her pink ball gown billowing in the wind.

When I close the door behind me, I run a hand through my hair. "What was that about?"

"Nothing. I'm just ... off today, I think."

I look over her. Aside from not having a lifted eyebrow in my direction, she looks fine. Maybe a little rumpled from her run here, but mostly okay. I wonder if me calling her a friend after dinner was the wrong move. Should I have kissed her instead? At the time, it seemed like the right decision, but I'm not exactly an expert on Quinn Sauer's thoughts.

"You know," I say, "if I didn't have to go wrangle guests after our disaster, I could ravage you right here."

It's a joke. Me trying to be playful. But she doesn't laugh. My face falls. It's like there's an ocean between us with rough waves and no Coast Guard.

Fine. I'll have to conduct my own rescue mission.

"Quinn, talk to me."

"You've got a job to do," she says, walking to the rack holding my security hat and tossing it to me.

I catch it midair.

I laugh. "What's wrong? You've been weird since the engagement party," I continue. "What's going on?"

She doesn't respond, only chews the inside of her cheek.

"Come on," I say with a chuckle. "No snarky comment?"

"I'm out of them today," she says. "Why don't you run along and go be security?"

"Run along?" I repeat with a breathy scoff. I tighten my hat in my fist. "Why are you starting a fight with me?"

She turns around, reaching at her side to unzip her dress. She's trying to end the conversation by literally turning her back to me. The zipper catches, and I sigh.

"Do you need help with that?" I ask, moving forward.

"No," she bites out. "No. And stop being so nice. You're always so nice."

"I like being nice to you."

"But that's not what we do," she says, dropping her hands. The zipper is still caught. "We're not meant to be nice. We argue. I push. You push. That's it."

I blink at her, but my irritation is bubbling up faster than I can stop it. I stare at the wall and bite my lip before looking back to her as she turns to face me.

"Was it the dancing?" I ask. "Was it too much?"

She pauses, thinking for a moment before saying, "Maybe."

That's not it. Her voice is too forced.

"Quinn ..."

My walkie buzzes.

"Fred for Landon."

The muffled sound makes my jaw clench. Quinn's eyes dart to my walkie, then back up, her eyebrows raised, as if expectant.

I sigh and press the button. "Go for Landon."

"Are you with Quinn?"

"Yes, sir."

"Can you send her to the offices, please?"

Quinn and I catch each other's gazes.

What in the world is going on in that head of hers?

"Yes," I answer. "Yes, I'll let her know. She'll be there soon."

I release the button and inhale, but the only words that come out are, "This conversation isn't over."

Quinn sucks in her cheek.

"I need to change, Landon. Can you please leave?"

I glance at her dress and nod.

I walk out of the dressing room with a, "I promise we'll keep talking."

39

Quinn

"We have an offer from a buyer."

"Oh," Lorelei says. She blinks where she stands, hands wrapping and fidgeting together. "Oh, wow. That's great, right? Is it great?"

I sit in the chair across from Fred's desk with my legs crossed. Honey is in the chair next to me, leaning back with her hands poised on the armrests. Her chin is tilted up. Her red lips pursed.

I fully expected to get in trouble for the act I'd pulled today at signings, but so far, they haven't brought it up. It makes me wonder why I'm even here. I'm not the general manager, like Fred, or the GM in training, like Lorelei, and I'm definitely not the creator of the park itself, like Honey.

So, why am I here?

I wonder if I'm getting promoted.

That would make the day at least a little brighter, especially when Landon's words keep echoing in my mind.

"This conversation isn't over."

I need to talk to him. At the end of the day, we're adults,

and he needs to know the truth about everything. If I'm not planning on dating him, he should at least know why.

"Quinn, are you listening?"

I blink back to the room.

"Hmm?" I ask. "What?"

Fred is behind his desk, standing now with his hands splayed on top. He looks from me to Honey and back again. I look around for Lorelei. I'm not sure when she left, but the door is now closed. I feel a tug behind my stomach.

Something doesn't feel right.

I look at Honey. A single penciled-in eyebrow is lifted. Her jewelry-laden arms are folded, one over the other.

"The theater department," Fred continues.

Or at least, I think it's a continuation. I have no idea what he was talking about.

"The buyer has ideas."

I shake my head with a blank stare. "I'll help out however I can, if needed."

Fred's eyes close, and he sighs.

A string in my chest pulls tight.

"I mean ... they have ideas on how they want our characters to be. And our department to be run."

My stomach feels the unease before my brain can process why. My breath hitches, but I swallow it down.

"And?"

"Standards that are similar to other parks," Fred continues.

The string is taut.

"Okay?"

Honey exhales a frustrated sigh and smacks her lips. "Queenie, after this season, you have to step down as Queen Bee."

I blink, but the words don't seem to penetrate. I try to

breathe, but the air won't come into my body. I want to move, but my legs are too heavy. I think Fred keeps talking, but my ears are ringing.

"Is this ... is this about today?" I ask.

"What happened today?"

Okay. Don't mention that.

I try a different route. "Is this even legal?"

"Yes," Fred answers with an exhausted sigh. "I'm told that *Bona fide requirements* on a job description can require a certain height for the role."

"Oh. So, they're going with height," I say. "Not the fact that I'm thirty?"

It's uncomfortable after I say it, but uncomfortable truths seem to be my specialty.

"If they were, could you blame them?" Honey asks.

My eyes swivel to her. My fists curl into a death grip. "What did you just say?"

She purses her lips. "I didn't mean it like that. Queenie, you can do so much more than just that part-time role."

"Yeah, you mentioned stage managing, right?" I ask Fred, ignoring Honey. "Or script writing?"

"The requirements are still there ..." Fred starts.

"What? You said they'd be too busy to notice. That my lack of a degree wouldn't matter."

"Yeah, well ... bigger corporations also mean bigger HR."

"You're kidding."

"Well, so we do have good news," Fred says. "They have scholarship options."

"Scholarships? Like going back to college? Fred ... you said ... you said ..."

Words are no longer coming freely to me. I feel like I'm sinking deeper into a pit.

"I want you here, Quinn," Fred says with a heavy breath. "But unfortunately, they're requesting a degree. I don't want to lose you though. Please think about it."

I swallow. "You know what happened last time I tried."

"And I also know that you're strong and you can do it."

My jaw clenches as I stand on wobbling legs.

It's hard to feel strong when your world is crumbling around you. But I don't say that. Instead, I turn on my heel, pass a look to Honey's pursed face, then leave the office.

40

Quinn

I take the rest of the day off.

I drive by Slow Riser to speak with the manager, Sean. I let him know I can be full-time after this season instead of just for my usual winter schedule, and I try to hide the bitter taste in my mouth when I say it.

Then, I come home and bundle myself in blankets, watching texts come in, but not bothering to open them.

Okay, maybe my will breaks a few times.

Landon sends me a *hope you're feeling better* text along with pictures of him throughout the afternoon at Honeywood. Him patting the Buzzy statue's belly with his wide, dimpled grin. Him pretending to sleep at his security desk. Him with his arms raised into fists, as if he's about to box the bumblebees in the Bumblebee Greenhouse.

I told him I'd left because I felt sick. I didn't mention me basically getting fired. So, he did his usual thing and became cute, which makes him difficult to ignore. I try to turn my attention elsewhere. I reread my mom's last text again and again. It's an opposite conversation to my and Landon's.

Mom: I won't disappear this time. I promise.

The unnerving thing is that it's too self-aware. I'm not sure what to make of it. She's not a self-aware person. My mom could be a cat and still claim to have opposable thumbs. Or a teapot and vehemently argue that she is not short and stout. I consider responding, but I instead throw the phone to the other side of my bed with a raccoon-like hiss.

I grab another blanket, creating a larger cocoon of comfort around myself. By nine o'clock that night, I've collected all the blankets in our house and graduated from rabid animal to glorified burrito.

As I watch reruns of an old sitcom on my laptop, I hear a car pull into the driveway, followed by the front door shutting and Lorelei's head poking in my doorway.

"Yoo-hoo," she says, knocking on the doorframe. "Best friend for hire. Wow, do you have on all the house's blankets or something?"

"I was cold," I lie. I'm actually sweating bullets under my fluffy home. "It's getting cold outside," I try to reason. "Bet it'll rain soon."

"Hmm, yeah."

"Cloudy outside."

"Yep. Uh, hey, Quinn?"

"Hmm?"

"We're talking about the weather," she says with a gentle smile. "You realize that, don't you?"

"Oh," I say. "Right."

Lorelei sits on my bed, curling next to me. I look to her, then down to my swaddled legs.

"I would let you into my blanket sleeping bag," I say, "but I genuinely don't think I can."

I push against the tight hold to prove my point. She laughs, then pauses the show on my laptop mid-audience laugh track.

"Hey, I was watching that."

"Are you okay?" she asks.

"Well, I'm losing my job, so ... no," I say. "Not really."

She twists her mouth to the side. "I'm sorry," she says.

"It's not your fault."

I already know whose fault it is.

Honey Pleasure. The woman selling this whole thing. The woman trying to retire, no matter the cost of the existing employees. But I don't say that. Instead, I watch Lorelei's face fall as she glances over me.

"Oh no. The buyout isn't affecting you too, is it?" I ask. "I know you were slotted for that GM role—"

"No! Thankfully, it's not," she says with an exhale.

Good. I think it would kill Lorelei if she was kicked out of Honeywood. But before I can say so, she slaps against my burrito fort.

"But, hey, stop it! This isn't about me. I can read you like a book, Quinn. Tell me what's going on."

"If I'm a book, what's my title?"

"Hmm," she muses. "*Blonde Girl Missing?*"

"Is it a thriller novel?"

"True crime."

"Do I get kidnapped?"

"Unsolved mystery," she says with a smile. "So, let's solve it."

I lean my head back and groan. "You're too good at bringing the subject back."

"I know. It's a talent."

I sigh. "I just need to finish out my last few weeks, is all," I say with a shrug. "Performances and stuff."

"Performances, like the one where you kiss my brother?"

I jerk my head toward her as quick as my blankets will allow. She's grinning ear to ear.

"That's gotta be the silver lining here, right?" she says. "What's going on with you two?"

I swallow and look away. "Nothing."

She laughs. "It's okay to like him."

"But I don't."

"Then, why are y'all going to parties together?" she asks, pushing my knee. "Hmm?"

"Lore ..."

"Come on. We never keep secrets from each other!" she says. "Why is this one any different? Because he's my brother?"

I don't know about *never*. I've still not told her about his friends' bullying. And that truth settles in my gut more than it should.

I sigh. "It's complicated."

"I can handle complicated."

"It's a lot."

"I'm a lot."

I swallow. "You ... you might not like him."

Her eyebrows furrow in. "Then, I definitely want to know."

"He ... well, his friends ... I guess," I start. It's harder to say than I thought it would be, so I just let it rip out of me. "I was bullied a lot more in high school than I told you. After Landon's friends found my diary, they left notes, whispered in the hallway ... and I was so ridiculously infatuated with your stupid brother that it hurt ten times worse. He told me I didn't have a chance in the world with him—"

"He didn't," she gasps.

"Well ... I thought he was involved after that. So, I hated him for years. Turns out, he didn't know about a lot of the extra stuff, and then he kissed me and said he should have done it forever ago, and then I found out he'd read all the books we used to read together and he was secretly into me, and now ... well ..." I reach for my phone and show her my text thread with Landon and the pictures he sent me throughout the day.

She picks it up, still blinking through the onslaught of my words. But her face lights up immediately when she sees what he sent. "Aw, he's so cute!"

"He's been trying to cheer me up," I mumble but still smile. "It's annoying."

She touches the screen to scroll and see more, and I instantly pull the phone back.

"Probably shouldn't read the texts before that."

"Why?"

I wince.

"Wait, are you sexting?" she asks, then gets serious. "Are you sexting my brother?"

I don't say anything, but I don't need to.

Lorelei gasps, as if the life got sucked out of her. Her elbow juts back, ramming into my dresser. She jerks it away, gripping the injury. But even as she winces, her mouth is still hanging open. Her eyes are as wide as saucers.

"Quinn!" she squeaks, hitting my knee.

"Told you it was complicated."

"How did this happen? Like ... you two ... I mean, we gotta talk about that bullying stuff, but ... you read together? I don't ..."

"There's a lot, I know," I say. I forgot she didn't know we were sorta, kinda friends.

"And now? You're just ... sexting?"

"And I've been hanging out with him after work too."

"What?!"

"He makes me dinner," I admit.

"Secret dinners?!" she squeaks.

"And milkshakes."

"Secret milkshakes?!"

Lorelei's mouth opens and closes. I give her time to process. Finally, she's able to form some words.

"So, what does this mean?" she asks.

The million-dollar question.

Landon and me. Me and Landon. I have no clue how to justify that our names are in the same sentence, let alone potentially intertwined.

My phone buzzes in my lap. I expect it to be another picture from Landon, but instead, my mom's name flashes across the screen again. Lorelei's eyes whip down, then back to me.

"She's still texting?" Lorelei asks. Her tone is almost a whisper, as if talking about my mom is taboo to the nth degree.

"At first, it was every few days," I say. "Now, it's almost every day."

Lorelei curls her bottom lip in to chew on it. "She's never been this persistent, has she?"

My stomach drops.

"No," I admit.

This is the part that aches the most. The idea that I can't even trust the signs in front of me that things might be different. It's my dad talking—the part of me that judges my mom for her past even though I know better. Now, I've been through what she went through, and I should be more understanding. But it's hard to be understanding when she was incapable of handling it in the past. When I'm still stuck on the memories of her missing plays, a graduation ... everything.

"Is she ... okay?" Lorelei asks. I can hear the implication. "Are you?"

We both know what she's trying to avoid saying. We never talk about my junior year of college, per my request. But it's always there, lingering in the background, like my own personal Dorian Gray portrait—a mirror image of a worse me.

My mom creeping back into my life feels like an omen— a reminder that every precaution I've taken might never be enough. That no amount of medication or therapy can prevent me from being the me I'm meant to be. I can't risk dragging Landon down with me into my inevitable future. But, more than that, I'm not even sure I trust that he wants to endure it with me.

"It's fine," I say, not indicating whether I mean my mom or me.

Lorelei nods more to herself than me, then sighs.

My phone buzzes again. This time, it is Landon.

"Are you gonna ignore that one too?" Lorelei asks.

"I'm just pretending my phone doesn't exist for now."

"Okay, well, as long as we're playing pretend," she says slowly, "how about we pretend we didn't just have pizza earlier this week and order some more?"

I can tell Lorelei wants to talk about it more, but she knows me better than that. With some people, talking is the key. For me, she knows I'd rather add another safety blanket to my collection.

And eat comfort food.

"That's my favorite game of pretend," I say. But as the words come out, I know it's no longer the truth.

My favorite game of pretend is playing a queen who falls deliriously and hopelessly in love with a certain forest ranger. That game of pretend is the best one I've played yet. And I need to face the music and tell him why it has to stay that way.

41

Landon

Dark clouds loom over Honeywood Fun Park. I wouldn't say I'm a superstitious person, but I will definitely avoid cracked mirrors and tall ladders today.

My sister already has her bad hip under her palm as she walks with me out of the employee offices. She looks up at the sky, and my gaze follows. The gray clouds are thick, but the air around us is thicker. There's a low groan of thunder, shaking to a rumble that echoes down the midway.

"It's gonna be a rough one," Lorelei says with a sigh. "I can feel it."

"Ten bucks we close," I say.

"I'd take you on that bet, but I'd lose."

We exchange grins and go about our day as if the sky doesn't look like hell is going to break through. But it takes two hours before we spot lightning, and another hour after that, fat raindrops start plunking down. With deliberation over the walkies, as I stare out the window into the white haze of rain, unable to see the roller coaster I know is only yards away, the park announces it will close due to unforeseen storms.

272

Unforeseen storms, my tight shorts. It looks like we're about to be on the set of a natural disaster movie.

I help clear the guests, trying to rush around under a yellow Honeywood poncho. Other team members do the same, handing out matching ponchos as guests exit past the Buzzy fountain. Another flash of lightning sends a wave of wobbling screams as they shuffle out faster.

I jog across the midway to the amphitheater, where the cast is trying to drag the set pieces backstage. Emily hugs one of the pumpkin standees to her chest.

"Here, let me," I say, popping it up into my arms and carrying it for her. But I pause in my tracks when I see Quinn standing in the wing.

I can tell by her parted lips that she wants to talk. But the same moment she opens her mouth, another crack of lightning pierces the sky.

I turn to see Lorelei walking down the aisle, waving her hand. The drooping canopy above is the only thing protecting her from rainfall. I go to the edge of the stage at the same time Quinn does.

"Hey, I've gotta go," Lorelei says. "This storm is too much for my hip."

"Makes sense. I can't leave yet though," Quinn says. "But I'll find a ride."

"I can drive you home," I offer.

Lorelei smiles at me, her shoulders rising to her ears, as if eager to hear that. Something tells me she knows about our *not* relationship. But when Quinn's face falls, my stomach shifts.

"I'll figure out something," Quinn says noncommittally. "I'll see you at home, lady."

Lorelei grins between us, then walks off. She probably thinks she did us a favor, that we'll spend the stormy day holed up in my house, boning like bunnies. That would seem like the better option than fighting, but I don't pick outcomes with Quinn. Her irritation is a wildfire, and I can only point the extinguisher and hope for the best. It's why I like her so much, but it's also why she'll be my downfall.

"I don't need a ride," she says to me.

"Quinn."

"I've got stuff to do."

"Yes, but I can wait for you in the parking lot."

"You have stuff to do too," she argues.

"If you finish before me, come to the security office. It's not an issue."

She pauses mid-step. "I'll find someone else."

The words cling to my body like static. The sound that leaves my mouth afterward is a mix between a laugh and a scoff.

"You know, you're doing a real good job of pushing me away."

"Landon ..."

"Are you trying to?"

Thunder booms above us, shaking the stage, the loose floorboard up front rattling in its place.

"Now, apparently, isn't the time," she says.

Irritated, I slap my hat to my thigh with a forced laugh. "Sorry, but that's crap."

A single eyebrow of hers lifts. "Fine. Let's talk. We were doing our jobs, and it got out of hand. That's what happened, and it shouldn't have."

"And our jobs include hanging out after hours?" I ask. "Texting? Sitting in a hammock together?"

"We were practicing lines," she says, turning away from me.

I reach out for her and spin her to me. "Quinn, be serious."

She blinks, her lips parted. Her eyes trail over my face, as if searching for something, until she finally says, "It's not going to work out."

I stare at her as the thunder rolling over the sky echoes through me.

My chest rises and falls.

"What do you want me to say?" I ask. "That I agree? It went too far? That I wish I hadn't accepted the Ranger Randy gig?"

"You needed the money," she says.

"Screw the money," I snap. "I've enjoyed every second of this little play with you. I love your sarcasm. Your attitude. The way you tell me to shut up."

"I'm a jerk."

I bark out a laugh. "You might not be nice all the time, but I love that about you. You don't know how it feels to be acknowledged by you. It's a privilege for those who earn it."

She swallows. "That's all well and good, but I won't even be here much longer."

I close my eyes and suck in a breath. "What are you talking about?"

"They're selling the park," she says. "And there's no room for me."

I pause. My whole body stills.

"Says who?" I ask.

"Honey."

I grind my teeth. "That's ridiculous."

"Is it?" she asks.

And I see something I've never seen in her eyes before. A shimmer. The start of tears as she jerks from my hold.

"Landon, I'm thirty, playing a twenty-year-old character. Let's be honest with ourselves. I'm not wanted here anymore."

"I want you."

She exhales and tilts her head to the side. "Well, you shouldn't."

"Tough luck. I do."

"Then, you're wasting your time."

Lightning crashes, and less than a second later, thunder booms. I see her jump.

"You should get inside," I say.

"I'll be fine."

So stubborn ...

I swallow and nod again. It's the only motion my mind can think to make.

"If you need a ride, I'll wait for you," I say.

She sighs. "Please stop waiting for me."

A piece of my heart flakes off right as the thunder rolls over and Quinn walks away.

42

Quinn

I was trying, trying, *trying* to do my job—the same one I'll be losing in a few short weeks. I helped hurry the set into the wings of the theater. I stacked chairs in the back. And lightning heralded thunder with each passing moment. Then, Landon had to show up.

My mind is whirling too fast to consider our conversation.

I'm angry with how much my heart craved to kiss him. How he said, "I love that about you," so casually, as if it were as easy as breathing.

I barrel down the midway and to the offices. I think I left my bag in Lorelei's office, but it isn't until I'm taking the stairs two at a time that I realize I left it in her car. And my phone is in there too.

Crap!

Okay, think.

If I'm lucky, Bennett might still be here. I can get a ride from him. Or maybe I can camp out in the offices? But what if the power goes out?

Then, my brain says, *You could always carpool with Landon.*

No. No, I can't do that. I've made up my mind.

I turn to leave to go find Bennett, but then I pause in place. Honey Pleasure is waiting for me in the hallway.

We stare each other down. My heartbeat pounds in my ears, almost as loud as the thundering booms outside. It might be from my sprint across the park, but something tells me that's not it at all. It's her. The woman in front of me who sold the park. The woman who is putting me out of a job.

She narrows her eyes, the wrinkles between her brows deepening.

"I don't want to talk to you," I say.

"Why not?"

"You're getting me fired," I respond, then blow out air through my nose. "God, I still can't believe it."

"That's actually very believable," she says.

I twist toward her. "It's my job," I say. "It's my livelihood. How do you not see that?"

She lifts an eyebrow. "I'm doing you a favor."

"A *favor*?! Are you kidding me? You don't even know me."

She shakes her head. I think she'd be rubbing her temples if she could reach them, but she's balancing her hands on a door handle behind her.

"I was stuck at your age too."

I scoff. "Is this your way of *guiding* me?"

"It's my way of pushing you out of the nest."

"Ha." It's bitter and anything but a laugh.

"You need this change."

"Who are you to come here and tell me what I need?" I accuse. "You think you can just show up and say, *Oh, wow,*

278

this woman needs to get her life together? What about you? Where have you been for years?" I ask.

"I wish people had told me then what I'm trying to tell you now."

"And what's that?"

"You need to let that chip on your shoulder fall."

"Real nice, coming from you. Real nice. What about the one you still have?" I ask.

"I'm fine with mine."

"Are you? What about the people you pushed away? You're selling the park you worked so hard for, and for what?"

"To be alone," she says. "I've spent my whole life running and pushing people away. And I don't have anyone now. And I've come to terms with that. I've stopped running. But you know what? I wish I hadn't in the first place. I wish I had someone to pass this park on to, but I don't."

"You ever consider that maybe you're still running?" I ask.

Lightning flares through the windows, and her jaw tenses.

"Queenie," she says, the word an unveiled threat.

"No, let's talk about it, huh? You're still running. You've just accepted your fate. You're just ... existing. It's like losing your husband and having some guy cheat on you were enough to break you. You preach to me about living, but what about you? Are you?"

I pause. My blood pumping. My heat rising. My entire being slowly igniting from my toes up to my chest until my head pounds.

She sighs. "Do me a favor, then."

"What?"

Julie Olivia

"Don't be like me."

I open my mouth to talk, then close it. I repeat the motion until I collapse into the chair in Lorelei's dark office. Until Honey walks off—maybe saying good-bye, maybe not—but she leaves me alone to the sounds of silence and the breaking storm.

43

Landon

I'm the last person in the park. I camp out in the security office, making a quick log of today's events and radioing to double-check all lines are dead to confirm everyone is gone. Then, I hustle the heck out of there.

I get to the parking lot, soaked to the bone, even with my poncho on, and my truck is thankfully the only one left.

Good. Everyone is out.

But before I can get too happy, I see one other person in the parking lot, shuffling under a large clear umbrella, going one mile an hour. I'd recognize that gait anywhere.

"Honey!" I call.

She pauses, turning on the spot. Her shawl whooshes in the wind. Her blue hair a contrast against the dark gray sky. Her umbrella wobbles in her hand.

I jog over to her. When I reach her, she seems angry.

"Hey, what are you doing?" I ask. "The weather is awful."

"No shit," she says with a snort. She looks done with the world right now. "I'm going home. I just need to go back to my hotel and think."

"Okay, well"—I look up to the sky and cringe—"let me help you."

I hold out my arm. She takes it. Thankfully, our on-site hotel—Honey's home for the time being—is only a few yards away. Uncharacteristically for Honey, she's quiet as we walk. And she's slower, which only increases my anxiety over the pounding storm.

When we're finally on the hotel's sidewalk—thankfully under the awning—I ask, "You all right?"

She sighs. "Queenie sure knows how to pick a fight, doesn't she? Really amps up your blood."

I let out a weak laugh. "Yeah, she does."

Then, my eyes widen as I process the words.

"Wait, did you just talk to her?" My voice has taken on a tone of panic that even I can't hide. "Is she still in the park?"

Lightning strikes too close for comfort, followed by immediate thunder.

"Yes, she was in the offices. Why?"

"Good Lord," I say, running a hand through my wet hair. "She doesn't have a ride."

"She doesn't have a ride?!"

"I need to go get her."

Honey's hand lands on my arm, and she turns around toward the park.

"No, no, I'll handle it," I say. My jaw tenses. "Go inside. I'll see you tomorrow."

She opens her mouth to talk, but I pat her back.

"Go, Honey," I say.

I don't wait for her to agree before I'm bolting back to my truck.

My body is soaked to the skin. I can barely see in front of me. It's just a battering ram of rain and white noise.

I consider my options.

I could hop in my truck and drive onto the maintenance roads, looking for her. But what if I miss her? The rain is coming down too hard to feel safe driving on the midway. What if I crash into a roller coaster? Or, God forbid, what if I hit Quinn?

I could also run to the employee offices.

Running it is.

My arms pump beside me as I sprint back to the employee entrance. Lightning illuminates the wash of rain in front of me as I struggle to key back in. When it beeps, I push through. My boots pound through deep puddles. The sound of the underground drains gurgle beneath me. The pinging of droplets on the roller coaster beams is my symphony.

Once I reach The Beesting, I finally see her.

A small figure in black, barely visible through the haze, walking in front of the Buzzy fountain.

I rush toward her, blinking past the drops tearing down my forehead. I ignore the way my clothes sag with the weight of water.

Quinn is shivering when I reach her. Her clothes are stuck to her like a second skin. She doesn't have an umbrella or a poncho. I lean in so that I'm hovering over her. The rain beats on my back, shielding her from the onslaught. The concrete sizzles around us.

Quinn tilts her head up, her chin wobbling. I can't tell if the streaks on her face are from rain or something else. It's the *something else* that shakes me to my core. I've never seen Quinn look so small. So frail.

"You're still here," she breathes.

I take her cheeks in my hands and nod.

"Told you I'd wait for you," I say. "Now, come on. Let's go."

I tear off my poncho, throwing it over her, and we both run—through the park, past the employee gate, which I fumble to lock behind me, and back out to my truck in the center of the parking lot.

I tug open the handle of the backseat, and she crawls in. She palms the seat behind her, scooting herself backward to make more room as I slam the car door behind me.

Quinn is already in a shivering ball. I scoot her to the side, so I can lie behind her, tucking my legs into hers, placing my palm on her stomach to pull her back against my chest. I rest my chin on her shoulder. She entwines her fingers in mine.

"What the heck were you doing out there?" I ask.

"Not preparing for a storm," she answers, her teeth chattering with the words. True to Quinn fashion, irritation flows through her, like *how dare* the weather do such a thing.

I chuckle, holding her tighter against me. "You sound like you're about to pick a fight with God."

"I might."

We lie there, the sound of the rain pounding the hood of the truck. It washes down the windows. Our bodies shiver together.

"Hang tight," I say.

I pull away, even when her hand clutches mine tighter, reaching over the console with my keys in hand. I crank the engine and turn the heat on high. I'm barely to the backseat again before Quinn is tugging me close once more.

My heart skips, and I pull her against me. I nuzzle into her wet hair. It smells like fresh honey and cool rain.

We lie there as the storm rages on around us. Flashes of

light illuminate the sheets of rain, followed by claps of thunder that have both of us jumping at the same time.

I laugh first. When her shoulders move against me, I think she might be laughing too. I run my fingers through her hair, rubbing circles with my thumb over hers.

Finally, when the truck is warmer and our skin less sticky, Quinn turns around and faces me. Our noses are inches away, and I can see the freckles dotting her cheeks as water catches her eyelashes. Her green eyes are swirls of emerald, mint, and light hazel. A mix of moods, just like her.

"I want to talk," she whispers.

My breath hitches, and I slide a strand of hair behind her ear.

"I'm ready to listen."

She pulls our clutched hands closer to her chest. "I'm sorry for what I said."

The words seem cold on her tongue, like an admission of guilt.

"Hey, you didn't—"

"Shut up."

I chuckle. Even when her eyes are lined in pink, she's ready to bite. Vulnerability obviously isn't her strong suit.

"Okay," I say. "Shutting up."

"So, this might be jumbled, and ... I'm not good at this whole thing, so just ... bear with me."

"Mmhmm."

"And don't interrupt with your little *hmms*," she says, raising a pointed finger between our chests.

I exaggerate another *hmm*, which makes her laugh.

"I don't want to push you away. I'm trying ... to ... well ... I guess the best way I can put it is that my life feels stitched together," she says. "It is stitched together so tight that I've made myself immovable. But it's like I'm just now realizing the stitches are only duct tape and glue. First, there's you, then my job, and my mom ... it's a lot of things that require me to be flexible, and I'm simply not built that way. But I want to try. I do. With you. Maybe with my mom too? I don't know. I'm not sure."

Her head shakes, and she closes her eyes.

"What's going on with your mom?" I ask.

"We're complicated. We always have been. She wasn't there for me a lot, growing up. And I know now, it was something she couldn't help. That if she'd just stayed on medication, she'd have been fine. But she'd always stop seeking help when she felt better. Then, she'd cycle again. She didn't want anything to do with me. She didn't come to my plays or musicals. She didn't come to parent-teacher conferences or anything a mom normally does. She didn't even come to my graduation. Nothing."

I think back to high school and all the times my mom insisted we go to Quinn's plays as a family. I also remember seeing Fred, Honeywood's general manager, sit next to us. His daughter wasn't even in the drama club. I remember thinking it was weird, but now that I think about it ... was it? Were they the parental surrogates for her life?

"My dad didn't understand," Quinn continues. "I don't think I even understood what she was going through until I went through the same thing in college. I just always said I wouldn't end up like her. I would be tough. Able to handle everything.

"But the funny thing about depression, which isn't actually funny at all, is that it sneaks up on you when you least expect it. And when it happened to me, I didn't know what was going on. I felt like I'd failed in being tough. Or that I'd failed in becoming someone different than her. I remember my dad saying, 'Hey, let's nip this in the bud before it gets worse.' I know my dad was helping, but it also felt like he was saying, *Hey, let's make sure you don't turn out like her before it's too late.*"

It's like glass shatters in front of me—a realization.

I swallow. "Your junior year of college."

I feel her nod against me.

"It was Lorelei who recognized the signs first. By the time it was all said and done, all I had to show for myself was a mishmash of class credits. I went to see someone, got on medication ... but I had already lost my scholarship. The important thing was that I was fine. I could get out of bed. Medication worked. But I'd be lying if I said I'm not terrified of it happening again. Because the cycles are what happened with my mom. She'd get off her meds and then leave. And ... who says I won't do the same? Who says I won't neglect everyone?"

"But you just said it's because she stopped working at it, right?" I ask. "I'm not saying it's not hard, but you're you, Quinn. You're the strongest person I know. You kicked ass, even before the meds, and I bet you kick even harder now. Like a roundhouse type of thing."

She laughs. "Yes, but ... I'm not that much different from her at the end of the day. I'm ... difficult. And a little broken. And a massive mess of a person. And ... I don't want to live through their divorce again. I don't want to be with someone, only for them to wake up one morning and realize what I really am."

I cup her jaw in my palms. She inhales as I stare into her eyes.

"But what you are is wonderful. You're honest and courageous and loyal. I mean, you punched a kid in the nose freshman year for making fun of my sister. When Lorelei

287

told me that, I didn't know whether I should be afraid of you or in love."

"You were afraid, weren't you?"

"So very, very afraid."

A smile cracks at the corner of her mouth. I swipe my thumb over her cheek.

"There's always a chance things don't work out in life," I say. "But you just have to place your bets on the ones that you enjoy and hope for the best."

"I'd bet on you," she says.

My heart swells, and it feels so overwhelming that I have to bark out a laugh to keep it at bay, to keep my heart from exploding out of me.

"Quinn, did you just say something sweet to me?" I ask.

"Momentary lapse of judgment. I take it back."

"No, no, it's out there now."

Quinn leans into my chest, burying her nose in the wet fabric of my shirt. I feel her warm breath as she sighs.

"I don't want to want you," she says. "But I do."

I shift on the seat. My heart pounds beneath my shirt. It's so loud, so wanting, as if it were desperately trying to touch her.

"You do?" I ask.

"Yes, but don't make me repeat it."

I chuckle. "I won't put you through that torture."

She laughs against me. I lean down as she looks up, pressing my forehead against hers. For a moment, neither of us says anything. We breathe in each other's air, her soul settling with mine.

When she tilts her head back and stares into my eyes, I can feel a piece of my puzzle clicking into place once more.

She opens her mouth and closes it.

"You look like you want to say something," I say.

A slow smile spreads on her face. "I want to *do* something."

"Oh yeah?" I ask.

The thunder rolls. The rain beats down above us. And with one single move, she leans forward and kisses me.

44

Quinn

I love how Landon cups my jaw when I kiss him. It's like
he's trying to keep me close, but I'm not running this
time.

Our kisses are needy but soft. Slow but purposeful. We
let the sound of the rain serenade us as we fall into each
other.

I wondered if I would regret telling Landon about my
mom, but instead, it's like something else happened entirely
—like a piece of my guilt flittered away. It didn't go far.
Landon was able to catch it in his palm and hold it close,
happily sharing my burden. And he didn't think twice
about it or ask for anything in return.

He listened. He understood. He did everything my dad
hadn't done for my mom.

I bury my nose into Landon's soaked neck, planting a
kiss right below his ear and another along the dip above his
collarbone, his beard tickling along my cheek.

He chuckles. The raspy sound in his throat is a balm to
my wounds.

"You're a natural at the *neck thing*, Quinn," he says.

My name on his lips is a chorus in my soul. A hymn.

Our touches go from kind and soft to quick and needy.

His hand slides up my wet stomach to my ribs as I push my waist against him. I hike a leg over his as he grips the outside of my thigh. I let out a small gasp, and his eyes dart down to my open mouth and back up. His expression is heady and wanting.

His large hand buries itself under my shirt. My tongue licks across his lips. Our mouths wrestle as he gains purchase on my clothes. He widens the hem to shimmy the sticky fabric off and over my head. I toss it to his front seat while he reaches around to snap my bra apart with one hand.

"That was smooth," I whisper.

He laughs and pumps his eyebrows. "I'm full of surprises."

He rips his own shirt over his head and tosses it to join my clothes. My eyes trail over his chest, lightly furred and all man.

He slides my bra straps down as I nip at his neck, my hands sliding over his wet chest. I throw the unhooked bra up front in the passenger seat.

It's an exchange of moans and small exhalations as we explore each other. Every time we come together and apart, we repeat it, as if we're desperately trying to experience first touches again. Like we're making up for lost time.

Landon leans back, staring down at my naked chest. He cups my breast in his palm, his thumb rubbing a circle over the peak. His lips part, and I've never noticed until now just how full they are beneath his beard. How pretty he is.

"Distracted?" he jokes.

"Maybe. You?"

"By you?" he asks. "Always."

His eyes dart back up to mine, peering up from the unchanged position of his head tilted down toward my chest. Meeting my gaze, he leans in and kisses the peak of my breast. I inhale a breath. His tongue flicks over me. He closes his eyes and hums, as if tasting heaven.

I feel down toward his pants, but his longer torso makes it difficult. It's farther away than I can manage.

"Take off your pants," I demand.

With my nipple still in his mouth, his tongue lapping over it, sending shots of nerves through me, he blindly works his belt buckle.

The clanking and hiss of it coming undone, combined with his low, "Yes, ma'am," sends goose bumps over my arms.

Landon kicks his pants to the floorboard, scooting up toward me so that I'm within reach. I stroke him in my hand, and the subsequent groan is enough to send me flying. Enough to almost make me annoyed. That he is everything I thought he'd be and more.

"You are the best annoyance," I say.

He chuckles, low and husky and warm. "And you are my favorite misery."

He undoes the button on my shorts and scoots them down my thighs. I pull them and my underwear the rest of the way so I'm fully naked. He grips my waist, picking me up like I'm light as air, and rolls onto his back. I land on top, straddling his waist. We fall into a rhythm as easy as remembering an old story, like it's a distant memory, as if we'd both practiced this before.

Landon removes one hand from my hip, using his middle finger to slide between our bodies and dip into me.

My head falls back.

"So perfect," he breathes. "So wet."

His other hand drifts up to my breast, pinching the nipple between his fingers. I grind with the sensations, pushing him further into me. He growls in his throat, adding a second digit, increasing the speed. I gasp as his fingers curl. The pressure builds in my stomach, my body buzzing, my thighs tightening around him.

"I want you to come for me," he says.

"You think you can make me?"

He laughs, but it's breathy, deep, like rocks grinding together.

"You think I can't?" he counters.

Nothing on God's green earth thinks he can't. But this is more fun.

"I'd like to see you try," I challenge.

His fingers curl on my command. Within seconds, I'm whimpering with the movement. The pressure balloons, slowly spreading over my pelvis and out to my fingertips. I'm on the precipice of begging for more, testing him to his limits, but it's too late. Whining, my eyebrows stitching in, I choke out his name as I let the orgasm wash over me.

"Oh God."

"So gorgeous."

"Inside me," I breathe. "Now."

He leans toward the front seat, feeling around for something, but I pat his chest impatiently.

"I'm on birth control," I say.

His eyes meet mine, and he freezes mid-movement.

I nod. "And I trust you, Landon. I trust you."

Landon opens his mouth to respond but closes it again.

He bends at the waist, moving up to meet me. He cups my jaw and kisses me hard. It's brilliant and deep and wonderful.

I reach behind me for the hem of his boxer briefs. I start

to tug his underwear down, and he removes them the rest of the way.

His palms grip my hips, and he lowers back to the seat, lifting me up to hover over him, his body flexing with the motion. I take in every ridge of his abs, the large convex curves of his biceps as he holds me, and the heat in his eyes as he watches me lower down.

Landon inches himself inside me slowly. So slow that it's agonizing. So slow that I could die right there.

His head falls back against the door's armrest, his chest heaving in and out, but his eyes stay on me the whole time.

"You are everything I thought you'd be," he breathes.

"I'm better," I say, grinding forward so that he's buried into me up to the hilt.

He chokes out a mix between a groan and a laugh.

"Yeah," he rasps. "Yeah, you're much better."

I rise and fall on top of him, assisted by his hands that grip my waist. The sound of the rain almost drowns out our noise. Our wet bodies. Our breathy exhales. His husky moans and my desperate whines I didn't even know I was capable of.

When my second orgasm comes, I don't expect it. It's a rush to my head, a sting of brain freeze, followed by the warmth of something else. And when Landon releases seconds later, he moans my name—not Queen Bee, not Barbie, but *Quinn*.

I fall down, settling my cheek against his chest, kissing every inch of him within reach. He clutches my hips tighter when I do, and part of me wonders if he's afraid I'll disappear in his arms.

I rest my chin on him and stare. His eyes are closed. He looks serene in that moment, at peace with the sound of rain. But his hands don't leave my hips.

The windows are foggy and wet. Outside, light rain pattering on the roof signals the storm's passing. Only the dregs of it remain.

"Can I ask you something?" I ask.

Landon lets out a low, sleepy, "Hmm?"

I bite his side to wake him up.

He squirms and mumbles, "Ow."

"Do you like it when I'm mean to you?" I ask.

His eyes open and wrinkle into a smile. His dimples peek through the beard.

"I like pleasing you," he answers.

"That didn't answer my question."

"I thought we didn't talk about feelings?" he asks.

"Were you not listening to a word I said earlier?" I say. "That was a lot of feelings back there."

He chuckles. "True. True." He tosses his head side to side, as if thinking. Then, he sighs. "When you say things, they feel honest. You don't sugarcoat anything. You make me feel real. I like that."

I plant another kiss on his chest and rest my cheek on top, listening to his heart beating.

It's taken me too long to realize how similar we are. That all either of us truly wants is to feel like the world is being honest with us. That we are safe.

"Okay, enough with the feelings today," I say, trying to ignore the sting behind my eyes.

"One more?" he asks.

"I don't know if I can handle it."

He laughs. "I'll be gentle then."

Landon reaches his large arm up behind me. Slowly, with tiny squeaks, he writes on the window's condensation.

I turn my face to the other cheek, and when I look up, I see the messy words.

I like you.

"You're so lame," I say. But even as I do, I lift my hand, trying to reach the window, and I add one word to the end.

I like you TOO.

Not a chance, my ass.

45

Quinn

Landon drove us back to his house afterward since the rain let up. I tugged him into the shower with me, even after he insisted on starting dinner. The chicken almost burned by the time we were done making permanent outlines of our bodies against the shower walls.

There was a coolness brought on by the storms—a feeling of autumn with new falling leaves and spice in the air. Some branches fell overnight, ripping through part of the amphitheater's canopy.

But, aside from landscaping cleaning up this morning, it doesn't mean the show won't go on.

That's the beauty of Honeywood. It's reliable and consistent. But I can't always lean on an unchanging Honeywood to carry me through life.

I sit backstage at Honey Pleasure Stage with my phone clutched in my palm.

Landon felt like the first step to becoming someone new. To being a woman who won't push people away, who might actually trust for once. He won't fix my life, but he is the start of a new future, a happier one. But he's not the only person I need to let my walls down for.

And those walls are tall and made of brick.

We're about thirty minutes from showtime. The stage is already in preshow mode, lit in greens and yellows and a soundscape of chirping birds and blowing wind. But I've been here for nearly an hour, looking down at my phone and watching the text thread from my mom, as if wondering if it'll do anything magical.

Pull a rabbit out of a hat? Show me the ace of spades I drew from the deck? Saw a woman in half?

It's basically cut my life in two already, hasn't it?

I wonder if she has changed. I wonder if she won't disappear this time. I wonder if I'm capable of trying something new.

Forgiveness isn't easy. It's as hard as looking at that Band-Aid and knowing you're about to rip out some hairs at the root. But sometimes, you need to feel the sting of pain to let the true healing begin.

I tap my mom's contact and let the phone ring. I don't know how long I sit there in silence, but when the ringing finally stops and I hear her voice, it's like the world stops with it.

"Quinn?"

My mouth feels dry as I choke out, "Hey."

"You called."

"I did."

I almost forgot what her voice sounded like. It's too much like mine. Raspy and harsh. Matter-of-fact yet with an undercurrent of speculation.

"How's life?" she asks.

"It's trying its best to knock me over. Is that normal?"

"What a silly question," she says with a laugh.

I can hear myself in that sentence. I can see the eye roll. The implied *of course.*

"I'm sorry for ignoring your calls," I say.

"I can't say I don't understand."

"It's just ..."

"You've been busy," she says. And it doesn't sound accusatory, but genuine. Curious.

"I have, and I haven't," I say honestly.

"Then, tell me all about it."

"I've only got twenty minutes or so."

"I'll take all I can get."

So, I talk to her. With trepidation, but still pushing through. I explain how my time at Honeywood might be coming to an end. Possibly. Maybe. It's still up in the air, I guess.

"Are you scared?" she asks.

"I'm ... not excited," I say.

"That's okay," she says. "It's okay to be scared."

"Easier said than done," I scoff.

"No, not really," she says. "Don't let what you believe you can or can't do hold you back. I learned that the hard way."

I let the words sink into me. The wisdom of a mother I needed so bad, coming so many years later.

"My therapist told me I need to change the things I can and let go of the things I can't."

Therapist.

"Is that why you called me?" I ask.

"Yes," she says. "Because I wanted to change this very badly."

I smile and mutter a small, almost imperceptible, "Good."

I decide I don't want to talk about myself more, so I ask

about her life. She says she's in one of the Carolinas now. Renting a place and keeping steady with medication. She's also been seeing a therapist for months now—something she didn't do when I was a kid—and it's sticking. It's working.

For a moment, I envy her. I envy that she doesn't fear change anymore, but embraces it. But then I feel relief—that being stuck isn't a permanent fixture for us. That there's hope if we try.

The music onstage swells. I almost forgot where I was. I glance backstage, and Landon is poised on the opposite side.

He's ready to go, peering at me with that dimpled smile, throwing a thumb toward his backside and mouthing, *Pizza butt.*

I laugh. "Listen, Mom, I've gotta go now."

"Will I hear from you soon?" she asks.

"I ... need to take it slow," I admit, and it feels good to set boundaries. Because that's real life. It's not a magical fairy tale with blissful endings and quick apologies. Real relationship mending takes time. "But, yeah," I finally say. "Yeah, I'll call you again."

She pauses and exhales. I can hear her smile over the line as she says, "Thank you. And I'll be here, waiting. I promise."

"Thanks, Mom."

I smile to myself, say good-bye, and hang up.

It feels like I'm tearing down the brick walls I've built, and though I'm bruised and scraped, every brick fallen feels right.

The backstage lights turn off, and Landon walks onstage, illuminated in greens and pinks and yellows. A watercolor painting of comfort and everything good in the world.

I'm so enraptured in him that it takes Emily pushing me

onstage for me to remember I need to act too. But then I'm waltzing on air.

I walk through my lines like Sleeping Beauty waking from a long slumber. Finally seeing the many colors of life and options before me.

I can do hard things.

Maybe I'll go back to college.

Maybe I'll fall in love.

Landon guides me through the performance with his voice. I barely pay attention. I'm drifting into his brown eyes. Watching his deft hands reach out as he gives an over-the-top Shakespearean performance I've grown to admire. It's ridiculous, but it fits Honeywood. It fits him.

I'm not good at this whole fairy-tale thing, but I can try. I will attempt a happy ending for him.

As the show comes to an end, as I stand more off-center than we should be, Landon walks toward me for the final kiss. His look is not hungry. It's not needy. It's wanting, a desperate plea for me to be his.

Landon's hands land on my hips, and he opens his mouth for his final line, but I interrupt.

"It's all gonna be okay," I say.

Landon's eyes widen.

Okay, bad decision.

Landon has never been one for improvisation, and it shows.

"Uh ... My Queen ..." he stammers out.

He fails at new lines. *Hard.*

I can't help the laugh that comes out of me. And it isn't Queen Bee. It's mine. Genuine and real.

I slam my heel down to make a point, saying, "Ranger Randy, I—"

Except I never get the chance to finish.

CRACK!
The air whooshes out of me, and down I go.

46

Quinn

I wake up with a start, like a pulled cord of a lawn mower.

"Christ!" someone yells.

My senses come to me. White walls. White sheets. Beeping.

Then, the memories come next. The fall. The underside of the stage. The gasps of the audience. Landon carrying me in his arms across the park. It happened so fast. I can get bits and pieces. It's not fully gone, but it's not fully there as well. And once I register where I am, I recognize the four people I love most surrounding me.

"I'm in a hospital?" I ask.

Lorelei smiles as Theo laughs. Bennett huffs out air through his nose, and Ruby leans her head on my leg.

"Yeah, you really showed the stage who was boss," Theo says with a fist pump.

"What?"

"The loose floorboard we've been working to get fixed finally gave out," Bennett says, cringing and patting my shin. "I'm so sorry."

Then, I realize that the pat sounded hollow.

I pull up the covers and see the bright pink cast on my leg. *Oh, right.*

My friends' initials are already scribbled along the sides. Lorelei's loopy signature. Bennett's scrawl. Theo's block letters. Ruby's tiny chicken scratch with a heart beside it.

And my heart sinks as I realize what this means.

"I can't perform on this, can I?"

Lorelei's face drops. "Uh, no. No, not really."

I feel off—something more than just the broken bone in my leg and the lack of work. It's like there's an extra person who should be here.

"Where's your brother?" I ask Lorelei.

A slow grin widens on her face. "He's bringing food."

"He hasn't left your side actually," Ruby says, upturning her lips into a sweet smile. "I mean, except now. But, you know, we had you covered."

As they always do.

"The quesadilla crew," Theo says.

"He's a mess for you, you know," Lorelei says.

"A garbage bin of love."

"A trash bag full of smiles."

"A dumpster fire of feelings."

Bennett glances to Ruby, smiling. "Nice one."

I notice Ruby and Bennett on the same side of the bed, shoulder to shoulder. Bennett is smiling down at her, but her smile isn't as wide. It's only when he looks away that her face completely falls.

The light from the hallway dims, and when I see who's standing in the doorway, my heart swells.

Landon leans against the doorjamb with his hands in his pockets.

"Mom and Dad have the food in the lobby," he says, his dimpled smile a gift to my weary heart.

All four of them look to me with eyebrows tilted inward.

"Oh, go eat, you vultures," I say, waving my hand and shooing them away.

As if on cue, the entire room explodes into *oohs* as they scatter to the door, like children having snack time in school. Landon steps aside to give them room to exit.

Lorelei lingers behind. "Be nice to him," she whispers.

"Old habits die hard," I say back.

Landon clearly overhears because his dimples deepen.

She walks out, knocking her elbow against his as she passes, and shuts the door behind her. The final closing click of the door echoes through the room.

Landon walks over to my bed, his steps steady and careful. He bends to one knee beside me, taking my hand and dipping his lips to kiss the back of it.

"Gross," I say.

"I'm feeling romantic," he says. "Get over it."

A smile spreads over my cheeks. They almost hurt, as if my body is still getting used to this level of happiness. That, or I bruised my face too.

"Feeling all right?" he asks.

"Feeling irritated that I'm in a cast," I say.

"Sounds about right," he says. "You haven't stopped talking about it."

"I haven't?" I ask. "Jeez, what else don't I remember saying?"

"Well, you begged for me to go down on you in front of everyone."

My heart stops, but his smile looks too crooked.

"You're kidding," I say.

"I'm kidding."

I hit his arm. "Jerk."

He feigns an exaggerated, "Ouch," as he shakes out his arm.

"Were you hoping for some kind of big confession of love or something?" I ask.

"Nah," he says. "You weren't on enough drugs."

"Good," I say. "Ain't gonna happen anyway."

"One can dream," he says with a shrug. He knocks against my cast. "Hating the pink?"

"I've been in pink for years," I say.

And just the thought of Queen Bee has my shoulders slumping.

"What'll they do about Queen Bee this season?" I ask.

"Emily is stepping up," Landon says.

Part of me feels possessive of the role. Like it's the only thing that was keeping me grounded. That Queen Bee was my lifeline to security, and yet ... I now know it wasn't. There is so much more, and one look at the bearded man in front of me tells me exactly that.

I can't play Queen Bee anymore. The shoe literally won't fit—pink cast and all.

"She deserves it," I finally say. "I mean, I'm out of a job now, but it was bound to happen soon anyway."

Landon smiles.

"You'll get through it," he says. "You always do. You're the strongest woman I know."

"You're so full of it."

He chuckles, low and raspy, and leans in to kiss my forehead. "Or maybe I just believe in you."

"Wait, is she gonna be kissing you?" I ask.

He barks out a laugh. "That's your concern?"

"You're still playing Randy, right?"

"Yes," he says, grinning. "*I'm* not the one who fell off the stage."

"I just know that ... you're saving for school and ..."

"Yeah," he says with a smile. "I'll be fine." Then, he plants a kiss on my forehead. "And I promise, you're the only queen for me."

And that soothes my aching muscles more than anything else.

47

Landon

Autumn leaves curl on the ground and crunch beneath our feet as the midway fills up with guests every weekend. We've opened the park to early trick-or-treating, having buckets of candy at each ride entrance, at the gift shop, and in little nooks and crannies. Kids run around with Buzzy the Bear masks and Bumble the Bee stingers. Some of the teenagers twist the stinger to the front and hump the air.

Ah, to be a teenager again.

Emily took to Queen Bee like a fish takes to water. We perform weekend after weekend, and I hold her where I need to and dip her after my final line. We turn our heads to the side to give the appearance of kissing without actually touching lips. It was Emily's idea, which is good because my only thought was just giving her a hug onstage or something.

Improvisation has never been my specialty.

I drop off little autumn tastes of Honeywood whenever I visit Quinn—hot honey tea, warm bumblebee pancakes, and cinnamon Buzzy Push-Pops. She's slowly hobbling around and throwing snarky comments again.

Since Emory is self-employed, he agreed to work out of their house and watch over her. I receive pictures throughout the day, where he looks like he's in hell and Quinn looks like she's enjoying making his life hell.

I'm in the security office when I receive the latest text. It's the two of them at the breakfast table. His arms are crossed. She has an exaggerated grin and a thumbs-up.

A rhythmic knock on the door breaks me out of my thoughts.

"Come in," I say.

A cloud of light-blue hair peeks in, followed by jangling jewelry.

"What are you doing knocking?" I ask with a laugh, standing to scoot a chair out as Honey shuffles in.

"I'm trying to be considerate," she says.

"Why would you do that?" I chuckle. "I like inconsiderate Honey."

She snorts, taking her seat. "That makes one of us." She seems distracted by something else. A spot on the wall or maybe even the books on the shelves behind me.

I look around. "Uh-oh," I say. "So, are we having a heart-to-heart or ..."

"I just want to think," she says. "And this is where people need me the least. Or hate me the least, I think."

I bark out a laugh. "I don't think people hate you, Honey."

"Queenie does."

"What did you say to her?" I ask.

It's hard not to feel protective over Quinn, but I know she doesn't need a pit bull to fight for her. She's her own guard dog. Which is why I place my hand over Honey's instead.

She exhales. "I said things that needed to be said, but maybe it wasn't my place." She shrugs. "I don't know if I should sell anymore."

"Well, look at you, with a change of heart."

"Don't make me feel like a hero." She says. "I like being the villain. I'm comfortable there."

I chuckle. "I won't tell anyone you almost sent Hansel and Gretel home."

Her eyebrows rise. "Almost?"

"It's okay to want to retire, Honey," I say. "I mean, sure, selling the park rearranges some things. But it's inevitable."

"I don't want to be a disappointment to more people," she says.

"It wouldn't be a disappointment if you chose a comfortable future you'd worked hard for."

"But I'd be doing what I always do," she says. "Abandoning something I love."

I bark out a laugh. I practically grab my stomach from laughing, and she squints.

"I don't see what's so funny. That was a serious comment."

"Well, you just sound a lot like someone else we know."

She smiles. "Ah, how is our queen?"

"Almost back to full sarcasm levels again," I say with a smile. "She was too sweet at first. Didn't feel right, hearing her say how thankful she was to everyone helping out."

Honey snorts.

"But she's doing great. She's figuring things out. Just like you."

"I should have been nicer to her," she says.

"She can take it. She'll be fine."

Honey sighs, leaning back in her chair and twisting her lips side to side.

"Maybe I should be around here more," she muses. "On the ground floor. Getting involved. You know I've never been much for involvement."

"Do what you wanna do," I say. "But you don't have to take us into account. We've got our own lives."

"But what if this old woman wants to change?" she asks.

I smile. "Then, by all means, I'm sure not gonna stop you."

48

Landon

I carry Quinn out of the passenger seat, and she's already pushing against my shoulders.

"Absolutely not. I'm perfectly capable of walking."

I laugh, placing her down as she grips the side of the door to keep balance off her cast-ridden leg.

We're at The Honeycomb to meet everyone for trivia night, and Quinn might still have a leg swathed in pink, but she's back to her dark humor and spitting comments. At least on the outside.

She might say through gritted teeth, "I swear if you try to escort me in, so help me ..." but she still reaches for my hand and entwines her fingers in mine.

"I'm not looking weak," she says with a smirk.

"You could never."

She's been anything but weak, stagnant, or unmotivated lately.

We stopped by Slow Riser on the way here, so she could collect her final schedule.

On the way out, she blurted, "I applied to college for next spring."

"You did?" I asked.

"The local college," she said, the rest of the words stumbling out in a mess of, "Only some of my old credits carry over, but if I can kick ass with this dumb cast, then I can kick ass without it and ..." She trailed off, then exhaled, as if the nerves needed to blow out with it.

"That. Is. Amazing," I said.

Pulling her jaw into my hands, I kissed her with too much passion for a small-town sidewalk, but I didn't care. Her back arched, and she lost her balance, but I caught her in my arms and carried her back to the car.

"Put me down," she said.

"It's way easier to just carry you," I grunted. "But just don't tell anyone I'm your pack mule."

We keep it a secret as she uses crutches to swing into The Honeycomb. I steady her along with Emory as she drops into her seat.

"Lager?" I ask her.

"You know it," she says.

I go to the bar, knocking on the counter, and Orson stands there, watching our table. And when I follow his line of sight, in the direction of Theo, I see his furrowed eyebrows.

"Orson?"

"Hmm?" he asks, shaking his head. "Yeah. Hey. What's up?"

"You all right there?"

"Fine. Uh, lager, right?"

"Yeah," I say.

I peer over at the table, watching Theo's eyes avert from the bar. Then, I notice Quinn laughing, and I smile.

"Tell me you've taken the plunge," Orson says from behind me.

I look back to Orson, who is leaning on his palm. "The plunge?"

"For Quinn," he says. "You're escorting her around like she's your world," he says. "Tell me you've locked it down."

"She'd have a heart attack if we tried to define this," I say with a laugh. "Do we want her back in the hospital?"

"Come on," he says. "Get her cold, dead heart, lock it in a box, and keep it."

"I'm not some evil queen, Orson."

"You love her," Orson says. He states it like it's fact.

I steal a glance over to Quinn, who leans back in her chair, arms crossed over her chest. A single eyebrow is raised at her friends, and when they all laugh, she joins in. Her eyes swivel to mine. She keeps smiling that same laughing smile without testing out a sneer. It's a new development, but one I'm quickly getting accustomed to.

Even when we admit we like each other, it's with a side of animosity or teasing. "You're cute," followed by, "You jerk," or, "That feels good," accented with, "Bet you can't make me orgasm a third time."

We're the most delicious type of fruit cake, topped with poison berries. My favorite dessert.

Orson holds his hand out, palm up. "Tell her you love her, man."

I shake my head. "She's got too much on her mind," I say. "She's figuring out things, and I don't want to create another wrinkle of complication. I just wanna be whatever she needs me to be."

"Coward."

I give him a side-eye, but the moment I look at the table again, Quinn is still smiling at me. Practically beaming. And I can't help but give a small wave back, which she instantaneously returns.

49

Landon

"Stop scaring the kids."

"What are you talking about?" Quinn asks. "I'm beautiful."

"You're disgusting."

"That's not a nice thing to say."

"Don't turn this on me. You did this to yourself."

"Ooh, I bet it'd be more fun if I hid in the bushes ..."

"Quinn!"

I swoop down, lugging her over my shoulder. She's cackling her raspiest witch laugh as I throw her back on the couch. She bounces off the cushions in a mess of pink fabric. She uses my popped collar to tug me closer.

I'm dressed as a Ken doll for Halloween, complete with a polo shirt and pomaded hair. Quinn is cheekily dressed as Barbie. However, she chose an alternative route to the costume. I wouldn't have expected anything less.

I laugh and groan as she rubs a hooked nose against my cheek. "Please stop that. You're terrifying."

Quinn, dressed completely in classic Barbie doll pink, decided to choose Hag Barbie—which is definitely *not* a

thing, but you try telling her that—complete with pros-
thetics crudely plastered to her face and a giant mole with
bits of hair sticking from it, topped off with bruising wrinkles and yellow contacts. It's scaring the kids away and
likely confusing them as well.

I bend down and kiss her firmly on the lips and avoid
the rest of her made-up face.

"What? You don't like the look?" she asks with a witchy,
wobbling, cracked voice. "You always call me Barbie ..."

"Oh, hush." I push her tight pleather skirt aside and trail
my hand over her thigh. "You drive me crazy."

I feel for Quinn the way you feel the change in seasons.
Nothing tells you it's autumn, but suddenly, you need a
sweater, you want everything pumpkin-flavored, and horror
movies demand to be watched. And I've loved Quinn for far
too long to know when it happened or when I started baking
pumpkin pies so often.

But regardless of my enthusiasm, we haven't discussed
what this is or what it should be. I can't make someone love
me, and I don't want to. Quinn looks at me like she wants to
punch me, only to kiss the bruise afterward. She shrouds
her emotions and makes it difficult to get in. But I wouldn't
change Quinn for the world. Her anger is half the fun
anyway.

The doorbell rings.

"I'll get it!" she says, fumbling her way off the couch and
to the door.

"You're gonna ruin this holiday for these kids," I mutter.

"Oh, it's all in good fun!"

She rips open the door and blurts out an over-the-top,
"BLEGH!"

The kids scream. She cackles and tosses candy into

their buckets. They don't even remember to say, *Trick or treat.*

"Good Lord, Quinn," I say, coming around the corner to crouch down to the kids' level with a smile.

Quinn joins me soon afterward and gives them extra candy. Eventually, they relax and laugh at her hideous makeup. Some people need a bit more time to realize she's not the villain, but that's all right.

We spend most of the night eating candy we're supposed to be giving out—me, chocolate; her, candy corn, which convinces me she's truly dead inside. Once it's too late for trick-or-treaters, we turn off the porch lights and go to Orson's house, where he's hosting his annual Halloween party.

We bypass groups of people, including Meghan, a yoga instructor at Yogi Bare, dressed as a unicorn. Frank, our local mechanic, dressed as ... a mechanic. *All right.* And Mrs. Stanley, dressed as a sexy witch with purple-and-black stockings that look like every other costume sold in a Halloween superstore. Except I don't think the designer intended an eighty-one-year-old woman to wear such a short skirt. Oddly, she pulls it off.

In the kitchen, we find the rest of our group.

Theo, in roller-rink shorts and skates, grins at Quinn's getup, saying, "Witchy Barbie? Nice."

But when Lorelei sees Quinn, she screams. "Quinn! Good Lord!"

"Cute, huh?" Quinn says.

Considering Lorelei is dressed up as a cowgirl, I'm willing to bet scary wasn't on her list of outfit ideas. Emory comes up behind her in a tight flannel and brown vest. He looks less than enthused to be a cowboy or rancher or whatever, but when Lorelei hugs his arm, he relaxes into it with a smile.

Emory lifts his thick eyebrow at us as my hand rests on Quinn's lower back.

"Knew it," he mutters.

"You knew nothing," Quinn says.

Emory shrugs. "I know what it's like to want someone and hate yourself for it."

"Softy."

"So I've heard," he says, his expression stilled back to seriousness.

"So, we're celebrating, right?" Theo asks, clapping her hands together. She skates over to the cups and rolls back.

"Celebrating?" Quinn asks.

"You getting into your program!"

Her eyes dart to me. "You told?"

I laugh with my hands held up. "You've got the wrong twin!"

Lorelei cringes and wraps an arm around her. "Oh, sorry for spilling the beans! We're just so proud!"

"Yeah, a thirty-year-old back in college," Quinn deadpans. "Whoopee."

"Oh, hush, it's fantastic," Lorelei says, pulling her into a side hug, which Quinn leans into.

"Ew. Gross," Quinn says. "Supportive friends." A slow smile creeps up her hag-like face.

Orson walks over in full disco gear with flared denim. His huge Afro wig adds enough height to make him slightly taller than Theo. She looks at him with wide eyes and laughs with her hand held up.

"Oh my God, same era! Heck yeah!"

They high-five, and then he turns to me, leaning in.

"So, the new fries have actually been doing great,"

he whispers. "Uh, would you wanna redo the whole menu at The Honeycomb? I can pay ya. Won't be free work."

"I don't know ..."

"Yes," Quinn says. "He absolutely would. Right?"

My heart swells, and I grin.

"I would?"

"Yeah. How else are you gonna pay for school? Be Ranger Randy next season without me as your queen?" She rolls her eyes. "Please."

I smile, and I hug her toward me.

"Oops, watch the crutches."

"Yeah," I say with a laugh. "Yeah, I'll do it."

Orson claps me on the back. "Attaboy."

Bennett and Jolene come around the corner. They're dressed as a caveman and cavewoman. Behind them is Ruby, also dressed as a cavewoman.

"Did y'all plan to have a threesome costume?" Quinn asks, lifting an eyebrow.

I curl my lips in to stifle a laugh. Her lack of filter is my favorite thing about her.

"It was an accident," Bennett says, rubbing the back of his neck, resting his bat over his shoulder.

Ruby bites her lip with a small shrug. "Great minds think alike?"

Jolene doesn't say a word.

"Okay, grab a drink, everyone!" Theo says.

All of us grab a red cup or a can of beer or whatever is closest and unopened.

"To Quinn and her future!" Theo says.

"To Quinn!" we all chorus.

I feel Quinn drag in a long inhale beside me. Goose bumps trail over her arm, and she swallows. I can tell she's overwhelmed with happiness, but being Quinn, she won't come close to admitting it.

"Y'all are so dramatic," she says with an eye roll and a smile.

"You fell through a stage," Bennett says. "I think we have every right to be."

"Well ... thanks," she says.

"Don't break your brain too bad, trying to be thankful," Theo says.

We all clink drinks. I squeeze Quinn's side, leaning in to plant a kiss right on her witchy mole.

"They're gonna freak when they find out its clown academy," she whispers to me.

I chuckle. "Now, we're talking."

She leans her head against my chest, and I rest my chin on the top of her head.

If this is all I get with her—a witchy Barbie and whispered jokes—I'll take it.

50

Quinn

The day after Halloween, I start back at Slow Riser. I decided to go in early so that I could help the manager, Sean, update the interior displays for winter. I'm slowly learning how to hop behind the counter without crutches, but it doesn't make prepping espressos any easier.

It feels weird, not being at Honeywood on the last day of the fall season. I know they're prepping the final show, just hours from packing away the set pieces in the ware-house for next season. I always enjoyed the final good-byes.

I'm only one hour into my shift when the bell over the door rings, and the clattering of bangles and jewelry follows.

"Hey, Queenie."

I glance up, and shuffling toward me is the one woman I partially hoped to avoid. I haven't seen Honey in weeks, and knowing that our last conversation wasn't exactly great makes me sick to my stomach.

"You're looking as slow as me nowadays," she says, glancing over the counter to my cast.

"I could still beat you in a race."

"You gonna make a break for it now?"

"I might," I say with a smirk.

"Well, I hope not. I'd like to talk. I ... well, I have an apology for you."

My stomach shifts. Some part of me knew this would happen. I've practiced this potential conversation in the shower—one of those discussions you run through, but never think you'll actually have. I guess this one is coming to fruition.

"I'm sorry," she says. "I shouldn't have snapped at you. I shouldn't have tried to push you out of the park."

"It's fine. It was a good decision for you," I say. "And it'll be good for me. I need to move on."

Honey sighs. "Well, I'm actually gonna be sticking around a bit."

"Why?"

"Why not?" she answers. She gives me a smile, the wrinkles lifting up in an almost-defiant grin. The challenge of banter. "I want to see what I've missed out on all these years. Make sure the new ownership doesn't completely mess it up. This place needs an old woman's touch," she finally says.

"Oh, so you're crocheting pillows and quilts?"

My manager, Sean, snorts from the display he's working on.

Honey grins. "And immediately outlawing dance too."

"Well, thanks. For the apology. I'm sorry too."

"Don't be too sorry, too soon. I have another reason for being here," she says. "I'm actually coming to collect you."

"Collect me?" I ask through a choked laugh. "Can you even drive?"

She snorts. "Of course not."

I lean over the counter to peer out the window, finally

eyeing a familiar car idling near the sidewalk. Inside is Lorelei, giving an excited wave from the driver's seat.

I cross my arms and squint at Honey. "What's the catch?"

"You have to work at Honeywood with a cast. That's the catch."

I laugh. "I'm not working there anymore. I'm not Queen Bee."

"I know. You're my mentee."

My heart stammers. "Pardon?"

"I want to take you under my wing," she says. "I need help writing the next season's shows. We'll have to work in Ranger Randy for all of them, and my old brain doesn't understand anything but a typewriter, remember?"

A slow smile spreads over my face. "That's right. You're totally useless."

"Exactly," she says with a pointed finger. "And with more attendance and the new budget, we'll need to start picking up more shows in the indoor theaters. We need stage managers for them, don't we?"

"That's ..." I laugh. "Are you serious?"

"Do you want a mentorship or not?"

I open my mouth and close it, trying to blink through my feelings and thoughts.

"I can't though. I don't have a degree."

"It's a *mentorship* under *me*," she says. "I can do whatever I want. Plus, I hear you're going to college in the spring."

I glance out at the car again. Lorelei is giving the biggest thumbs-up.

"Snitch," I mutter.

"Good," Honey says with a clap of her hands. "So, we agree. Get your crutches. We're leaving."

I blow out air, looking from Sean loading up coffee bags for the display, then back to her.

"I can't just leave my job," I say.

"What if I said we could cycle between you and Emily next season?" she offers. "You wouldn't fully lose your Queen Bee gig."

I bark out a laugh. "I'm not asking you to sweeten the deal. I'm saying, I am currently at a job. I can't just leave."

Sean glances from Honey to me.

"Just go," he says with a shrug. "I can hold down the fort."

"What?"

"Yeah, yeah." Sean waves his hand. "It's the last day of the season. You should be there anyway. Go, go."

"You're serious?"

"Don't ask the man twice," Honey says. "Come on. Let's pick up the pace, Queenie. Let's blow this Popsicle stand."

"It's a coffee shop."

"Whatever."

Honey shuffles to the door, the bell ringing again as she swirls her finger to Lorelei.

"Start the engine!"

Being backstage feels odd when I'm not in a poofy pink dress.

"Wish you were out there?" Emily asks.

"Maybe," I say. "But it's time I passed the torch."

Emily is gorgeous in her Queen Bee outfit. She fits in the ball gown like it was tailor-made for her. Her hair is more golden blonde than mine, more fitting for the youth of the character. She looks ethereal. There's no way I ever looked that ethereal.

The stage door opens behind me, and Honey shuffles in, the usual symphony of too much jewelry.

"Emily, you look gorgeous. Queenie ..." She looks me up and down. "Eh, you're all right."

She elbows me, and I roll my eyes with a smile.

"Much better suited for being my right-hand woman," she says.

It's hard to imagine how things are both different yet the same after just a few months. I'm standing in the same spot, yet now, I have a future. I have a text from my mom dinging in my pocket, confirming my plans for a video call for later tonight. I have some old coot next to me, who is already murmuring set changes for the spring.

And I have Landon, who is smiling at me across the stage in his Ranger Randy getup.

"You know what I'd do if I were you?" Honey whispers to me.

"What would you do?" I ask.

"I'd storm over there and confess your undying love to that man," she says. "Make a complete fool out of yourself. It's the only logical solution."

"From dragon to fairy godmother," I muse. "You're really stepping up."

"I gotta put this magic to good use somehow."

It does feel weird, not being onstage with him, kissing him silly and falling deeply in love with him each day.

Ew. Even the thought makes my skin crawl. But not nearly as much as it sets my soul alight.

I cross to the back of the stage.

"Wait, what are you doing?" Emily asks.

"Doing something foolish," I say.

I can tell Emily wants to escort me, considering I'm still in a cast, but I shoot her a look that says, *Touch me, and you'll die*. It's very different from my Queen Bee glance, but, hey, I'm stage manager—or something like that. I can look as menacing as I want.

I press against the wall, shimmying side to side with my crutches so that they don't touch the curtain. I've learned Landon's lesson from months ago. No falling for me.

Landon grins when I emerge on the other side. He chuckles to himself, arms crossed over his chest and his short shorts showing off those stellar thighs.

It's time I gave my pink-braces fourteen-year-old self her happily ever after.

51

Landon

Seeing Quinn hobble backstage is both a pleasant surprise and a concern. Though I'm trying to veer toward the pleasant surprise category.

"Come with me for a second," she says, tugging me by the tie toward the stage door.

I already knew when she hobbled up that I was going to do whatever she asked.

"Yes, ma'am."

We emerge from the theater, closing the stage door behind us and standing in a secluded clearing, concealed by trees and brush.

"Barb, what are—"

But I'm interrupted by Quinn dropping her crutches, rising to the toes of her good foot, and pulling me down to kiss me.

I smile against her mouth, scooping my hands under her thighs, lifting her up so that her free leg wraps around my waist. I walk forward until her back is pressed against the theater's exterior. It's passionate. Wonderful. A fantasy come to life. Though, when I try to hike up her cast more and fail, she laughs into my mouth.

That laugh.

I plant one more kiss on her lips, deepening it for as long as she allows.

I rest my forehead on hers and chuckle. "What was that for?"

"I want to be the only Queen Bee who kisses you."

I plant a kiss on her chin, her cheek, and her nose. One right after the other.

"Are you jealous?" I tease.

"Oh, get over yourself."

"Just admit it," I say, propping her chin up with my forefinger.

"I mean, if you're gonna *make* me."

"I couldn't make you do anything, Barb."

A slow smile spreads over her face as she tilts her head to the side.

"I want you," she says. "If you want me."

"*If you want me,*" I echo with a breathy laugh. "What a silly sentence."

I press my mouth against hers, exhaling into her, kissing until neither of us can barely breathe. Our mouths move effortlessly, as they always have.

And right up against her lips, I say, "Of course I want you. It's always been you."

She sighs into me, placing another kiss on my lips. I tuck her as close to me as she can get, moaning into her mouth.

She pulls away.

"If you break my heart, I will end you," she threatens.

"Oh, hush," I mutter, capturing her mouth once more.

I can hear the music from the theater swell, and Honey's head pops out the side door.

"All right, show's on, Randy!"

Quinn pats my shoulder repeatedly. I don't put her down. I hold her under the pits of her arms, swinging her out like a sack of potatoes and plopping her into my arms, bridal-style.

Maybe not now, but definitely one day.

She laughs that laugh again, and if I wasn't pressed for time, I might kiss it right off her face once more.

"You're really playing up the royal treatment for me, huh?" she says.

I pause right before I can pull open the handle to the theater, scanning every bit of her—from her light-tan freckles to the button nose and into those deep green eyes.

"Quinn," I say, "you will always be my queen. And don't ever think you're anything less."

For once, she doesn't answer with a snippy remark. She only smiles.

I carry her over the threshold as she leans her head against my chest. I only drop her down once we're at the edge of the wing.

I bend at the waist to look her in the eye. "Tell me you like me," I say.

And without hesitation, she says, "I like you."

Quinn leans in the same time I do. But our mouths haven't even touched before I hear a loud *RIP*.

I reach for her waist right as the threadbare curtain tears down, and we both topple backward. I turn and clutch her tight against me so that she lands on top of me instead of crushed underneath. I might have saved her, but the damage to the stage is already done.

The curtain is ripped. The stage lights are on. The audience is full.

And with Emily still backstage, it looks like Ranger Randy just fell with an off-duty Queen Bee.

"I *knew* it!" a voice yells from the audience.

When we both look up, hair a mess and our limbs tangled together, we see little Mike and his friend pointing at us with still fingers.

Emily hisses at me offstage. I glance over right as she tosses me the crown from off her head. I catch it midair, looking from it, then to the woman on top of me.

"My Queen," I say.

A slow, elegant smile rises on her face as I set the crown atop her head.

"Ready for a final performance?"

"Let's do this, Ranger."

Real life truly is stranger than fiction.

Epilogue
Quinn

One Year Later

"Landon for Quinn."

I unclip my walkie and press the button on the side.

"Go for Quinn."

"I've got a fire-breathing dragon who needs slaying in the amphitheater."

I groan. Lorelei sits on her desk as Emory clacks on his keyboard behind it. Both of their eyes peer up at me.

I click the side of the walkie.

"That old bird is gonna be the death of me," I say into it. "Be there in ten."

Sometimes, the queen needs to save her ranger.

I twist on my heel toward Lorelei. "Care to join?"

"Nope," she says with a pop of the *P*. "Honey is your problem."

"Leave it to her to wreak havoc before we leave for the weekend," I mutter.

Emory snorts. I point a finger at him in a mock threat.

"Well, I'm probably gonna head out after this," I say.

"Have fun with your mom!" Lorelei says. "Tell her we said hi!"

"Mama Arden had better save us some roast," I say.

Lorelei laughs. "You know she'll have enough to feed y'all for a year."

I lean in to hug her good-bye, then fist-bump Emory before taking the stairs from the offices down to the midway.

It's weird, not being in my Queen Bee ball gown as I walk past the Buzzy fountain. It's even weirder, being here in late November when the water isn't running from the spout. Full-time employee perks.

But even with it being the off-season, it's far from calm. It's practically a madhouse as we navigate through the restructuring. There's hammering and whirring as we build a new roller coaster. Parts of the midway are blocked off as we lay down new blacktop. I hear we're even getting better lighting for The Canoodler. But one of the bigger renovations is that we're getting a better outdoor amphitheater.

No collapsing stage for us anymore.

No, sir.

I walk down the aisle of the amphitheater with a grimace. Landon is at the bottom of the stairs, hands on his hips. Beside him is Honey.

"I said I wanted the moving platform," she says.

The construction crew raises their eyebrows to me, as if pleading for her to go away.

"They're working on it," I tell her.

"And the thing," Honey says, waving her hand. "Where's the stage curtain thing?"

"They're doing that," I insist. "But, listen, we can't micromanage the construction team."

She *hmms* with a low grunt. I roll my eyes. Landon chuckles.

This past season has been a whirlwind with Honey. We rewrote all the park plays together, hired in more Queen Bees and Ranger Randys to do multiple performances, and got a big enough budget to hire a songwriter for an upcoming musical. Landon and I get to jump in as characters every so often, though he's started a new habit of trying to see if he can make me break character. Fred isn't so fond of it.

My mentorship has been ninety percent stage managing, writing, and overall theater department maintenance. But the other ten percent has been wrangling my mentor.

"What are you even doing here?" I ask Honey. "Go enjoy the holidays."

Right as I say that, my phone buzzes in my pocket.

Speaking of holiday plans ...

I pull it out, the screen displaying a picture of me and a fellow short blonde woman who looks similar to me but with far more lines on her face. My mom defies aging, which gives me hope for the future. In the picture, we're both hugging Buzzy the Bear.

I bring the phone up to my ear. "Hey, Mom. We're heading out soon."

"Well, I'm looking right at the frozen turkeys right now—"

"Mom! I told you, Landon's got the turkey handled."

"Okay, but what about the gravy?"

"Yep, all in his wheelhouse, I promise."

I glance to Landon, who shakes his head with a smile. I reach out to entwine our fingers. He finds my mom amusing, but this is the same man who finds me and Honey endearing. I have a theory that he just likes difficult women.

"So, no turkey?" my mom asks.

"Nope. Covered."

"Okay, but—"

"Mom, if we're gonna make it before midnight, we gotta go," I say. "Okay. Uh-huh. Bye," I continue through her sounds of, "I'll get mac and cheese," and, "You still like sweet potatoes, right?"

I hang up and pocket my phone.

"We should hit the road, Ranger," I tell Landon.

He chuckles. "Let me get my stuff, and we'll go."

"Tell your mom hi for me," Honey says as she wraps me in a side hug.

"She would love for you to come too, you know."

"Can't. I've got a hot date," she says with a pump of her eyebrows.

Honey is spending Thanksgiving with Fred and his daughter, Jaymee, and Jaymee's husband. Don't ask me how Honey finagled her way into their family events. I'm still confused how she did it with me and Landon. It turns out that Honey prefers chocolate milkshakes, so we now have Neapolitan Friday nights, full of rants and arguments that normally end in hugs.

It works for us.

I moved in with Landon back in April. Bookshelves full of old fables and fairy tales line our living room walls, but the kitchen is still the centerpiece to the house. I guess that's what happens when your boyfriend is in culinary school. There's a consistent mess of flour, sugar, and recipes scattered across the counter.

I've been taking my own classes for two semesters now. A lot of my previous credits didn't transfer over, but it's fine. I have a feeling it'll be a different journey this time around. Especially with Landon next to me.

We collect our bags from the security office and walk hand in hand to his truck, stuffing the backseat with luggage. I buckle in right as he reaches into the cooler, pulling out two thermoses.

"Milkshake?" he asks, handing it to me.

I grin, not even asking which is which. Vanilla, strawberry ... it's all the same to me. He couldn't make a bad shake if he tried.

Sometimes, it hits me just how far I've fallen for him. How I've turned into a swoony mess of feelings for my best friend's brother. How, if I had a diary, I might be writing *Mrs. Landon Arden* all over again.

Landon leans across the console, pressing a kiss to my forehead before starting the engine. We rumble down the street, right toward the open sky, filled with hues of pinks, purples, and oranges.

If I were a sappier woman, I might admire this moment —this beautiful scene, where I'm riding off into the sunset, bluebirds chirping, a curtain of pine trees on either side, and my own Prince Charming smiling in the driver's seat. I might, but I'd rather admire it for exactly what it is.

No queens. No princes. No fantasies. No fake relationships.

Just me, Landon, and our very real slice of happily ever after.

Also by Julie Olivia

INTO YOU SERIES

Romantic Comedy

In Too Deep (Cameron & Grace)

In His Eyes (Ian & Nia)

In The Wild (Harry & Saria)

—

FOXE HILL SERIES

Contemporary Romance

Match Cut (Keaton & Violet)

Present Perfect (Asher & Delaney)

—

STANDALONES

Romantic Comedy

Fake Santa Apology Tour (Nicholas & Birdie Mae)

Across the Night (Aiden & Sadie)

Thick As Thieves (Owen & Fran)

Landon's Recipe Book

Now available at
The Honeycomb!
— Orson

Beer Battered Fries

Ingredients

- Oil, preferably peanut or grapeseed, for frying
- ¾ cup white rice flour
- ¼ cup cornstarch
- 1 teaspoon paprika
- ½ teaspoon baking powder
- ½ teaspoon garlic powder
- ½ teaspoon onion powder
- ⅛ teaspoon cayenne
- Kosher salt and freshly ground black pepper
- 1 to 1 ¼ cups light beer, such as pilsner
- 3 pounds russet potatoes, peeled and cut into batons 3 inches long, ½ inch wide and ¼ inch thick, soaked in cold water

Instructions

Special equipment: a deep-frying thermometer

1. Fill a small Dutch oven with 3 to 4 inch of oil and heat over medium heat until a deep-frying thermometer

inserted in the oil registers 325 degrees F. Line a large plate or baking sheet with paper towels.

2. In a medium bowl, whisk together the flour, cornstarch, paprika, baking powder, garlic powder, onion powder, cayenne, 2 teaspoons salt, and ½ teaspoon black pepper. Add 1 cup of the beer and stir until smooth, adding more beer a tablespoon at a time if necessary until the batter is the consistency of heavy cream. Set aside.

3. Using kitchen towels, dry the potatoes thoroughly. Working in batches, slide the potatoes into the oil, being careful not to crowd the pan, and cook until lightly golden, about 5 minutes. Use a slotted spoon or skimmer to remove to the towel-lined plate and sprinkle with a few pinches of salt.

4. Raise the oil temperature to 350 degrees F. Dip the partially cooked fries a few at a time in the batter to coat. Using a fork, slide the coated potatoes 1 at a time into the oil, about 6 or 8 in a batch so as not to overcrowd the pan. Use a metal skimmer or tongs to keep them separate, as they tend to cling together. Cook until deep golden brown, 2 to 3 minutes. Remove to fresh paper towels to drain. Serve immediately.

Landon's Notes:

There are 2 advantages to double-frying the fries. First, you ensure that they are cooked through without burning the batter. Second, you can do the first fry in advance and hold them, par-cooked, for several hours. Batter them up for the second fry right before serving, and they will be hot and crispy to bring to the table. Then prepare to have your crush fall in love with you, or something like that.

Spaghetti and Meatballs

Ingredients
- 1 pound spaghetti noodles

FOR THE SAUCE
- 2 tablespoons olive oil
- 1 small onion diced
- 4 cloves garlic minced
- 28 ounces whole Italian tomatoes canned
- 28 ounce crushed tomatoes
- 3 tablespoons tomato paste
- 1 teaspoon Italian seasoning
- ½ teaspoon crushed red pepper

FOR THE MEATBALLS
- 1 pound lean ground beef
- ½ pound ground pork
- ⅓ cup seasoned bread crumbs
- ¼ cup onion finely diced
- 1 egg
- ½ teaspoon basil

Spaghetti and Meatballs

- 2 tablespoons fresh parsley chopped
- ½ teaspoon salt & black pepper to taste
- ¼ cup parmesan cheese shredded
- 1 tablespoon olive oil for frying

Instructions

1. Cook onion in olive oil over medium heat until tender, about 5 minutes. Add garlic and cook 1 minute more.

2. Reduce heat to low, add remaining sauce ingredients with 1 cup of water. Simmer covered 60 minutes.

3. Meanwhile, combine all meatball ingredients (except olive oil) and form 18 meatballs.

4. In a large pan, heat olive oil over medium-high heat and add meatballs. Brown on all sides until golden (they do not need to be cooked through), about 10 minutes.

5. Add meatballs to sauce, cover and simmer 30 minutes. Uncover and simmer until sauce reaches desired consistency.

6. Serve over spaghetti.

Landon's Notes:

For a full-bodied sauce allow it to simmer for a minimum of an hour and cook the meatballs right in the sauce. Be prepared for too many 'meatball' jokes from your partner.

Pot Roast

Ingredients

FOR THE POT ROAST
- 1 (4 pound)(2kg) chuck roast
- 1 teaspoon onion powder
- 1 teaspoon garlic powder
- salt and pepper to taste
- 3 cups (750ml) beef broth
- 2 teaspoons- 1 tablespoon beef bouillon (I like better than bouillon brand)
- 6 whole carrots; peeled and cut into large chunks
- 2 pounds potatoes; washed, peeled (optional) and cut into large chunks

FOR THE GRAVY
- 4 tablespoons butter
- ¼ cup all purpose flour
- 2 cups beef broth (from the crockpot)

Instructions

1. Pat roast dry with paper towels. Heat a large skillet over medium-high heat. Add a little oil and sear the roast on all sides. Place roast in the bottom of a 6-quart slow cooker. Deglaze the pan with a little beef broth scraping up all the browned bits and add to slow cooker.

2. Sprinkle with onion powder, garlic powder, salt, and pepper. Mix remaining broth with the bouillon and add to slow cooker. Place carrots and potatoes around the roast. Cover and cook on LOW for 8 hours. **I don't recommend cooking on high**

3. To make gravy, remove 2 cups of beef broth from the slow cooker and set aside. In a medium saucepan melt the butter over medium low heat. Stir in the flour and cook for 2 minutes stirring constantly. Slowly pour and whisk in the reserved beef broth. Simmer while stirring until thickened. If the gravy is too thick, stir in a little more broth.

Landon's Notes:

Choose a chuck roast that is very marbled with fat for the most tender result. Thicker carrots will withstand the cooking a little better and not be quite so soft. Recipe adapted from Mom's family recipe. Don't tell her I made changes.

Thanks, Etc.

Honeywood is my happy place, and I'm so excited y'all have joined me for another visit! But creating this theme park is only possible due to the wonderful, supportive people around me.

First, to you, the reader! For picking up another book of mine (or, if this is your first: hi!) For supporting my silly theme park ideas. For saying "sure, I'm on board" when I tell you that there's a character with short shorts and thick thighs. Y'all make dreams come true.

To my sister-in-law and best friend, Jenny Bailey. Thank you for everything. For reading this book twice before I sent it to the editor. For bringing Landon's recipes to life (!!) For letting me loiter at your house on Thursdays. For being you. I thank you every book, but it never feels like enough. You deserve the world.

Thanks to my dad, who is endlessly supportive. You track my Amazon rank more than I do! I can't imagine a release without your five a.m. screenshots and constant cheering.

To my brother. We may not have a *twin thing* like Landon and Lorelei (at least, I assume not, considering we're five years apart) but I'm so thankful we're as close as we are. You'll always be my hero.

Allie. Thank you for listening to my rants, reminding me that my books don't suck, and insisting that my boss (me) is trash for making me work so much. She totally is trash.

To my editor, Jovana. Thank you so much for your flexibility with this book! I'm constantly amazed by how thorough you are. I still can't believe you did a continuity check on the name of Honey Pleasure's children books. I want to keep you forever.

My beta team!! I'm in awe that y'all agree to read my early drafts time and time again! I'm so lucky to have such a great group: Jenny Bailey, Allie ("Zaddy Harry's #1 Fan"), Carrie, Emily, Elizabeth, Angie (my PT queen!), Jenny Bunting, and Kolin. Y'all are amazing. These books grow so much after you read them, and it is solely because of your feedback. Thank you so much.

To my reader group, the Feisty Firecrackers! Y'all are so supportive of each other and it brightens my heart every time I see y'all cheer each other on. Thanks for being so wonderful.

To every reader and author I've met through Instagram. I feel so at home on that silly little app. Plus, the fact that some of y'all like to vent about Twilight with me is the best.

Finally, to my husband. You're my dream man. My partner. And every romance trope I love wrapped into one person. I always said my ideal husband would be the man that I wake up laughing with, and I've used more than a few of your morning jokes in these books. Thank you for listening and helping me brainstorm plots. Thank you for ensuring the dudes in my books actually sound like dudes. Thank you for knowing I can do this even when I think I can't.

And, as the dedication at the front of the book mentions, this story is for everyone who thinks they're not enough. Quinn's plot was a bit personal to me for a variety of reasons. I won't go into it, as I feel I've already addressed it all by writing this story. But it's nice to see the conversation around mental health and boundaries finally shifting to one without stigma. I just hope I addressed these subjects with care. And I'm so sorry if someone ever convinced you that you're not enough. Lucky for you, they're wrong.

About the Author

Julie Olivia writes spicy romantic comedies. Her stories are filled with quippy banter, saucy bedroom scenes, and nose-snort laughs that will give you warm fuzzies in your soul. Her phone's wallpaper is a picture of the VelociCoaster. Her husband has come to terms with this roller coaster obsession.

They live in Atlanta, Georgia with their cat, Tina, who does not pay rent.

Sign-up for the newsletter for book updates, special offers, and VIP exclusives!: julieoliviaauthor.com/newsletter

facebook.com/julieoliviaauthor

instagram.com/julieoliviaauthor

amazon.com/author/julieoliviaauthor

bookbub.com/authors/julie-olivia

Printed in Great Britain
by Amazon

14760729R00210